Campaign
Ruby

Jessica Rudd, 27, had three career changes in as many years—law, PR, politics—but she is now going steady with her life as a writer. She is based in Beijing.

Jessica Rudd

Campaign Ruby

TEXT PUBLISHING MELBOURNE AUSTRALIA

Reading group notes available at textpublishing.com.au/resources

textpublishing.com.au

The Text Publishing Company
Swann House
22 William Street
Melbourne Victoria 3000
Australia

First published in 2010 by The Text Publishing Company
This edition published in 2011

Cover design by W.H. Chong
Text design by Susan Miller
Typeset by J&M Typesetting
Printed in Australia by Griffin Press, an Accredited ISO AS/NZS 14001:2004
Environmental Management System printer

Ebook ISBN: 9781921799600

National Library of Australia
Cataloguing-in-Publication entry:

Rudd, Jessica.

Campaign Ruby / Jessica Rudd.

ISBN 9781921758652 (pbk.)

Australia--Politics and government--Fiction.

A823.4

While window-shopping on New Bond Street during one of my career crises, Mum turned to me with love in her eyes and said, 'Just write something.' So I did, and dedicate this book to her.

Not quite the boot I wanted

An email popped into my inbox. There was no subject.

Received: Wednesday, 24 February, 9.15 a.m.

To: Stanhope, Ruby (Emerging Markets)

From: HR Department

Dear Stanhope, Ruby (ID: 521734EM)

You will be aware that the company recently entered into a consultation process with some of its Merger & Acquisition and Emerging Markets staff at Analyst and Senior Analyst level.

That consultation process is now complete. Regrettably, your position has been made redundant.

As such, attached is a detailed description of the redundancy package we would like to offer you. Please reply to this email, acknowledging receipt and confirming that the terms are acceptable to you.

There are two boxes labelled with your employee identification number in the staffroom on level seventeen:

the first for your personal possessions to assist with your homeward journey, and the second for company items provided to you during your employment. A full list of those items is set out in the attached document.

The second box should be left on your desk. You need not return the first box.

Thank you for your service to this company. You may leave the premises at your earliest convenience.

Regards

HR Department

Fuck.

A wave of rage swept over my body. How dare they? In this climate I, more than any of my colleagues, had defied gravity. I had brought in thrice my annual worth in as many months. Yes, they were smaller deals than those before the economy fell arse over tit, but they were deals, and billions of kilojoules of my energy had been spent on making them happen. Missed opportunities flashed before my eyes. I'd left my sister's wedding reception before she did so that I could wake early for a conference call with Slovakia. I'd swapped a holiday in the Seychelles with my ex for a €40 million Kazak pipeline plan that required my input in Amati. Countless yoga classes and family dinners had gone unattended, rays of sunlight unabsorbed by my pores. Vegetables had turned flaccid in the fridge. It was a life unlived.

I shut my eyes—partly out of exhaustion from not having left the office until two that morning, partly to conceal a tear. It was more the humiliation than the pain, similar to when I slammed face-first into a glass door during a party my parents threw in Bellagio last summer.

Prada Wayfarers askew and dripping with Mojito, I was shocked and then mortified—I ought to have anticipated the door. I should have seen it coming.

My phone rang. 'Delivery for you,' announced Sean from the level-three mailroom.

They had arrived. I'd ordered them online at Net-a-Porter to congratulate myself for sealing the Hungarian telecommunications deal. Downstairs, inside an elegant box adorned with ribbon, waited a pair of Mr Louboutin's tallest matt, black, leather ankle boots complete with signature red underbelly. They were meant to take me to my next performance review. Now they would prop me up in the queue at Job Centre Plus.

'Thanks, Sean. I'll be down shortly.'

I swivelled my high-backed leather chair in chorus with at least eight of my colleagues, all reeling from the same email.

Those spared had already formed a small coalition in the corner. Overcome with survivor's guilt they would forge new alliances with old enemies over takeaway macchiatos. I knew this because I used to be one of them, having been retained in the last three 'headcount control phases'. Sebastian and George were nowhere to be seen. Once sworn adversaries, they were probably already at St Paul's tavern enjoying a round of congratulatory backslapping over a cheeky pint and a bowl of deep-fried common interest. 'I'm not terribly surprised that Ruby's head's finally on the chopping block,' Sebastian would sneer. 'Quite,' George would reply. 'She's always assumed she's untouchable because of her father—that'll be a tense family dinner at the club next week.'

Slap, slap; chap, chap.

Stop wallowing and get your shit together, counselled my head, so I drafted a To Do list.

1. Pick up Louboutins from mailroom
2. Collect boxes from staffroom
3. Place in Company Items box:
   3.1 BlackBerry
   3.2 Swipe card
   3.3 Company lanyard
   3.4 Corporate credit card
   3.5 Corporate umbrella
   3.6 Laptop
   3.7 Business cards
4. Place in Homeward Journey box:
   4.1 Coffee mug
   4.2 Yoga mat
   4.3 Peace lily
   4.4 Travelling Toolkit, including:
      4.4.1 Spare pants
      4.4.2 Spare bra (including One Cup Up enhancers)
      4.4.3 Dental hygiene pack
      4.4.4 Razor and shaving gel
      4.4.5 Shower in a can
      4.4.6 Plasters
      4.4.7 Shoe cushions
      4.4.8 Kleenex
      4.4.9 Tampons
      4.4.10 Sewing kit
      4.4.11 Double-sided tape
      4.4.12 Spare phone battery
      4.4.13 Make-up remover wipes
      4.4.14 Industrial-strength concealer
      4.4.15 Hand salve

4.4.16 Lavender refresher mist

4.4.17 Travel-sized moisturiser

4.4.18 Vitamin B

4.4.19 Whiteboard marker

5. Reply to email from HR

6. Get coat; leave.

I made my way to the lifts and hit the down button. Ping. Out fell Sebastian and George as if I'd scripted it. Wankers. Sebastian sailed straight past me, but George cocked his head. 'Sorry about all this, old girl.'

'Old girl?' I walked into the lift. 'What are you, an Edwardian vet about to put down a sick filly?'

Satisfied with my response, I was alone in the lift. I glanced up at the tiny television monitor. Today's entertainment was a Charlie Chaplin film set to a track from *Birds of Paradise II: Sounds of the Amazon*—porn for ornithologists. The film cut to a sequence of Charlie with a hand on each cheek, his mouth agape. 'Scream,' said the white text on the crinkly black screen. Good idea, I thought. I stomped my feet and screamed, drowning out squawking macaws and ribbiting tree frogs. At level ten, I didn't hear the lift ping. The doors opened like curtains to reveal me harmonising with the howl of a lone spider monkey. My decrescendo wasn't fast enough. I cleared my throat. The tea lady readjusted her trolley.

'I might wait for the next one, love.'

You're already psychotic, said my head. *You'll be a cat lady in days.*

At level three, I drifted into the mailroom.

'That Mr A-Porter must be quite keen on you,' said Sean, presenting me with a long black box.

Tears spilled without warning. Poor Sean didn't know what to do. 'I didn't mean it like that. Someone's out there for you, poppet.'

I was crying too hard to explain that the problem wasn't my lack of man so much as my lack of employment. Then I began to laugh-cry. Sad sobs followed by short snorts then sobs again. I could barely breathe, but it felt good.

'Treasure,' he persevered, 'if I weren't a raving homosexual, I'd make passionate love to you on this mail counter. Right here, right now.'

More snorts, more sobs.

He swept the mail off the counter onto the floor and growled. Yes, growled—like a camp tiger. 'I'll lock the door and get the lights. Why don't you slip into something a little more...'

My legs failed me. I slid down the side of the counter onto the floor.

'I've lost my job,' I managed between snorts.

'Cock,' he said. 'You're fucking kidding me.'

'Nope.'

'But you never sleep. You just buy shoes and work.'

'Not helping,' I sniffed. More tears dripped as I told him the story. About the consultation, the deal, the endless hours, the missed opportunities, the Louboutins, the email and the boxes.

'Darling,' he said. 'I'm not sure how best to say this so I'm just going to come out with it: you're covered in snot.'

I caught a glimpse of myself in the stainless-steel counter. He was right. My usual halo of shoulder-length, strawberry-blonde waves was now a limp slick covering each ear. My alabaster complexion was specked with hot, pink patches spanning brow to neck. The whites of my blue eyes looked like someone had scribbled on them in red pen. My long thin nose was the centrepiece, expelling snot like Vesuvius would lava. My unhelpfully pink collar was covered in foundation. Tears had dripped onto my pitiful excuse for a chest. I looked like a lactating man. The neat silver-grey Hugo Boss skirt suit which usually elongated my petite frame had crumpled and crept up: a casualty of the Amazonian mosh pit.

'Christ.'

'There's only one thing to do,' he said, nudging the elegant box in my direction. 'If you are to cling to the integrity you have earned in this godforsaken cesspit of a bank you must deflower these Louboutins. Prontissimo.' Sean knelt and slid off my Steve Madden pumps. He loosened the black ribbon, removed the lid and unfolded the tissue paper. Inside was, quite possibly, the *perfect* pair of boots. 'Let these be your glass slippers.' He unzipped the right boot and fitted it to my foot. The left followed. Their curve spooned my arches. I zipped them up and let Sean pull me off the floor.

It's amazing what four inches of height can give you. Sean handed me my pumps and kissed my cheeks. 'I'll miss you, darling girl. But you mustn't miss this place. Let this be the making—not the breaking—of Ruby Stanhope.'

Fifteen minutes later, there were tiny ticks next to Items 1 through 4 on my list. I was looking forward to Item 5 with keen anticipation.

To: HR Department
CC: All in London Office; Global Board
From: Stanhope, Ruby (Emerging Markets)

Dear HR Department,

I have received your profoundly ill-mannered email. I'm astonished that you have the audacity to enforce monthly 'Internal Communications' training sessions, and didn't think to inform me in person or even via telephone that certain global investment decisions have had an uncomfortably local impact for me and eight of my esteemed colleagues. I work two floors away from you.

If the restructuring process hadn't been masterminded by incompetent nincompoops like those found in your department, we might have seen some very positive organisational change, such as the permanent outsourcing of all HR and IT services to Mumbai. Alas, it wasn't to be.

When I was here at 1.20 a.m. today, eating lukewarm teriyaki salmon alone at my desk to the sound of vacuuming—having missed yet another dental appointment, another gym session, another dinner with my sister, another opportunity to meet a future partner—I was comforted by the knowledge that while I might die fat, friendless and alone of a tooth infection, I would die a valued employee of this bank, which employed my father and his before him.

Once, this institution showed me loyalty. Now, it is showing me the door.

I accept the redundancy package you offer and thank you for the free box.

Regards

Ruby Stanhope

Former Senior Analyst (Emerging Markets)

Tick. Tick. Ping.

The Tube was as empty at half eleven in the morning as it was at half eleven at night. I picked the bluest and therefore newest of all the available seats and put my free box next to me. At the other end of the carriage a suited man was on the phone, taking advantage of the only reliable thing about the Hammersmith and City line—it offered at least ten minutes of uninterrupted mobile signal.

'You assured me that you sent them my CV,' he fumed, presumably to a recruiter. 'Do you have any idea how embarrassing it is to turn up to an interview like that without a CV?' He caught me staring at him and lowered his voice. 'Do you have any idea how embarrassing it is to turn up to an interview like that without a CV?'

Why, I pondered, do people reiterate sotto voce the things they've already shouted? It's nonsensical. First, you've already broadcast it. Second, it draws the attention of people like me to the very thing you're trying to keep private. Anyway, what kind of airhead would go to an interview without a copy of his CV?

My stomach writhed, reminding me of my new reality. I was now that guy. I was unemployed. Soon, I too would be pacing between stations, blaming my predicament on a recruiter.

Did I really just send an email to the entire bloody office and the global board? If I did, I was also unemployable. The faces of the old men at my parents' thirtieth wedding anniversary shuffled through my mind. Many of them were still on the board, including Andrew Leigh, the chairman. I imagined the chairman's secretary knocking on his open door. 'Andrew, you've received an email from Roger Stanhope's daughter, Ruby—shall I print it for you?' I couldn't even remember what I'd said. I grew clammy as I searched through my bottomless pit of a handbag for my BlackBerry. Shit. It wasn't my BlackBerry anymore. Shit, shit, shit—it was in the other box.

I pulled out my rickety personal mobile to text Sean. There was a message.

> Brill email, sweet cheeks! Everyone talking. My contact at the mailroom in Paris wants to meet you. Wear those Louboutins tonight to celebrate. Sean xxxxxxx

Good grief.

> Paris? Merde. I only copied in London and the board. Can you hack my account and hit recall? Password: Rueful. R x

'The next station is Ladbroke Grove,' the Tube Lady announced.

My niece, Clementine, explained to me last Sunday on the way home from Covent Garden that there is a magical lady who lives inside the Tube. She is a very small, very busy lady, 'like Tinkerbell, but with a very big voice'. She runs around at light speed in the ceiling of each carriage giving everyone the information they need. Because there are so many different lines and she is getting old, she has asked her friends to help her, which is why you sometimes hear a man's voice instead of a lady's.

Clem insisted on greeting the Tube Lady and thanking her for the friendly reminder to mind the gap. 'Thank you, Tube Lady, I certainly will.'

Almost five years ago, just as I entered the workforce, my sister Francesca left it to have Clem. She was a fearsome litigator at a magic circle firm and was on the brink of making senior associate after leading a messy trademark dispute for a major retail client. The firm urged her to take paid maternity leave when she discovered she was pregnant, a few months after marrying Mark, but she was determined to be a parent first. We all found this news shocking, especially Mark, who probably expected he'd have to fight for my feisty sister to take any leave at all. 'I was good at my job,' she maintains, 'but I didn't love doing it; whereas I'm a good mother and love being one.'

My phone.

Too late for recall, gorgeous. Paris got it from Dubai who got it from Facebook. You've gone global! S xxxxxx

Fuck.

The freezing February breeze stung my nose and ears at Ladbroke Grove Station. The salt on the platform from the morning's frost crunched under my new boots. I swiped my Oyster Card at the turnstile before commencing the short journey to my neglected flat in Elgin Crescent. The sky was the colour of my formerly favourite white shirt, ruined by washing it in haste with a new black bra. The wind played havoc with the long line of skeletal trees in my street. It didn't worry me that it was so bleak outside: it was a nod from God acknowledging my bad day.

My legs carried me up the three flights of stairs without buckling. Thank you, legs. I unzipped my boots, peeled off my clothes and stood under the shower. As always, I glanced up at the waterproof digital clock suction-cupped to the tiled wall, but this time was different. Euphoria set in. I had nowhere to go and nothing to do. I could exfoliate, shave even. I flipped open my face scrub with abandon. I didn't have to use a hair dryer because it wouldn't matter if my hair was frizzy tomorrow. I could use a face mask fearless of spots, watch the extras on my *Love Actually* DVD, drink and stay up all night. Tomorrow's hangover wouldn't matter; I could sleep all day.

The buzzer interrupted my sudsy fantasy. I ignored it. Nobody is home at lunchtime on a Wednesday, not even the old lady next door. It rang again. Bugger off, I willed it. No such luck. I rinsed, wrapped myself in a towel and went to the intercom. 'Hello?'

'Delivery.'

I peered through the window to see a courier van and a man with a big box. 'Sorry, I'm not expecting anything.' I hung up. Buzz. I picked up again.

'Yes?'

'Are you Ruby Stanhop?'

'Sort of.'

'Delivery from Blurrybross.'

'Listen, I don't know a Blurrybross. I suggest you take it up with Dispatch.'

'My sheet says delivery of one case of Austrian peanut noise to Mrs Ruby Stanhop at this address—this is flat 302, isn't it?'

'Peanut noise?'

'Says right 'ere, Austrian peanut noise to be delivered to—'

'Hold on a minute.' Wringing the drips from my hair, I yanked a pair of perilously under-elasticised sweat pants over my damp skin, and grabbed a cardigan, buttoning it up on the way down the stairs.

'Look, who did you say the sender was?' I asked, breathless.

'Blurry-Bross-And-Rudd, delivery of one case of Austrian peanut noise to Mrs Ruby Stanhop.'

'It wouldn't by any chance be a case of Australian pinot noir from Berry Bros & Rudd, would it?'

'That's what I said.' He pushed past me with the box.

Five minutes later, straddling the wooden crate on my living-room floor, I knew this was one of life's intersections. My instincts told me to get the flat-head screwdriver and jemmy the lid.

Leave the crate alone, said my head. *This wine represents an investment: the kind you might need to rely on now that you're unemployed.*

My head had a point. It was 2005 Toolangi Estate pinot noir, destined for better drinking in a couple of years. Luckily, a suite of excellent counterarguments came to me, so I sat up to present them for the benefit of my sceptical head.

1. I must ensure that each bottle has arrived unscathed
2. I was dumped by my employer today on the eve of certain promotion, so it is fitting to open a bottle and drink it before its time
3. You, my dear head, only favour the No camp for dread of your own pain in the morning. Red wine is known for its holistic benefits—it would be unfair to listen only to the voice of the self-interested lobbyist on my shoulders.

*But...*my head protested. Triumphant, I leaped up and began rummaging through the kitchen drawers for the screwdriver.

The afternoon was productive. I called Cool Monkey, ordered, had delivered, and demolished their delicious Thai red duck curry—a perfect match for the peanut noise, which I sampled in abundance. I unpacked the crate and tucked each of the remaining ten bottles into my temperature-controlled wine fridge. I even put on a load of washing. Nearing the halfway mark of my second bottle of peanut noise and still impressively sober, I decided to call my sister. The phone rang twice.

'Good evening, Clementine speaking, how may I subsist you?'

'Good evening, Clementine, it's Aunty Ruby. Would it be possible to speak with your mother?'

'Hello, Aunty Wooby, kindly hole for one minute and I will see if she is abailable. ARE YOU ABAILABLE, MUMMY? AUNTY WOOBY IS ON THE PHONE FOR YOU AND SHE'S DOING FUNNY VOICES!'

Footsteps.

'No need to yell, darling,' said Fran. 'Hello, how are you?'

'Slightly deaf. Just thought I'd call for a quick—'

'Just a second,' said Fran, covering the receiver. 'Clementine, could you please brush your teeth and choose a story—I'll be there in a minute.' She uncovered the receiver. 'Sorry, we're attempting to enforce a seven o'clock bedtime because she talks herself hoarse if she's awake until eight and Mummy will go bonkers and get alopecia if she doesn't get an hour of alone time. What's on the desk menu tonight? Teriyaki salmon or teriyaki chicken?'

'Actually, it was red duck curry.'

'You've already eaten? I'm impressed, Ruby. I'm surprised they haven't sacked you.' She laughed.

'That's why I'm calling.'

Her laughter petered out. 'Seriously?'

'According to an email from HR this morning my position has been made redundant.'

'Oh, Ruby...wait, did you say email? That's a disgrace!'

'That's what I said in a rather too angry email to HR copying the entire office and global board.'

'Well, it's no wonder you're doing funny voices.'

I could hear heavy breathing. 'See, Mummy.'

'Clementine Genevieve Gardner-Stanhope, if you do not hang up that phone right now there will be no story for you tonight or any night.'

Darth Vader disappeared with a clunk of the bedroom extension. I giggled.

'I'm so sorry, Ruby,' Fran said, perhaps not knowing whether I was laughing or crying. 'What utter nobs they are. How much have you had to drink?'

'Almost two.' Bottles, not glasses, but she didn't need to know that.

'Why don't you come over? We made cupcakes today. They taste prettier than they look. I'd come to you, of course, but bloody Mark isn't home yet.'

'No, I think I might just go to bed.'

'Okay, don't worry about this—we'll sort something out.'

'Goodnight, Aunty Wooby,' breathed Darth, risen again.

The deterioration of my hand–eye coordination was the only thing clear as I emptied the last of bottle number two into my glass and wandered over to the computer at my desk.

Googling aimlessly about wine, I was bewitched by a photograph of grapes on a vine. Toolangi seemed to be somewhere near Melbourne. How did those frosted purple, spherical Australians become this complex liquid in my glass in Notting Hill? Despite the amount of time we had spent together, I was yet to meet Mr Noir in his fruity flesh. We were like those couples in the tabloids who've had an entire relationship online before marrying at their first date. I heard my thoughts grow stranger with each sip.

Drink a case, pack a case

Fuck you, Ruby, said my head. *Yeah, fuck you, Ruby*, the rest of my body chimed in.

Morning had broken and entered my flat. I could see its orangeness through my sealed eyelids. I groaned, pulling the duvet back over my head. This was supposed to be a day of sleeping with possible cupcakes in the afternoon, but blood pumped through my veins with the grace of a snowplough. My liver flapped and floundered, mopping up toxins. *Go to the loo*, urged my bladder. The carpet of tannins on my teeth and tongue felt ghastly. I couldn't remember my last glass of water and was certain I hadn't brushed my teeth. I was parched. How I made it to bed was a mystery.

The intrigued part of me wanted to get up and assess the damage; the other part knew that the slightest movement could disrupt my equilibrium, resulting in certain vomit. I caught a glimpse of my clock radio out of the corner of one eye: 12.48 p.m. Not a bad effort.

With little warning, my head span, my mouth watered, my stomach churned. These telltale pre-purge signs were not unfamiliar to me. *Ignore them at your peril*, warned my head. I rose, slowly enough to prevent upchuck, but fast enough to make it to the bathroom. I sent a quick prayer to the plumbing gods in the hope that my Georgian loo would cooperate, along with my liver. Briefly, the cool slate of my bathroom floor comforted me. Alas, what followed was inevitable.

After what felt like a marathon, I got up. Loo flushed, teeth brushed, toothbrush buried, I exited the bathroom.

The pungent stench of expelled grapes and curry polluted my flat. I reached for a favourite candle and matches, learning quickly that sick overlaid with gardenias is less pleasant than sick alone. Instead, I opened the windows in the living room and kitchen.

An icy gust gave flight to some sheets of paper in my printer tray. I couldn't remember printing anything. I stepped over three empty wine bottles and gathered them.

My credit and debit cards were scattered across the kitchen bench next to my laptop, presumably from when I ordered the Thai curry. I needed hydration and rest. I went to the fridge, took out the bottle of Evian I had left there in case I ever made it to a yoga class, and sipped.

A cursory glance at the printouts puzzled me. It seemed I had printed a Wikipedia page about pinot noir, another about the Yarra Valley and one about Melbourne. En route to the sofa, my body felt the shock of chilled liquid. I had missed my mouth and poured the Evian down my front and onto the pages. I carried the soggy mess to the kitchen sink and wrung the damp from each sheet.

And there it was.

To: Ruby.Stanhope@gmail.com

From: etik@qantas.com

Thank you for choosing to fly with Qantas.

Your e-ticket itinerary and receipt are attached. Print this document and carry it with you when travelling.

We may use this email address to contact you about flight updates up to three days before your first flight out.

We look forward to welcoming you onboard soon.

Surely not. But the next page was more alarming. 'QANTAS BOOKING CONFIRMATION,' I read aloud, 'BOOKING REFERENCE GCU9263...MS RUBY STANHOPE...QF30... LHR–HKG; HKG–MEL...26 FEBRUARY...0020.'

I dashed to the bedroom as best I could, stubbing my little toe into the Samsonite suitcase on the floor. My toe throbbed in unison with my head. I flopped on the bed, reached for my phone and looked at the date.

Today was the twenty-fifth of February. It was now 1.12 p.m. I appeared to have booked a flight to Melbourne via Hong Kong departing in eleven hours. Fuckity fuck. I clutched my toe. *Calm down, Ruby*, said my head, still pounding. *Take deep breaths*.

'Welcome to Qantas,' said a friendly lady when I dialled the number. 'If you're a Qantas Frequent Flyer, please enter your membership number, followed by the hash key.'

My fingers mashed my number into the keypad. I hobbled to the freezer and pulled out a bag of frozen peas for my swelling toe.

'That is not a valid membership number,' said the lady. 'Please enter your—'

I silenced her and re-entered my number.

'I'm sorry, we couldn't find that membership number,' she said. 'Please choose from the following options.'

'Don't pretend to be sorry—you're not sorry at all.'

'Please hold the line. A customer service representative will be with you shortly.'

'Thanks for your patience; we're currently experiencing longer than normal wait-times,' said someone with Hugh Jackman's voice. Hugh would have sympathy for my situation.

As the peas thawed against the heat of my feet, I worked on my excuses. 'You see,' I rehearsed, 'I've broken my toe and it is so swollen that I can't wear shoes and it would be unsafe to travel without shoes.' This excuse had merit because it carried an element of truth.

Hugh's spiel came to an end and a new lady answered the phone. 'Welcome to Qantas. This is Mara.'

'Hello, Mara, my name is Ruby Stanhope and I'm calling from London.'

'How can I help, Miss Stanhope?' asked Mara. She was much nicer than the first lady.

'Well, I'm glad you ask, Mara,' I said, channelling my mother's charming I'm-about-to-ask-you-to-do-something-for-me voice. 'You see, yesterday I was made redundant. I went home, got terribly drunk on some very good Australian wine and appear to have inadvertently booked myself a flight to Melbourne. I need to cancel that flight. Urgently.'

'Do you have a booking reference number, Miss Stanhope?'

'It's GCU9263—GCU probably stands for Giant Cock Up.'

Mara laughed, which I took as a good sign. 'I'm going to place you on hold for a minute, Miss Stanhope, while I pull up your booking.' More Hugh. 'Miss Stanhope, thank you for holding. Regrettably, as your flight is due to depart in less than twenty-four hours, I am afraid we're unable to cancel the booking without it incurring a fee. Alternatively, you could postpone your booking, but this would also incur a fee.'

'Right,' I said. 'Did I mention my Frequent Flyer number?'

'No, Miss Stanhope, would you like me to attach it to the booking?'

I read her the number.

'Thank you, Miss Stanhope. Now, what would you like to do?'

My hope was dwindling. 'Is there no special...you know...is there anything that can be done given my... er...membership status?'

'No, Miss Stanhope,' Mara said politely. 'You have booked an inflexible ticket. I am happy to offer you a cancellation with a fee or a postponement with a smaller fee.'

'You see, Mara, I don't even have a visa for Australia, so it's simply impossible for me to board the flight.' I bent down to collect runaway peas. 'It's probably better for everyone involved if it's just cancelled. It was an administrative error anyway.'

'I'm afraid our system requires customers to confirm that they have a visa before they proceed with the booking,' she explained. 'So we are unable to refund customers when they have, as you have, confirmed that they possess a visa for the destination, even if they booked

20

under the influence of alcohol and didn't intend to.'

I wasn't sure I liked Mara after all. 'I see, but this was my first BUI offence and I really don't want to go to Australia. It's not that I don't want to ever go there,' I backtracked. 'I'm sure it's a lovely place. In fact my aunt lives there and she adores it. It's just that I don't want to go there *right* now because I have no job and I need to find another.'

Mara was silent.

'How much is the cancellation fee?' I asked.

'It's £1,340, with a five per cent fee for credit card transactions,' she said as if she hadn't just asked me to pay more than twice the value of a Mulberry Bayswater bag. 'Postponing your booking would cost £894.70, with a five per cent fee for credit card transactions as well as any additional cost for the new ticket, but you would have to make that booking for a flight departing London no later than the third of March.'

'How much was the total booking?'

'Actually, you managed to find an excellent deal,' said Mara. 'You paid a total of £1,864.45, which is very competitive as a last-minute booking.'

'So essentially, my choices are: I can go to Australia without a visa tomorrow and be detained for unlawful entry, or I can pay a fraction more than £890 and do the same thing next week, or I can pay slightly more than £1,340 and pretend this never happened.'

'Yes,' replied Mara, 'but if you're a citizen of the European Union, you can arrange an emergency visa online that can be processed in a matter of hours.'

I took a moment to reflect. I couldn't remember any of this so how was it possible that I'd been sufficiently lucid to complete an internet transaction?

'Your return leg has more flexibility,' Mara continued. 'It's in three weeks' time, so you can make changes to your itinerary until a week beforehand.'

'It looks like I'm going to Melbourne, doesn't it, Mara?'

'Well, Miss Stanhope, if it's any consolation, I was chatting to my mum in Melbourne tonight. She said yesterday was a stinker, but today it's cooled down to thirty-eight degrees. Is there anything else I can help you with?'

'No thanks, Mara.'

I returned to my bedroom, peas, phone and laptop in hand, and buried my head in the bed. The duvet muffled my scream. The events of last night returned in dribs and drabs. My passport number was scrawled across my palm in blue ink next to a smiley face. The huge suitcase next to my bed contained the items of my free box, alongside an old bikini, an array of footwear from Birkenstocks to Louboutins and the latest *James Halliday Wine Companion*.

'Francesca speaking.'

'Fran, it's me,' I yawned into the receiver. 'I'm going to Australia.'

'Oh, don't be melodramatic, darling. Today's papers line tomorrow's litter trays.'

'What?'

'Some North Umbrian will find a tarantula in his pantry today and you'll be yesterday's news.'

'What on earth are you talking about?'

'Hello, Aunty Wooby,' said Darth Vader. 'You wrote an email in the newspaper.'

'Good grief.'

'Hang up, please, Clementine,' said Fran. 'I'm so sorry,

darling, I thought you knew. Look, it's not *that* bad and it's an excellent email.'

'Which paper?'

'The pink one and the rude one,' puffed Darth.

'I'm in the *FT*?'

'Yes, there's a mention of it in the diary pages and a larger piece in the *Sun* on page eight. Very positive, actually. "RUBY'S REVENGE: LAID-OFF BANKER STINGS HR 'NINCOMPOOPS'." Here it is. Blah, blah…"Stanhope's email went viral in City circles yesterday. An estimated nine hundred thousand people had read it within two hours of it being sent. The bank declined to comment on its headcount control plans, but maintains its internal communications methods are in line with industry standards." Only a small mention of Daddy.'

'Fuck.' I plugged my dead mobile phone into its charger and switched it on. Forty-three text messages. Nineteen missed calls. 'Well, it's a very good thing I'm going to Melbourne tonight.'

'Sorry?'

'I got wankered on wine last night, woke up and discovered I'd booked and partly packed for a trip to Melbourne leaving at about midnight.'

'As in *Ramsay* Street?'

I held the phone away from my throbbing head. 'Yes, as in Ramsay Street.'

'Cancel it, Ruby.'

'I can't. Well…I can, but there's an exorbitant fee attached to the privilege. I haven't had a holiday in…' I couldn't remember my last holiday.

'You don't take holidays, darling. You couldn't even come to our wedding without feeling the need to return to work,' said Fran, with an ounce or two of resentment. 'We're coming over with cupcakes. Is there anything you need me to do?'

'Could you put on your lawyer hat and determine whether I'm eligible for one of those online visas?'

'I'll do that. Call Aunt Daphne, darling. I think she lives near Melbourne or Sydney or something. She'll be able to recommend somewhere to stay. See you soon.'

I hobbled around my stinking flat in search of a pen to jot down a To Do list. On the back of a gas bill, I wrote:

1. Call Daphne
2. Shower
3. Ice toe
4. Dispose of empties; spray Air Wick
5. Confirm visa
6. Pack
   6.1 Pack Toolkit
7. Go to airport
8. Buy newspaper
9. Inform parents.

My mother's sister, Daphne, is our family's black sheep. Mummy, the eldest of their clan, is a judge. Her brother, Benjamin, is in private practice. My late grandfather, who was a silk, was the son of an attorney-general.

Daphne 'owns a bakery in the colonies' (according to Grandma) and is a lesbian to boot. At Christmas, hers are the purple tissue-wrapped parcels adorned with koala gift tags, clashing with the cream and gold theme of my grandmother's eight-foot fir. Mummy has long phone calls with Daphne where they laugh and reminisce like Fran and I do, but the rest of the family whisper her name as if she's deceased.

A barking dog answered Daphne's phone. 'Shut up, Pansy!' said a harsh Australian accent. 'Hello?'

'Daphne?'

'Who's calling?'

'Ruby.'

'Hold on a minute.' Stomp, stomp, stomp. 'Daph, phone. If it's a telemarketer tell them to fuck off or I'll report them. It's almost midnight.'

'Daphne speaking,' sang a voice that could easily have been my mother's.

'Hello, Daphne,' I said, 'I'm sorry for calling so late. It's Ruby...your niece.'

'Ruby? How lovely to—' The barking continued. 'Shoosh, Pansy!' Silence. 'Sorry about that. My dog's pregnant. The vet says it's normal for her to bark at imaginary things. Ruby, how are you? Is Charlotte all right?'

'Mummy's fine. She and Daddy are at a human rights forum in Paraguay, I think.'

'She's wonderful, your mum. Now tell me about you, Ruby. I think the last time I saw you was when you reversed into the letterbox at Daddy's wake. Or was it Francesca?'

'It was Fran,' I said, recalling the look on my grandmother's face. I was sixteen and in the passenger seat. That was eleven years ago, when I was full of promise, not a notorious unemployed alcoholic banker.

'Your mother tells me you're doing very well at the bank. Your father must be very proud. How are you finding it?'

Ouch. 'As it happens, I'm no longer with the bank.

I'm going on a holiday. To Australia. Melbourne actually. Tonight. Arriving Saturday. Hence the call. Do you have time to catch up for a cup of tea while I'm there?'

'Of course. How wonderful, Ruby. I'd love to see you. Where are you staying?'

'I haven't booked anywhere yet—this trip is quite spontaneous. Is there somewhere you'd recommend?'

'With me, of course.'

'No, I wouldn't want to impose.'

'Nonsense, I won't have you being polite with me. I insist. Stay with Debs and me. She's just bought a nice house in the Yarra Valley. We're going to spend a couple of weeks out there.'

None of us had met Daphne's partner—'her beau', as Mummy puts it. 'Well, if it's not too much trouble,' I said, 'I'd love to go to the Yarra Valley.'

'No trouble at all,' she said. 'Text me your flight number and I'll pick you up from Tullamarine. Can't wait to see you. Love to Fran...'

I had made it to Item 4 on my list when Fran arrived. Clem's riotous ringlets sprayed out from under a rainbow beanie that captured every colour on her person from the orange *Dora the Explorer* pyjama top to the pale pink tutu and navy-blue ribbed tights.

'Clementine decided to dress herself this morning,' said Fran, pulling the long, dark-blonde hair I used to plait from the collar of her Burberry mac. 'You're going to be fine, Ruby,' she convinced herself, shifting her gaze from my left eye to my right. 'Everything's going to be fine.'

'Mummy,' said Clem, crouching on the floor, 'Aunty Wooby's toe is fat.'

26

'I kicked it,' I said.

'It looks like the cupcake I made you, Aunty Wooby.' Clem pulled out an old cake tin bearing the Queen Mother's rusty face and unveiled a squat cupcake smothered in red and yellow icing. 'See?' She handed it to me. The resemblance was uncanny.

'You need to ice and elevate this,' said Fran. 'Immediately. Sit down. I'll make you a cup of tea.' She waltzed into the kitchen, wincing at the sight of my lime-encrusted kettle.

Fran morphed into the kind of big sister she was when I was three—enabling and incapacitating all at once. While Clem jumped and then slept on my bed, Fran arranged a visa, registered my whereabouts with the Foreign Office, packed a change of clothes, strapped my toe, fed us a homemade supper, refilled my ice-trays and separated like items into labelled zip-lock bags.

'I'm not going on *I'm a Celebrity...Get Me Out of Here!*' I reminded her. 'Melbourne is a rather large city.'

'Remember to thank me when you can find a clean pair of pants in an instant,' said Sister Superior.

Clem was snoring like a wild boar by the time we were ready to go to Paddington. Fran buckled her nasal pixie into the car seat as I switched off the boiler and bounced my suitcase down the stairs.

We passed the kaleidoscope of sorbet-coloured houses on Elgin Crescent, the young couples at trendy Westbourne Grove restaurants, the late-night walkers with their iPods and knapsacks at Lancaster Gate before pulling in at Paddington Station.

Fran turned to me from the driver's seat. 'I'll miss you, Ruby.'

'Me too,' I said, attempting to suppress the anxiety building beneath my sternum.

'Bye, Aunty Wooby,' yawned Clem from the back seat.

I reached back to kiss her forehead. 'You look after your mummy for me, won't you?'

'Say hello to Kylie Danone,' yelled Clem out the window as I wheeled my bag inside.

I looked back and caught a glimpse of my sister blotting away a tear.

Meet the family

The man at Immigration was called Bruce. I shouldn't have laughed, but in my jet-lagged delirium I remembered Daddy's impassioned re-enactments of the Bruce sketch from Monty Python. This Bruce didn't appreciate my good cheer.

'I can't see your visa here, Miss Stanhope.' He flipped through my passport and scratched his mousy beard.

'Oh yes, sorry, I almost forgot—I have a printed receipt here. It's one of those emergency ones for citizens of the EU.' I removed it from the zip-locked bag marked 'Important Travel Documents' in my sister's handwriting.

'I see.' Bruce turned a page. 'You've written here that you're staying at Aunt Daphne's in the Yarra Valley. Do you have an address for this aunt of yours and maybe a surname?'

Having slept for much of the 23-hour journey, I'd only got around to completing the paperwork mid-queue, resting on the dreadlocked backpacker in front of me.

'Um, no, I don't have an address for her, but she's just outside—I could call and ask if you like. Her surname is Partridge.' I was smiling like an idiot. 'Unless...I don't think she's married. She could have taken her partner's name. Do you have gay marriage here yet?'

Bruce scrawled 'Partridge' on the form.

'What's the purpose of your visit?'

'I was made redundant, so I'm having a holiday while I figure out what to do next.'

'Unemployed?'

'Yes, but I was a senior analyst at a very reputable investment bank until quite recently.'

Shut up, Ruby, counselled my head.

'Right, so when are you going home?' asked Bruce, perusing the Kazak visa in my passport.

'I've booked a flexible return leg, so who knows? I could be grape-picking in the Yarra Valley by sunset!'

Bruce closed my passport and looked me in the eye. 'No, Miss Stanhope. This is not a working holiday visa. It does not entitle you to pick anything. And if you are not on a plane by the time your visa expires, you will be in this country unlawfully. Do you understand me?'

Don't react, Ruby. Just say yes, said my head. 'Yes,' I said.

'Good.' Bruce tapped his stamp in the ink pad twice and slammed it on a blank page in my passport. 'Welcome to Australia.'

It hadn't been the smoothest of border experiences. My subconscious had expected someone resembling Alf Stewart from Summer Bay to give me an affable 'G'day, love' before helping me with my luggage and discussing our latest Ashes loss. I'd always assumed Australians were a friendly people, forgetting that we were responsible for the development of their bureaucratic systems.

In the arrivals lounge, Samsonite in tow, I scanned the crowd. A news crew was conducting an interview with a grey-haired man in chinos. A woman crouched down to her two children, pointing out their travel-weary father; they ran to embrace him. A businesswoman on her mobile phone manoeuvred her luggage towards a chauffeur with a sign bearing her name. That used to be me.

There stood my aunt. She hadn't noticed me. She was a taller, younger version of my mother. She wore a long lavender linen dress with a baggy white shirt open over the top of it. Her skin was tanned, particularly around her décolletage and sandalled feet, where the sun had wrinkled it. Her long, dark-blonde hair was plaited loosely and tortoiseshell-frame sunglasses kept it from her face, revealing a pair of dangling earrings: blush-pink blister pearls encased in silver. Her kind eyes caught mine and I picked a path through the crowd towards her.

'Ruby!'

When I reached her she placed a hand on each shoulder and examined my face as if she was looking for something. 'Hi, Daphne, you look well,' I said, leaning in.

'You're just like Charlotte, except with your dad's chin—which, believe me, is a good thing. You don't want this chin, my girl.' She kissed my cheeks. 'Gorgeous.' She took off her shirt and grabbed one of my bags. 'Now, I want you to prepare yourself, Ruby. You're about to experience heat. When I say heat, I don't mean the kind we have in London every second June when everybody takes their clothes off and goes to Hyde Park. I mean proper heat. It will feel foul at first, but then you'll get used to it.'

She marched towards the sliding doors. I followed, thinking it was an offensive presumption that in all my twenty-eight years I'd never experienced a Mediterranean summer.

Then it hit me. It was not dissimilar to the feeling you get when you open a fan-forced oven to check the progress of a roast dinner; but I couldn't close this oven. The hot wind chapped my lips and sucked every last teaspoon of moisture from my skin. 'Oh my God,' I squeaked.

My aunt took one look at me and commandeered the luggage trolley. Feet hot in my leather ballet flats, I cursed myself for my choice of outfit: black leggings and a pale pink tunic with three-quarter-length sleeves. It had seemed a perfectly good idea at the time—a cotton-blend dress with cotton tights—but now, it felt like a parker in the afternoon sun. My hair, made frizzy by the Hong Kong lounge shampoo, stuck to my neck like a mohair scarf. I could feel my face turning dark red.

'We're almost there now.' My aunt pointed to a nearby car park. 'Mine's the four-wheel drive.'

The white van was like a mirage in the desert. I got a surge of energy as I strode towards it. 'I'm going to unlock the doors,' Daphne said in the tone of a rescue worker talking someone through an un-anesthetised amputation, 'but we need to cool it down before we can get inside.'

She opened the door, put the keys in the ignition, turned on the air-conditioning and then stepped back. I wanted to yell at her. Inside the car couldn't possibly be any hotter than outside.

'Right, it should be cool enough now,' she finally said.

With a polite smile plastered on my face, I heaved my Samsonite into the boot and leaped into the car. The air-conditioning blasted my face and began to dry the dark pink sweat patches under each arm and on the back of my tunic.

'You'll get used to it, darling.' She handed me a bottle of water from a cooler box in the back.

I gulped insanely. As we pulled onto the freeway I spotted a road-worker sitting on a folding chair, jiggling a teabag in his thermos, with his feet up on an orange traffic cone. Close by was a blue sign reading EMER-GENCY REFUGE AREA—SOS PHONE. *Why isn't he using it?* my head wondered.

Aunt Daphne laughed at my empty water bottle and handed me another.

'Thanks. Is this normal?'

'Not really,' she replied. 'It's been a stinking hot summer. It's nice to be in the company of a compatriot who shares my pain. Debs says I'm a sook.'

Even with leftovers of her accent, most of my aunt's Englishness had gone. It was strange. She was a sort of hybrid.

'Tell me about Debs,' I said, catching a glimpse of my sweaty face in the side mirror. I was living up to my name.

'She came into my bakery one Monday. I remember it clearly. She was wearing a tailored black pant suit and killer suede heels. I knew instantly she was a lawyer, but figured she was a straight one.

'She was on her mobile when she approached the counter. I tell my staff not to serve people who are on the phone because I think it's poor manners on the customer's part. She pointed to a sandwich and a flat white on the menu and put twenty bucks on the counter. One of my staff asked her to step aside. Debs demanded to see the manager.

'When I got to her, she was still on her phone. She had the audacity to hold her finger up to silence me. "Listen, all I want's a fucking sandwich and this little prick won't give it to me because he's got some precious bullshit attitude about me being on the phone."'

We turned off the freeway and down a bustling suburban street.

'I just shook my head and pointed to the sign on the wall, which says FINISH YOUR CALL, THEN ORDER. By this stage, Debs was really aggro.'

'Aggro?'

'Aggressive. Anyway, she chucked a tantrum and threw her folder on a nearby table, which knocked a bottle of homemade chutney all over her beautiful shoes and my sandals. "Mother fucker!" she screamed.'

'She sounds lovely.'

Daphne laughed. 'I offered her a kitchen wipe, dustpan and brush and asked her to clean up the mess and leave. She did. After work that day, I was locking up and she was outside. She apologised and offered to buy me a drink...'

Outside, Melbournians were enjoying their Saturday. A sun-kissed couple in flip-flops wandered across the pedestrian crossing in front of us. Underdressed on account of the heat, they linked arms; he carried a picnic basket. At the next lights, a lady drove past in a Range Rover full of sweaty six-year-old footballers sipping from McDonald's takeaway cups. Before long, I was off in the land of nod.

A falsetto version of 'Land of Hope and Glory' blaring from my aunt's phone woke me from my slumber.

'What?' she said. 'Calm down, darling. She's *what*? Oh dear. We're almost there. Just get some hot towels ready.'

'Pansy's in labour,' she said, picking up speed. 'The vet said it was at least a week or two away. Debs isn't much of a dog person.'

'Are we meeting them at the hospital?'

Daphne laughed. 'It's a home birth.'

I texted Fran.

Arrived safely—thank you for zip-locked travel documents. Unfathomably hot. In car with Daphne, en route to Yarra Valley. Her dog is in labour. Love to Clem xo

We left the monotony of smooth bitumen for a narrow, rough, dirt road. Branches from wayward silver-leafed trees scraped against the car as we drove uphill through dwarfing eucalypts. Soon, across a vine-lined valley, I could make out the shape of a house with a corrugated-iron roof.

We pulled up and Daphne leaped out of the car. 'Sorry Ruby,' she called over her shoulder. 'Help yourself to a shower and the fridge.'

I dragged my luggage across the gravel, onto the vast deck and into the cool house. Glossy floating timber floors spanned the open space. Off-white walls were decorated with exotic masks and reclaimed doors. Two beaten, cherry leather chesterfields sat alongside a crisp white egg chair underscored by an intricate Turkish rug.

A statuesque woman padded barefoot down the hall towards me. Debs. She was quite a bit younger than my aunt. Dark, arched eyebrows, huge brown eyes. Her olive skin was wrinkle-free. Glossy, straight black hair cut with deliberate unevenness hovered above her shoulders. 'G'day Ruby.' She rolled up the sleeves of a white tuxedo shirt. 'Let me show you to your room.'

I wasn't prepared for what I saw there. Pansy, a white bull-terrier with a black eye-patch, shivered, shook and gasped for breath, her stomach swollen and writhing. The polished floorboards were slick with thick, kelp-green slime. Pansy was using her front paws to slide around the four-poster bed. Daphne, sitting on the floor, seemed to be facilitating a Lamaze class for her pet. It looked like a *House & Garden* Halloween shoot.

'Ruby,' said Daphne, panting in unison with Pansy. 'Thank God you're here. Debs is as useless as tits on a bull. Be a dear. Go to the computer in the study down the hall and find out from the internet if there's anything I need to do to assist Pansy with the delivery.'

'Tits on a bull?'

'I'll get the wine,' said Debs.

Relieved that she hadn't asked me to mop up, I ran to the room at the end of the hall and Googled 'my dog is in labour what should I do?'

'Go to the vet, you moron' was the first result. Then I found something useful. 'Okay,' I yelled, 'the green slime means the placenta has detached and the puppies are about to be born.'

'Go on.'

'Puppies are usually born within twenty minutes of each other but bitches can have a bit of a break between deliveries.'

'It seems wrong to call a pregnant lady a bitch,' Debs interjected, joining me in the study with two glasses of chardonnay.

'Shut up, Deborah,' called Daphne, 'you're not helping. Go on, Ruby.'

'Apparently,' I continued yelling, 'the pups will probably

come out tail-first, so you should cut your nails and make sure they're filed in case you've got to help pull one out.'

Debs groaned, gulping her wine on the recliner beside me.

'The house is lovely, Debs. How many bedrooms are there?' I had just read a paragraph about the importance of leaving the bitch and her litter undisturbed in their whelping room.

'Just the two,' she said. 'Daph's and mine, and yours and Pansy's.'

'Oh.'

'I think the first pup is coming,' squealed Daphne.

Debs and I scampered back to my bedroom, spilling wine on the way.

'That was a bit of an ordeal,' yawned Debs an hour later. She helped Daphne off the floor, where Pansy was licking three fairy-floss-pink pups in her makeshift nest. We tiptoed out of the birthing suite and onto the vast deck, where we topped up our wineglasses and watched the sun sinking into the Yarra Valley.

Debs' house topped a hill dwarfed by faraway mountains. I could see the undulating ground for miles around us, the landscape dotted with houses, vineyards and the occasional distant steeple. As the light dimmed to a yellower hue, kangaroos sprang like shadow puppets from the darkness, bounding in time, a trio of silhouettes across a distant ridge. 'Look,' I pointed, and my hosts smiled at me the way parents do when their children show them planes in the sky. Over smaller hills to my left, the remaining light formed pathways between symmetrical rows of vines, like a catwalk for the grapes. The sunset collaborated with the sprinkler system to create peach fairy lights in the mist above the garden bed. Then, for the finale, the sky reddened before settling into twilight.

An intoxicating smell pulled me out of my trance. I inhaled. 'What *is* that?'

'Bread,' said Daphne, breaking its crust against the wooden chopping block she had just carried from the kitchen. 'It's a new sourdough recipe I'm trialling.'

'Smells fucking incredible,' said Debs, kissing my aunt's cheek.

More people should have bakers for aunts, I thought as I sank my teeth into warm bread dunked in extra virgin olive oil.

'Shit.' Debs broke the peace. 'We forgot about Benny's party.'

'He'll understand,' said Daphne. 'It's not every day your dog gives birth.'

'Benny?' I asked.

'Benedict Jones,' said Daphne. 'A local winemaker.'

Debs checked her watch. 'I said at least one of us would be there, but with Pansy imploding I completely forgot. I don't feel like going, do you?'

My aunt shook her head. 'Ruby could go in our place,' she suggested.

They both turned to me.

'I'd love to,' I lied, 'but I was thinking about getting some shut-eye, what with the jet lag.' My eyes were having a hard time staying open.

'Great idea.' Debs didn't seem to have listened. 'You're into wines? This guy runs a boutique joint. Bit of a pants man, but not a bad bloke. He'll show you around—might even take you to the vines if you're interested.'

'What does he make?'

'Pinot, mainly,' said Debs. 'Good stuff.'

Don't even think about it, cautioned my head.

'You mustn't think you *have* to go,' said Daphne, slicing more bread, 'but if you do want to take a nap, the only place is the couch now that Pansy and her brood have taken over your room.'

I squeezed my eyes shut. 'Count me in,' I said in the spirit of spontaneity, my head's disapproval palpable.

'Great,' said Debs. 'I've got a bloody work call, but I can easily do it in the car. Let's leave in half an hour. Suit you, Ruby?'

I nodded and hurried to the shower, wondering why they bothered installing a hot tap when the cold alone was so balmy. As I towelled off, I saw a new text message on my phone.

> Glad you're safe. C has new fascination with Tooth Fairy. Wants me to assess wobbliness of each fang before bed. D got a call from chairman about The Email—M & D send their love. Channel 4 wants an interview.
> Miss u. Fran x

Bollocks. Putting my face on in the bathroom, I called Fran on loudspeaker.

'Good morning, this is Clementine, how may I erect your call?'

As I laughed I drew a charcoal stroke from left nostril to earlobe in eye-pencil. 'Shit.'

'I *beg* your pardon?' demanded Clem.

'Clem, it's Aunty Ruby, sorry—I just accidentally drew on my face.'

'Well, hello, Aunty Wooby, I am sorry about your face but that is no reason to say square words.'

'Sorry, Clem. Is Mummy there?'

'MUMMY! AUNTY WOOBY IS ON THE PHONE AND SHE SAID "SHIT"!'

'Ruby, you didn't,' said Fran, on the bedroom extension.

'Clem said "erect",' I defended myself, dabbing at my calligraphy with make-up remover.

'Hang up now, please, Clementine.' Clunk.

'I should thank you, I guess,' said Fran. 'Perhaps a new love for profanities will replace her obsession with the Tooth Fairy.'

'Surely it's just a little bit sweet,' I said, imagining my niece standing on 'tipsy toes' at the bathroom sink, watching for wiggles in the mirror.

'Sweet? No. Annoying? Yes. We're off to the dentist this morning. Poor man. I'm a bad mother if I don't constantly check for loose teeth and I'm a bad mother for propagating the fallacy that a small, very generous lady is known to spend her evenings breaking into homes to look beneath children's pillows, taking discarded bodily items for a few quid. Why do we do it? She's going to hate me when she discovers the truth.'

'She'll hate you if she's the only little girl at school who doesn't get money from the Tooth Fairy,' I said. 'Is Daddy very upset?'

'No, not about the email. In fact, Mummy forwarded it to her colleagues on the bench. She couldn't be prouder. Daddy's furious with the bank. They are understandably hurt that you didn't call them to say you'd lost your job and absconded to Australia.'

'I just haven't had time,' I said, 'and besides, they're in Paraguay.'

'Uruguay.'

'I get my guays confused.'

'You are staying with Mummy's sister, Ruby. The least you could do is send her a text. They said they emailed but you didn't reply.'

'That's because my email address belongs to my former employer. I'll call them tonight. When are they due back?'

'Next week. Tell me, how's Australia?'

'Lovely. Flight was great. I slept all the way. Quite sure I drooled on the man next to me. I don't have a room here because Pansy used it to deliver her pups. Very sweet little pink fluff-balls. I'll take a photo for Clem. The Yarra Valley is breathtaking.' I took her off loudspeaker. 'Aunt Daphne seems very happy with Debs.'

'What's she like?' I could hear her filing her nails in the background and felt homesick.

'Debs is about as graceful as a Hummer but looks like Cleopatra on a date night,' I whispered, vigorously brushing the knots from my hair. 'Daphne's like a relaxed, younger version of Mummy and clearly loves being a baker. We had fresh sourdough for supper. How's Mark?'

'Fine.' The filing accelerated. 'If you *like* that sort of thing.'

I stopped brushing and put her back on loudspeaker. 'What sort of thing?'

'Absenteeism,' she sighed. 'Clem hardly sees him. He's always "in conference" according to his PA. Last night he got home at half three and left at seven. When do you think *you'll* be home?'

'I only 'ust 'ot 'ere,' I said, blotting my lipstick. 'I'm going to a party tonight at a local winery. The Immigration man wasn't particularly pleased by the idea of me overstaying my visa.'

'Nor am I.' It hadn't occurred to me that she might miss me, but a blip in her voice told me she did. 'Make sure you stay away from that peanut noise tonight,' she joked.

'Talk soon.'

I pulled on the sky-blue maxi-dress I bought during the Net-A-Porter sale last year and left the bathroom feeling refreshed. A hint of sunlight had already kissed my cheeks and the in-flight sleep had erased the grey circles beneath my eyes. The dress, which I had only just cut the tags off, made my irises appear bluer and whites whiter. It also made the molehills on my chest appear even smaller, so I rifled through my Toolkit for the One Cup Ups and made mountains of them, even if they were day-hike mountains as opposed to the more exotic altitude-sickness-inducing ones my ex used to climb for fun. It might have worked if he'd spent more time mounting me. I stepped into tan Miu Miu wedges—the open toe freeing my still-swollen digit—and fastened the clasps on the coral earrings Daddy had bought me in Positano.

In the fogged-up corner of the bathroom mirror, I wrote:

1. Call parents
2. Check email
3. Buy bronzer
4. Stop writing To Do lists—you're on holiday.

The party's party

A gunmetal-grey Aston Martin grumbled as it pulled up in front of the house. Its mechanical roof lowered, revealing Debs. 'Shit, you scrub up all right,' she said. 'Jump in. I've just muted this conference call—client wants to embark on an IP dispute with a Chinese JV partner—mind if I do this on speaker while we drive?'

'By all means.' I knew she was a successful lawyer, but her personality lent itself more to hard hat than wig.

The sound of an under-populated boardroom on speaker-phone was familiar to me. Debs cut in across a distressed middle-aged man. 'Listen guys, I could spin you a whole lot of bullshit about how we could stop these fuckers, but I'd be lying. Bottom line is this: Australia doesn't have a reciprocal enforcement of judgment treaty with China, so even if we took 'em to court here and won, which would take time and cost millions, we'd end up with a bit of paper worth less than a square of loo roll in China. The Chinese have got a billion people to think about, so they couldn't give a flying fuck about a bunch of Aussie lawyers with their undies in a twist. Here's my advice: hang up, go forth and enjoy the rest of your weekend. Let bygones be bygones, gentlemen.'

They took her advice. It was poetic: the best counsel I'd ever heard.

'When I was a banker, working on big deals,' I said, hating the past tense, 'I'd have called the lawyers every day if they gave commercial advice like that.'

'That's the general idea,' said Debs, plugging her iPod into the car and selecting some opera. 'I love my clients and my clients love me cos I don't bullshit them.'

We zoomed around the valley, the high beams spotlighting a host of hand-painted signs pointing to tiny wineries. We stopped at one.

'Call us when you're ready to be picked up.'

'Aren't you coming in?' I was suddenly nervous.

'Nah,' Debs said, 'you'll be right—just find Benedict Jones.'

I walked up the drive and was greeted by a gentleman wearing a hideous pinstripe suit.

'Finally,' he said. 'There's a delivery drop-off point at the back of the building. Leave it there.'

'Excuse me?'

'The raffle prize.'

'I'm not a courier.'

He held his hand up to silence me and pointed to a tiny bluetooth headset in his left ear.

'Sorry about that,' he said, 'we've been waiting on a delivery.'

'I'm looking for Benedict Jones.'

'You're here for the fundraiser?'

I wondered whether my Miu Mius would take me back down the drive fast enough to catch up with Debs.

'Miss...'

'Stanhope. Ruby Stanhope.'

'I don't have you on my list—who are you with?'

'Myself,' I said. 'I was to be here with my aunt Daphne Partridge, and her partner Debs, Deborah...' I didn't know her last name.

'Sorry, I don't have you here.'

'Look, Pansy had puppies today, which was unexpected, and neither Aunt Daphne nor Debs was able to make tonight's party so I've come instead. They said to speak with Benedict Jones, so if you could show me to him I'd very much appreciate it.'

He pointed to his headset. I fantasised about ripping it from his ear and crushing it under a Miu.

'Hi,' said a voice behind me.

I swivelled and another unsuitably suited man extended his hand to shake mine. 'Hi,' I said, 'Ruby Stanhope.'

'Luke Harley. You'll have to excuse my colleague, Ruby; he was just checking you're not press, which you're not, are you?'

'No. Recovering investment banker, actually.'

'Good.' Luke walked me under an arch crawling with star jasmine and along a candlelit path towards a suited congregation in the vineyard. It looked like a vine-side funeral.

'Nobody told me the dress code was lounge suit,' I said, embarrassed by my tropical goddess outfit.

'It's not supposed to be,' said Luke. 'It's just that most of us don't own anything else.'

'The man at the door said this is a fundraiser. What's the charity?'

He laughed; then his phone rang. He gestured towards a Clooneyesque man, with substantially more salt than pepper, and centurion pecs. 'GI Joe senior over there is Jones. I'll be back in a minute.'

The only other person at the function in civilian clothes wove through the vines towards me.

'I don't think we've met.' Benedict Jones extended his hand.

Pants man plus jet lag equals regret, my head reminded me.

'I'm Daphne Partridge's niece, Ruby.'

'Pleased to meet you.' He shook my hand. 'Welcome to Benedict Estate.'

'Thank you, it's lovely to be here.'

'Your accent is cute,' he said. 'Let me guess—English?'

Psychic, groaned my head.

'Yes, I'm from London.'

'I'm told I have a very good ear.' He lowered his voice. 'Shall I show you my vines?'

I tried to keep my eyes from rolling and accepted his arm. 'So what do you grow here?' I glanced around at the tailored monochrome and wished I didn't look like a big blue parrot.

'Pinot,' he said, 'and a little chardonnay.'

'I hear pinot's plagued with problems. Or is that just a vinicultural legend?'

'It is tougher to grow than any other grape,' he said, 'but it's worth the chase.'

Groan.

He picked a single grape for me from a perfect bunch.

'Eat it,' he directed, dropping it into my mouth. It didn't taste like I'd imagined. I could taste the spices, but not the fruit.

I unhooked myself from his arm. 'Tell me, do you often have parties like this?'

'Just for Max. We go way back.'

'Is it his birthday?'

'You're charming, Ruby,' he chuckled, until he realised my question was genuine. 'Max Masters is the Leader of the Opposition.'

'As in a *politician*?'

I felt like a dill. There I was assuming I would meet a bunch of grape-lovers. Instead, I would spend the evening with a bunch of apes in suits expecting me to know who they were. The only politicians I knew were the ones I detested for taxing luxury goods and capping bankers' bonuses.

'Mingle!' directed Benedict, looking over my shoulder at a short-skirt suit. I found the bar in the marquee and mingled with the wines, where I was rudely interrupted by a woman sporting big teeth and a too-tight ponytail— think rabbit with an up-do.

'Christine,' she announced, thrusting her hand into mine.

'Ruby.' I felt her hand deftly deal me a business card.

'I work for the property development industry.'

'I see.' I skimmed her card. 'In what capacity?'

'Well, you know, helping them out here and there with a few bits and pieces.'

'No,' I said, 'I don't know. What kinds of bits and pieces?'

'Well, when there's an issue that is dear to the industry, I represent its viewpoint.'

'So you're their lobbyist?'

'Not exactly,' she said impatiently. 'Tell me about you, Ruby. What do you do?'

'I'm an astronaut.'

'Aviation, then?'

'No, that was a joke.'

She cocked her head to one side and scrambled for the abort button. 'It was lovely meeting you, Ruby.'

'And you, Christine.' One down, seventy to go. I went back to a fresh and zesty sauvignon blanc, hoping it might wake me up a bit, but the hum of dull conversation lulled me. My body slumped against the cushioned bar.

'Ruby?' said Luke, rescuing me from an imminent bout of narcolepsy.

I smiled, trying to wake myself up.

'What brings you here?' He loosened his tie, which reminded me of a banana tree on account of its yellow, brown and green stripes. It was a poor match for his ill-fitting, three-button charcoal suit. Come to think of it, banana trees make a poor match for most things. I wanted to flip it over and note down the maker. Nut-brown socks didn't inspire hope, especially when tucked into scuffed black shoes with plastic-tipped nylon laces: the kind I'd worn at school. Aside from that, he was pleasant to look at. Kind green eyes, a square jaw, albeit in need of a razor, like his overgrown buzz cut.

'My aunt's dog went into labour this afternoon just as I arrived. She and her partner were down to go to this function, so they asked me to go on their behalf.'

'I meant, what are you doing in Australia?'

'Oh, I'm pinot-hunting through the Yarra Valley.' It sounded so much better than the long version.

'So you're in the wine business as well as an investment banker?'

'No,' I said, 'three days ago I was an investment banker—in emerging markets, actually—and I was made redundant. Economically speaking, things are a bit grim. I got riotously drunk on an incredible Toolangi pinot noir—'

'Good choice,' he interrupted.

'I know,' I said, 'and, in the midst of my inebriation, booked myself a ticket to Melbourne. My aunt and her partner have a place in Warburton. So here I am.'

'So all in all, a sizable couple of days.' Luke sipped his wine, then gestured towards a man in the corner. 'That's my guy.'

Luke hadn't exactly struck me as gay, what with the banana tree. I took a closer look at his partner. He occupied visual space as if he was spotlit. It wasn't that he was attractive: average height, thin grey hair, an ecru complexion. He wouldn't have looked out of place at an auditors' convention, and yet there was something magnetic about him. He was the guy you listened to at a dinner party or who caught your eye at a gallery.

Benedict Jones took to a stage made of upturned wine crates and tapped his glass with the end of a fork. 'Friends,' he said, 'we're here tonight to show our support for Max Masters.'

People clapped politely.

'Max is a great friend of ours. A proud Melbournian. Max has been engaged in this community and others all over Australia for most of his working life. He has been a military man, a small-business owner and a mayor, and now he's in Canberra working in some building with a flag on top.' People laughed.

'What many of you probably don't know is that he was once a grape-picker, but in the Barossa, which is probably where he went wrong.

'Unlike most pickers, Max isn't just here for the harvest; he's here when it's tough too. After the bushfire season when we lost some of our vines, Max was the guy who'd call every week to offer his help. Come to think of it, he's not just a friend of the wine industry; he's a friend of all Australian businesses. He understands us. He understands that some times are great and others are a real struggle. But he's there with us, all the time, to help make it better.

'So, it's my privilege tonight to host this function for the man I hope will add another line to his CV at the election next year. Give it up for Max Masters, Leader of the Opposition and next prime minister of Australia.'

Profuse clapping filled the open space and Luke's guy took to the stage.

'Thank you all for coming, not that many of us needed encouragement when we heard our wonderful host would be putting on a dinner with matched wines from all around this beautiful valley.'

Benedict Jones nodded appreciatively to more applause. Max continued: 'But this valley, which is full of great Australian businesses, has had its fair share of turmoil. When bushfires swept across it, we all wanted to do something to help. And we did. Many of you here—in fact, probably all of you and the businesses you represent—have made some contribution to help this community pick itself up and dust off the ashes.

'I'm proud to see how far the Yarra Valley has come. I am proud to see businesses, homes and lives rebuilt. Because *we* did this. All of us.'

Approving nods moved like a Mexican wave across the room.

'That's a nation I want to lead. That's an energy I want to harness. That's a community I want to serve.

'Now, as I walk around this room tonight, I look forward to hearing from you about how we can make this nation even better. That's enough from me; enjoy the wine—in moderation, of course!'

More applause fizzled, replaced by loud, individual conversations as Max worked the room, followed closely by Luke.

No one will notice if you leave now, said my head. Edging closer to the loos, I looked to see if there was a side door somewhere.

'Trying to escape?' asked Luke.

'Yes, but it's difficult when you're dressed as a Smurf.'

'I can imagine,' he said. 'Look, I'd be a little offended if you left now. I've rearranged things so we can sit together. I've had a gutful of fundraisers—one every night this week—so it'll be fun not to talk shop.' He paused. 'If you're willing to stay, of course.'

'Why not? All that waits for me at home is a couch and a pair of lesbians.'

'I wish I could say the same for my hotel room,' he laughed.

'So you're, as it were, ambidextrous?'

'Huh?'

'It's quite unusual to meet a gay man with a penchant for girl-on-girl action,' I pointed out.

'Huh?'

'Didn't you say the Opposition Leader is "your guy"?'

'He's my *boss*,' he said, losing colour.

'An office romance?'

'Good grief.' He was mortified. 'I'm straight as a rod. Not that kind of rod.' His colour returned and darkened. 'Straight as a cricket bat, a really manly cricket bat. It's the suit, isn't it?'

'No, the suit has the opposite effect.'

'Thank Christ—this is my only clean one,' he said, mistaking my insult for a compliment. 'I'm going to need another glass of wine.'

We moved to a table writhing with property developers, each of them rocking back on their chair to get closer to Max. This left Luke and me to chat about the Australian wine industry over dinner. He talked me through the various challenges it faced, courtesy of both the wildfires and the global financial crisis, for which he blamed 'my people'. When a pair of leggy lobbyists strutted towards him, Luke had me call his mobile just in time to excuse himself from an odious entree of name-dropping.

As I cracked the surface of my crème brûlée, I gave him my precis of what was happening to the economy back home. Then we discussed everything from the timing of the Australian federal election, due the following year, to our host's wine selection; our brutal tasting notes included 'chewy' and 'hints of wet dog'.

A few raffle draws later, Luke stopped mid-sentence and stood up. 'I just got the nod—he's ready to go.'

'The nod?'

'When he's ready to go, Max gives me a sign so that I can pave a smooth exit. Otherwise, he'd never leave these gigs—everyone wants a piece of him.'

'So you're going too?' His departure would take the fun out of fundraiser.

'Yep,' he said, 'we've got an interview first thing in the morning, so I'll be up at sparrow's fart to read the papers.'

'It's been a pleasure meeting you.'

'You too, Ruby.' He reached into his pocket for a card. 'If you've got time to come up to Melbourne next week, I'd like to have a chat with you about working as a financial policy advisor on our team.'

I choked on a sip of sickly sticky. 'You're kidding.'

'Here's my card,' said Luke. 'Come to Melbourne for a coffee.'

I smiled awkwardly, partly because I didn't know what to say and partly because a globule of dessert wine was tickling my trachea. Tears welled in my eyes as I tried not to cough.

Luke stared. 'You're choking, aren't you?'

I nodded. Max joined us.

Excellent, my head enthused.

'Max Masters.' He shook my hand.

'Ru...' My lungs failed. I reddened like a chameleon at La Tomatina.

'Nice to meet you, Roo,' he said, moving towards the door.

'Are you all right?' asked Luke, torn between his boss and me.

I nodded.

'Awkward,' Luke observed, then he winked. 'See you later.'

I tried to wink back, but it felt more like a glistening, one-eyed squint, followed by a loud bark and pig-like snort. Thankfully, Luke and Max were disappearing into the back seat of a white saloon.

On the driveway as I waited for a lift, in a jet-lagged haze at the end of my first day in Australia, I stood beneath the vivid night sky and tilted Luke's card towards me. The moonlight hit each embossed letter. Luke Harley. Chief of Staff. Office of the Leader of the Opposition. My head caught me considering his offer. *What are you doing, Ruby?* it asked. I couldn't answer.

The morning after

Feeling seedy thanks to the putrid blend of day-old jet lag and matching wines, I awoke the next morning to the sound of oven trays clashing. I peeled myself off the hot couch.

'Hope I didn't wake you, darling,' said Daphne, tying a white apron over her lilac nightgown.

'Not at all.'

Debs was on the deck reading the papers. I wandered out to join her in my pyjamas and sunglasses. She folded the corner of the *Herald* and craned her long neck to greet me. 'Morning, kiddo.'

'Thought we might have a little Turkish bread for breakfast,' said Daphne, bringing a steaming rustic loaf to the table. 'Go and grab the poached apricots and ricotta from the fridge, darling.'

'That's my girl,' beamed Debs.

I followed Debs' billowing silk gown into the kitchen.

'So, how was the shindig?' she asked.

'Weird—it was a political fundraiser.'

'Shit, yeah, I should've told you.'

Yes, she should have, said my grumpy head. I carried a cafetière back out to the deck.

'Should have told her what?' asked Daphne, serving the hot bread on earthenware plates.

'That it was a fundraiser for Masters.'

Daphne sighed. 'Anyway, as it turns out, Ruby was offered a job.'

'No I wasn't; he was just suggesting a coffee.'

'Don't be bashful, Ruby. He said he could *use* someone like you.'

'Jesus Christ, that's bolshie,' said Debs. 'I had a feeling Benny would have a crack at keeping you around.' She shot me a cheeky wink.

'It wasn't Benedict,' Daphne said. 'It was Max Masters' Chief of Staff.'

'You're shitting me.' Debs' lips were encrusted with ricotta. 'Isn't little Lukey Harley working for Masters now?'

'You know Luke? He's the one who asked me for a coffee.'

'Luke's a good bloke. He used to be my clerk when I was senior associate. Bright kid: cute one, too. Terrible suits. He was a Melbourne Uni medallist, worked for me while he finished his degree, then as an associate to a High Court judge. When he finished his associateship he got a gig as a policy advisor to someone. That must've been about ten years ago.'

Daphne piled her bread with preserved apricot cheeks and drizzled them with syrup. 'Masters will probably get in at the next election. I can't imagine anyone will be able to stomach another three years of Hugh Patton.'

'Me neither,' Debs agreed. 'Masters is the first half-decent Opposition leader we've seen in a decade. Before now it didn't matter how sick to death people were of Patton. No one's going to jump ship when the economy's gone tits up, not when the alternative's a leaky boat. Masters is different, though.'

'He's a good speaker,' I said. 'I was impressed. The audience was full of sleazy industry types and yet he seemed to connect with everyone there. He was real.'

'You going to take the job then?' asked Debs.

I laughed. They didn't.

'Serious question,' said Debs.

'Look, I'm here on a tourist visa. The closest thing I've had to political experience was competing with my sister for my parents' Chelsea flat when I finished university. I'm an investment banker. I don't even know which party he's from, or which party is in government, or how the system works here—or anywhere for that matter. He hasn't offered me a job and...I'm supposed to be on holiday!'

'Codswallop.'

'I'm sorry?' Now I was annoyed.

'Means horse shit,' Debs explained.

'It might surprise you, but I do in fact know what codswallop means,' I muttered. 'It's an English term. And I appreciate your intentions, but that's not who I am. I'm *me*. I live in *London*. I have a lovely flat in *Notting Hill*. And I'm an *investment banker.*'

'No, you're not,' said Debs.

'Deborah!' My aunt lowered her sunglasses to reveal the full force of her glare.

'Settle, petal,' said Debs. 'Just telling it like it is. There's a wine glut in Australia and an investment banker glut in the UK—you're a dime a dozen, kiddo.'

She wasn't wrong. When I returned to London, I, like thousands of my former colleagues, would march zombie-like to interview after hopeless interview without finding a comparable job. Emerging markets no longer existed. Most markets were well and truly *sub*merged. My future flashed before me. My parents would call everyone they knew, desperate to find me respectable work. I would get some rubbish, back-office contractor role in a two-bit bank and spend every six months begging for renewal. I would be forced to surrender my flat and share a room with Clem at my sister's. I'd have to eBay my wine and my Louboutins.

My aunt's hand on mine broke the panic. 'It doesn't hurt to have coffee with him, love,' she said gently. 'Who knows, politics for you might be like bread for me.'

I channelled my mother for a bit of polite conversational transition. 'I've never asked how you got into baking in the first place.'

'At school,' she said, drizzling syrup from the apricots over her breakfast, 'I was certain I'd become a lawyer. I didn't want to be particularly, though I'd have been quite good at it.

'When I was reading law at university, I had a falling out with your grandmother about my sexuality. I rebelled a bit and took some time off. One night, when I was walking home from a club, I passed a bakery.

'It was about four in the morning and there were three people inside, working away. I envied them. They had their own peaceful, beautiful-smelling world away from the hubbub of normal trading hours, like Father Christmas and his elves.'

'Farver Cwistmiss,' teased Debs, attempting to mimic our accent.

Daphne ignored her. 'Better still, they created bread. Everyone loves the smell of fresh bread. It's primal—a simple, common staple. It meets people's needs. Nobody feels that way when they pay their lawyers.

'So I got an apprenticeship at a French patisserie and deferred my studies. Daddy was delighted, which surprised me. Mother wasn't. Anyway, I love what I do, I'm good at it and it makes money. I own two shops and I'm about to open a third.'

'I've got a meeting in town tomorrow,' said Debs, clearing the plates. 'If you did want to meet up with little Lukey, I could drop you off.'

That evening, I emailed him.

To: Luke.Harley@aph.gov.au

From: Ruby.Stanhope@gmail.com

Luke

Good to meet you last night.

As it happens, I'll be in Melbourne tomorrow and thought I might take you up on that coffee if you're free.

Hope the interview with 'your guy' went well this morning.

Kind regards

Ruby

A few seconds passed.

To: Ruby.Stanhope@gmail.com

From: Luke.Harley@aph.gov.au

R

Come to the CPO (4 Treasury Place) at midday. Ask for me and they'll point you in the right direction.

My totally platonic boss did fine this morning. Doorstopped this arvo too. Check out the six o'clocks.

L

I went looking for Debs and found her lying on the floor talking to the pups. Pansy thumped her tail against the floorboards twice to greet me, alerting Debs to my presence.

'I was just going through some emails.' She grabbed her BlackBerry.

'No, you weren't,' I said, 'you were doting.'

'I don't dote.'

'I know a doter when I see one.'

'They're pink,' she observed, 'like little marshmallows.'

'Indeed. Have you named them yet?'

'Fuck, no.' She sat up. 'You shouldn't sneak up on people.'

'I wanted to ask you a question.'

'Shoot.'

'Luke has asked me to meet him at something called the CPO tomorrow. He also said to watch the six o'clocks and that he had doorstopped. Do you know what any of that means?'

'I think the CPO's the Commonwealth Parliamentary Offices up at Treasury Place.' She stood up and tiptoed out of the bedroom.

I followed her to the kitchen, where Daphne was cooking dinner. 'These are the six o'clocks,' said Debs, flicking on the telly to a balding man with the skin tone of an Oompa Loompa. 'There are three main commercial stations, two of which broadcast the news at six. This is Channel Eleven.'

She opened a bottle of red. 'Ruby's off to have coffee with Luke tomorrow,' she told my aunt.

'Wonderful,' clucked Daphne.

I was drawn to the screen.

'First on tonight's bulletin,' said the Oompa Loompa, 'Prime Minister Hugh Patton participated in a fun run for charity in Canberra today. But Opposition Leader Max Masters suggested that his opponent is a skilled athlete, having had much experience "running away" from his political reality. Senior political correspondent Oscar Franklin has more of the story.'

The report began with footage of a perspiring Prime Minister in a pair of unflatteringly short shorts. Smiling through his exhaustion, he stumbled across the finish line to half-hearted applause.

'With thirty-six degrees on the barometer here in Canberra,' said the even hotter reporter, 'organisers of today's annual Fun Run for Prostate Cancer Awareness were delighted but surprised when the Prime Minister's office called early this morning to say that Hugh Patton was eager to participate—causing speculation that, however severe the temperature outside might be, nothing quite compared to the heat inside the government's party room.

'For at least a fortnight there have been mutterings from prominent government backbenchers that his party is no longer confident Mr Patton can deliver a fifth consecutive win at the next election, due in eighteen months.

'Senior government figures, including the Health Minister, were this morning forced to defend their leader and call on detractors to put up or shut up.'

A confident and relaxed Max Masters stood open-collared outside radio studios surrounded by journalists and fluffy microphones.

'There's Luke.' I spotted the bad suit in the background.

'Mr Masters,' said a journalist, 'the Prime Minister is at a fun run today—are you going to wish him luck?'

'Of course I wish him luck,' said Masters, 'but he doesn't need it. He's a practised athlete—he knows how to run away from a political reality.'

'Tellingly,' said Oscar Franklin, in a voice so manly it made Russell Crowe sound like Shirley Temple, 'Treasurer Gabrielle Brennan was unavailable for comment. It should be an interesting week in parliament. Back to you, Peter.'

'I wish that Oscar guy would wear a tie—he's the only political journalist in the country who never bothers,' said Daphne.

I, too, was staring at his open-necked shirt. 'In Oscar's case,' I murmured, 'I'm not sure many other women would agree with you.'

'He's fucked.' Debs muted the television.

'Who?' asked Daphne.

'The Prime Minister?' I asked.

'Yeah,' said Debs, 'not a good look to go on a fun run when your backbench is plotting against you.'

Daphne carried a platter of roast chicken to the table.

'Masters' analogy was clever,' I said.

'You're going to be great at this.' My aunt patted my shoulder.

You're in way over me, said my head.

'It's just a coffee.' I helped myself to peas.

'You know,' Daphne said, 'afterwards you should spend the night at my place in the city. It'll give you a chance to look around—unless you'd prefer to come back here with Debs.'

I contemplated her offer. Having admired the work of a few Australian designers online, a quick shop wasn't out of the question. Mmm, Bettina Liano, Kirrily Johnston, Akira, Scanlan & Theodore, Fleur Wood...

'Actually, I'd love to spend some time in Melbourne.'

And sleep on a bed.

While Daphne watched *Australian Idol*, Debs and I did the washing up. 'Do either of you have a belt I could borrow for tomorrow?' I handed her a soapy dinner plate.

'I'll lend you a belt if you don't make a big deal out of me spending time with the pups,' she said under her breath.

'You mean doting?'

'Whatever you want to call it,' she said. 'I don't want Daph thinking I want to keep those little critters, because I don't. They're nice 'n' all, but we can't have four dogs running around here.'

'Deal. I promise not to tell Daphne that you're a hopeless puppy-doter.'

'You're dangerously close to missing out on my cream, waist-cinching Stella McCartney.'

Dishes done, I packed an overnight bag. For some reason when we packed Fran and I had images of sandy beaches, the outback and quaint towns. Anyone looking at my suitcase would be forgiven for concluding I had picked from the washing lines of Miss Universe and the cast of *Australia*. For tomorrow, I settled for a watermelon shift dress with capped sleeves, the Mius and the Stella belt.

I switched off the living-room lights and lay down on the couch. On the back of a boarding pass, I wrote:

1. Set alarm for seven o'clock
2. Get up; have breakfast
3. Wash hair and shave legs
4. Pack toiletries
5. Call Fran
6. Buy newspapers
7. Find out meaning of 'to do a doorstop'.

Yarrawhatla?

I was in the public gallery in what looked like the House of Commons with Daphne and Debs. On one side sat British members of parliament. On the other, a raft of rowdy Australians. Dame Edna Everage was Thatcheresque in a skirt suit; Rolf Harris wore a wig and robes; Kylie Minogue sat in the prime minister's seat and chatted with fellow frontbencher Dannii.

Max Masters stood. 'Thank you, Mr Speaker. I invite members of the gallery to do The Doorstop.' The lights dimmed and a disco ball lowered from the ceiling. The members stood back and hung their heads.

Then two huge trap doors opened, sinking both front-benches and the table between them. In their place, a giant, wedge-shaped wooden doorstop slowly emerged. Covered in rich green leather, its highest point reached the balcony of the public gallery and its lowest stopped just short of the Speaker's chair.

The galleries cheered. 'Order, order,' said the jowly Speaker, before breaking into song. 'Keep on, do The Doorstop,' he grooved, 'don't stop 'til you get enough.' The MPs joined a conga line, led by Alf Stewart. Back in the public gallery, two Qantas flight attendants in roller-skates stood on either side of The Doorstop. Rolling in time with the music, they pointed towards it with spirit fingers.

Daphne pulled out a life jacket from underneath her seat and put it on. 'Come on, darling,' she shouted, 'that's our cue.' She kicked off her sandals, stepped up onto the railing and slid effortlessly down The Doorstop. When she reached the bottom, she looked back at Debs and me. 'Come on, darlings!'

'Your turn,' said Debs. The flight attendants flashed their torches at me, creating a spotlight.

'I don't want to.'

'Ruby, get up,' she said, putting on her life jacket.

I gripped the seat.

'Come on, Ruby, it's time.' She kicked off her shoes.

'No.' I turned my head.

'Ruby!' Debs shook me. 'You slept through your alarm—we have to leave in twenty minutes!'

'Bollocks.' I leaped off the couch. 'I had the weirdest dream.'

'You can tell me about it in the car.'

I scrambled for my list.

'One,' I read aloud, 'set alarm for seven o'clock. Fuck. Two, get up and have breakfast.' I ran to the kitchen and put two bananas in my handbag. 'Three, wash hair and shave legs...'

'No time, sunshine!' yelled Debs from her bedroom.

'Bugger, bugger, bugger. Four, pack toiletries.' I raced for the bathroom and began packing before catching a frightening glimpse of the spot on the tip of my nose. 'You bastard,' I said to my skin, plastering it madly with concealer. I brushed my teeth, zipped my wash bag, squeezed into my dress, grabbed my handbag and over-nighter and ran back to the kitchen, stepping into my wedges on the way.

'Five, call Fran; six, buy newspapers; seven, find out meaning of "to do a doorstop".' I sprayed myself with deodorant.

'No time!' yelled Debs.

'Leave her alone, Deborah,' scolded my aunt. 'This is a very important day for Ruby.'

'It's an important day for me too.'

'Maybe you're right,' barked Daphne, seemingly out of nowhere. 'Maybe you're not right for this—it's not all about you.'

My head cringed. *You know you've overstayed your welcome when people start fighting in front of you.*

'You look lovely, darling,' said Daphne, trying to avoid staring directly at the hideous creature on my nose.

Debs grabbed her briefcase and went to kiss my aunt goodbye, but she was rejected. She turned to me. 'Right, we've got to...what the fuck happened to you?'

'Deborah!'

'It's fine,' I said, 'she's just telling it like it is.'

'See, *she* understands me.' Debs stormed out the door.

I kissed my aunt goodbye and slinked into the car, where I lowered my sunglasses and thanked the fashion gods that huge frames were in.

Once we were on the open road, I dared to go there.

'Is everything okay?'

'Fine.'

Don't pry, Ruby, urged my head.

'It's just that,' I paused, 'well, things didn't seem fine.'

'Daph's driving me up the wall. She keeps going on about babies. Babies, babies, babies.'

I should have listened to my head.

'If I wanted to be a mum, I'd be a mum. Clearly, I don't.'

'Is that...practicable?'

'You mean getting knocked up?' We purred onto the highway.

I nodded.

'Guess so. I haven't really looked into it—it's Daph's agenda, not mine—but it'd have to be me. And I don't want to have to lug another person around inside me and then on me—I like being unencumbered.'

I let it go for a while but couldn't help myself. 'For what it's worth, I think you'd be great parents.'

'Bullshit. We both work too hard to be able to incorporate another person. Anyway it's all totally hypothetical.' She dialled in for a conference call. 'There's no point in discussing it.' While we listened to the hold music, she turned to me and summoned her most diplomatic voice. 'You don't look that terrible.'

'Thank you.'

'No worries,' she smiled, thinking she'd fixed things. 'Listen, I have a friend who works miracles. Not that you need a miracle because you don't look terrible. But if you did need a miracle, she'd be the one to go to.'

'Right, excellent.' I had no idea what she was on about.

'Her name is Olga. When I've done an all-nighter and I look like hell—not that you look like hell—but when *I* look like hell and need to go to court I see Olga in the morning and she fixes me for the day. I'll call her for you after this call and you can see her first up. Okay?'

'Okay.'

Four conference calls and a banana later, we were on the outskirts of Melbourne, when Debs rang her.

'Olga, it's Debs.'

'Da,' said Olga.

'My niece needs you.'

'Da?'

'She needs'—Debs looked at me intently—'hair washed and styled.'

'Da, da.'

'Brows waxed. Legs waxed.'

'Da.'

Debs lifted my right arm. 'Pits waxed.'

'Da.'

'Bikini?' she asked me. I shook my head.

'Da,' pre-empted Olga.

Good grief.

'She needs make-up, a manicure and pedicure. I'll drop her off at your place in twenty minutes. Okay?'

'Da.'

'Sorted.' Debs hung up. 'She's real nice. She's Russian.'

Not Japanese?

We soon pulled up at a rather grotty block of flats. 'Go to the first floor,' Debs said, 'press the buzzer and Olga will come and get you.'

'Right.'

'Daph told me to give you this map and keys to the apartment, but it's a bit confusing, so just call her when you get there and she'll tell you how to get in. I'll drop your bags off there this arvo. Gotta go, kiddo.'

Abandoned, I pressed the buzzer. Footsteps bounded down the stairs towards me and then a pint-sized blonde lady appeared. She looked like an Olympic figure skater.

'You must be Olga,' I said. 'I'm Ruby.'

I followed her into a sitting room. Olga took my handbag and reached into it for my phone, which she switched off. She handed me a robe and glass of water and showed me to one of the smaller rooms.

'I'm on quite a tight schedule,' I said. 'I need to be at Treasury Place by a quarter to twelve at the latest.' Olga looked at her watch. 'Da.'

'You want me to lie down?' I asked.

'Da,' she smiled.

Another woman joined her, and as they chatted incomprehensibly, they waxed, plucked, scrubbed, washed, buffed, dried, moisturised and painted me.

In two hours, I was a new woman. My spot had vanished, my hair bounced and my legs slithered.

Back in my dress, I grabbed my things and thanked them profusely. 'Da,' they said and showed me the door.

'Four Treasury Place,' I said to the cab driver.

'Righto, love, you off to something special?'

'I guess,' I said. 'I have an interview of sorts.'

The driver eyed me in the mirror. 'You'll get the job for sure.'

At Treasury Place a police officer appeared to be guarding a row of white Edwardian buildings.

'Press?' he asked.

'I have an appointment with Luke Harley in the Leader of the Opposition's office.'

'Right, I'll call and find someone for you. As you can appreciate, it's pretty hectic in there at the moment.' He picked up a radio and said, 'G'day, is Luke Harley there? Yeah, there's a lady here to see him; she reckons she has an appointment. Let me ask. Are you Ruby Stanhope?'

'Yes.'

'Yep, that's her. I'll escort her in.' He put on his hat and stepped down from his post. 'This way please, ma'am.'

I followed him down a narrow pathway to a nondescript office where a receptionist who could have auditioned for *Golden Girls* sat at a cluttered desk.

'Ruby?'

'Yes.'

'I'm Beryl. Did you get our messages?'

'No,' I said, remembering Olga had silenced my mobile. 'I've been in appointments all morning.'

'So have we, mate,' she said. 'We've been trying to call you to reschedule. Things are pretty fraught in there.' She pointed towards a pair of heavy oak doors.

'Big day?'

'You haven't seen the news?'

I didn't have the heart to tell her there was lipstick on her teeth. 'I haven't had a chance to read anything this morning,' I bluffed, smoothing a wrinkle in my dress.

'There's been a spill,' she said.

'Oil?'

'No, mate, a spill in the government.'

'Is someone...er...cleaning it up?'

She laughed. 'The PM's been toppled by the Treasurer and the new PM's on her way to Yarralumla.'

I longed for subtitles. 'I've just been down at the Yarra Valley,' I hesitated, 'it's a beautiful place.'

'No sweet 'art—*Yarralumla*. The GG's place. She's gonna be sworn in and we're being told she's calling an early election.'

I was still lost.

'How about I put the telly on and get you a cuppa?'

'That would be lovely.'

She turned on the antique television on her desk and swivelled it towards me, ushering me to a coffee-stained office chair. 'Voila,' she said. 'How do you have yer tea?'

BREAKING NEWS: PM PATTON OUSTED—BRENNAN TO BE SWORN IN AS PRIME MINISTER, streamed across the news ticker at the bottom of the screen. 'I'm standing here on the road to the Governor-General's residence at Yarralumla,' said an elegant, almond-eyed journalist, 'where, any minute now, the new Prime Minister, Gabrielle Brennan, is expected to be sworn in to her new role. At this stage, we are unsure who will take her position as Treasurer. Peter?'

'Thanks, Anastasia,' said Peter, back in the studio. 'Do we have any idea whether Prime Minister, sorry, *former* prime minister Hugh Patton will be standing again in his inner-Sydney seat at the next election?'

'At this stage, Peter, we don't, but it's highly unlikely that he would serve under his challenger and successor. This was a swift and seamless move on the part of Gabrielle Brennan and her co-conspirators. Very few people expected this day would come quite so quickly, if at all. Everybody is stunned. Peter?'

Peter pressed two fingers against his earpiece. 'Right, thank you, Anastasia. Senior Political Correspondent Anastasia Ng there, live in Canberra. We're hearing now that Hugh Patton is going to doorstop on the steps of

Old Parliament House'—bingo—'evoking vivid memories of the dismissal of Gough Whitlam in 1975. We'll cross live to that press conference now, where Oscar Franklin'—yum—'has the latest. Oscar?'

Beryl arrived with my tea in a chipped *Flintstones* mug, interrupting my Oscar-related daydream.

'Thanks.' I cleared my throat. 'What happened to Whitlam?'

'What do you mean, love?'

'Well, why was he dismissed?'

'Where are you from?'

'England.'

'Oh, that makes sense. In a nutshell, the GG dissolved the House of Reps and the Senate and put Fraser in as caretaker. It'd be like the Queen sacking your PM.'

'What's the significance of Old Parliament House?'

'Why's that?'

'Because Patton is about to do a doorstop there.' I hoped I had used the term correctly.

'Shit, that's dramatic.'

'I should just go,' I said, grasping the significance of the event.

Beryl shook her head. 'Luke wants you to stick around, if you're interested.'

Hugh Patton stood on a flight of white steps. He was emotional, supported by his wife, her hand firmly on his back.

'Ladies and gentleman, people of Australia—they say thirteen is an unlucky number. For my colleagues, my staff, my family and me these thirteen years have been the luckiest of our lives. We have been lucky enough to serve this country—to serve you.

'We've made some changes in health, defence, tax and education. We've been a force for good and, of that, I am proud.

'Sadly, someone else got lucky today. I wish her and her team—my party—well. I bear no resentment. No animosity. Because the fact remains I will always have those thirteen lucky years and that is thanks to them.

'Now, I'm going to spend some time with my family—if they'll have me.' His lip quivered, then his wife's grip spurred him on. 'To my constituents in Sydney, I hope you'll understand that this makes it difficult for me to continue to serve you well.

'Thank you to everyone who supported me and everyone who didn't but put up with me anyway.'

Journalists laughed.

'God bless,' he said and walked with his wife down the steps, into a waiting car and away from his career.

Oscar Franklin broke the silence. 'And that was the man of the moment, Hugh Patton, soon to be former prime minister of Australia. It's a solemn moment here at Old Parliament House—none of us quite knows what to say. Peter?'

'Well, don't, Oscar,' said Luke behind me.

'Luke.' I stood to greet him.

'Hi.' His phone rang. 'Listen, mate,' he said into his BlackBerry, 'I know it's a big ask, but I need you lot to pull your finger out and tell me when you can have it done by.'

It was a different Luke. He hadn't slept. He picked up my tea and started drinking it. Scratching his neck and loosening his tie—this one an insipid orange—he disappeared behind the oak doors.

Now we were back to Anastasia in Canberra. 'Peter, the new Prime Minister has just driven past on her way to Yarralumla to be sworn in. This is a historic day. She will be Australia's first female prime minister. The groundswell is unlike anything I've witnessed in my twenty-odd years in this job.

'School kids have come out to watch the cars go by. Workers are here for their lunch break. They're cheering her on, at the same time mindful of having lost one of the country's greatest prime ministers. Peter?'

'Thanks, Anastasia. We've just heard that Gabrielle Brennan is likely to seek the Governor-General's permission to go to an early election. She is due to hold a press conference in forty minutes. We'll cross now to our correspondent in Melbourne, where Opposition Leader Max Masters is understood to be bunkered down. Penny, do you think the Opposition knew this was coming?'

'I think that's unlikely, Peter,' said Penny. 'Max Masters is here with his team at Treasury Place, probably watching things unfold on TV like the rest of the nation. They'll be knocked for six by this news.'

I could see her standing out on the street.

'Get back from the window, darl,' said Beryl.

We watched the drama unfold, occasionally flicking between stations. When Gabrielle Brennan held her press conference, the phones stopped ringing and the nation listened.

At a lectern, flanked by her husband and three sons, she spoke. 'I stand before you today the newly sworn-in Prime Minister of Australia. I am enormously proud to hold this office, but saddened that it has happened this way.

'Hugh Patton has been this country's greatest champion for thirteen years. I have been blessed to serve alongside him.

'The Australian people have been telling us for some time now that change is needed—not a change of government, but a change of leadership. Australia, we heard you, and came—albeit reluctantly—to make that change.

'In public office, I swore an oath. The oath was to serve the Australian people. Today, I renew that oath.

'If we haven't made the right decision then the people of Australia will tell us so at the ballot box on Saturday the third of April.

'I might be new to this office, but I am the same Gabrielle Brennan you have trusted as captain of this robust economy for thirteen years. I'm the mother of school-aged kids, the wife of a council worker, the daughter of a war widow. I've been a university student, a community worker, a lawyer and a businesswoman, and I bring each of these experiences to this office.

'I'll take a handful of questions now, but then I've got work to do. Cabinet announcements will happen tomorrow.'

Back at Treasury Place, the oak doors clapped open and out spilled about fifteen people, all on phones, except for Max Masters. Beryl turned off the TV.

'Right,' said Max, 'where are we doing this?'

Phones were flipped shut. 'We've got a room set up next door,' said a slim redhead in red stilettos, fielding two mobile phones.

Luke stepped in. 'It'll be lectern, flags, suit, tie. Shelly's on her way from the airport. She'll be beside you. You'll speak, then you'll take their questions. Brennan is only taking a few, so I think you should feed them until they're full. Make-up's in twenty minutes, so you need to eat and then we'll get you ready.'

'Fine.' Max returned to his office and shut the doors behind him.

The phone calls resumed.

A minute later, he came flying out. 'I forgot to shave,' he announced. 'Have we got a razor?' He banged his head repeatedly against the door like an animal in captivity.

As always, I had my Toolkit in my handbag, having been advised as a teenager by my sister that no girl should leave the house without factoring in the possibility that she mightn't return until the following morning.

'Um,' I squeaked, through the silence. *Shut up, Ruby.*

'I know you?' said Max, resting his head. Everyone turned to face me.

'Ru...' I stuttered.

'That's right. Roo. You were choking at the winery.'

Way to make a first impression, said my head.

'This is Ruby Stanhope,' said Luke. 'She's a possible financial policy advisor who I was due to talk with today: a former investment banker—'

'So, Roo, do you have a razor?' asked Max.

'Yes,' I said, 'and cream.'

'Thank the good Lord for Roo.'

'Wait until you see it before you thank me.' I offered up a purple glittery razor complete with Almighty Avocado sample-sized shaving cream.

He seized it. 'What the fuck is an almighty avocado?' he asked, quite reasonably.

'I'm not sure,' I said. 'It came free with a magazine. I presume it's better than a normal avocado. More... almighty.'

That clears things up.

He held the sparkly razor up to the fluorescent light. 'My daughter has a skipping rope like this. Anyone else have a razor? Or cream?'

People shook their heads.

'What, no Legendary Lettuce or Captivating Cucumber in the room?'

'How about Ravishing Radish?' said Luke.

I alone laughed.

'Well,' Max said, 'it looks like I'm going to smell like an almighty avocado for the most important fucking press conference of my life, but thanks to Roo here at least I won't be stubbly.' He retreated to his office.

Everybody resumed their calls. Beryl gave me the thumbs up. I added 'buy replacement razor' to my To Do list, 'and cream.'

In came a petite, luggage-laden lady with an angular face and long dark hair. 'Where's Max?' she asked, as only a spouse could, dumping her bags on the floor.

Luke rushed over to her. 'Fine-tuning his speech. Make-up in fifteen. You'll both go in for the presser.'

'Fine,' she said. 'Abigail has a band concert this afternoon and she's flute solo so she couldn't come. I've asked Sally's mum if she can pick them up. She'll spend the night there.'

'There'll be plenty of time for pics later,' said Luke. 'We've got thirty-three days of this.'

She nodded, vanishing into the room with the oak doors. Luke followed her, texting furiously.

The mood was sombre, which was interesting given the huge opportunity the Opposition had just been presented with; but what did I know?

Then two broad-shouldered men marched into the room, removing their Oakleys. Beryl was answering other people's mobiles; red-stilettoed redhead was lying on the floor in the hallway attached to a phone charger; and an older man appeared to be fighting with a photocopier in the corner.

'I'm Charlie Flack, from the Australian Federal Police,' said one of the Robocops, brandishing his badge. 'Where is Mr Masters?'

No one looked up.

'I'm sorry,' I said, 'they're all a bit busy at the moment. Is there something you need?'

'The parliament has been dissolved and we're now officially in an election campaign. As such, Mr Masters is the alternative prime minister and requires immediate protection. I need to brief him and Mrs Masters immediately.'

'Right. Can I get you a cup of tea?'

'Ma'am, I realise you're all busy, but I need to see either Mr Harley or Mr Masters.'

'Wait here, please.' I took a deep breath, approached the double doors and knocked.

'Yep.'

'Luke,' I yelled, 'it's Ruby.'

Go in, you idiot, said my head.

'Come in,' he said.

Max and his wife were sitting on a sofa drinking tea. They looked up at me inquisitively.

Luke came to the door. 'What is it, Ruby?'

'I'm sorry to interrupt. There are two gentlemen here who say it's their job to provide security to Max. Apparently they need a word with you rather urgently.'

'Security?' asked Max.

'I don't think we've met,' said Shelly, standing to greet me.

'Shelly,' said Luke, 'this is Ruby Stanhope, our new financial policy advisor.'

No she's not, said my head.

'Ruby, this is Shelly Masters.'

'Pleased to meet you,' I said, extending my hand and suppressing the urge to curtsey.

She shook it and then returned to sit beside her husband. 'Something over here smells like—'

'Almighty Avocado,' Max finished her sentence.

'Smells better than I thought it would, actually,' I said.

'I was going to say salad,' said Shelly, closing her eyes and taking another whiff.

'Now,' said Max, 'what's this about security?'

Luke permitted me to brief him with a nod.

'Something about dissolving and the alternative prime minister...'

'They briefed me about this when I first got the gig. I don't want it.'

'Yes,' I said, 'it's just that the feeling I got from Mr Flack was that it's not exactly an optional service.'

'As in cop the flak?' Max checked.

'Ruby, would you mind showing them in?' asked Luke. I went to get them.

Before they had a chance to introduce themselves, red-stiletto lady hung up both phones and pounced on Max. 'We're on in ten and you need make-up.'

'You know, Di,' said Max, 'I'm going to try not to take that personally.'

'Shut up,' smiled Di, attacking him with a powder puff, 'or it'll go in your mouth.'

As Di dabbed a little concealer under his eyes, Max asked Flack the Cop a few questions about their role.

'So, you're not going to come with me everywhere I go, are you?'

'Yes, sir, we are.'

'What if I'm in the toilet?' Max asked through gritted teeth while Di dusted him with translucent powder.

'We will wait at an appropriate distance to give you maximum privacy.'

'How will you know whether it's appropriate?' he joked.

'Experience, sir.'

'And what if I'm at home?'

'We are in the process of setting up equipment so that we can monitor your home, sir.'

'And what if I'm at home but Max isn't?' asked Shelly.

'The surveillance team will remain in place to monitor any untoward activity, but the idea is that wherever your husband goes, we go.'

'Thanks, everyone,' said Max. 'I need to focus on what I'm saying for a bit, so I'll see you outside in two minutes.'

Everyone except Shelly left the room. The two men stood on either side of the door. I grabbed my handbag and put on my sunglasses—it was time for me to get out of there.

'Ruby,' Luke called out, 'where are you going?'

'This has been very eye-opening and thank you for inviting me here but you have a lot to do so I should leave you in peace.'

'Look,' he said, 'I don't have time to talk you through it all, but I'd really like your help over the next few weeks. Come to Sydney with us tonight and I'll explain on the plane.' His phone rang again. 'Talk to Beryl, Ruby.'

I went to the Ladies to think it over.

You don't have a working visa, Ruby, lectured my head as I sat on the loo lid. *You're supposed to be having a holiday. Some man with terrible taste in ties asks you to go to Sydney and you're actually considering it? What's got into you? Whatever happened to Bettina Liano and Fleur Wood? You don't know the slightest thing about politics, let alone Australian politics; and you're an investment banker.'*

'No, I'm not.' I flung open the stall and hurried back to the office in time to see Max, Shelly, Luke and Di stride into the adjacent conference room to a drum roll of frenzied photographers. A small crowd gathered around Beryl's telly. Max took to the lectern, Shelly beside him. Luke and Di moved out of shot.

'I'd like to pay tribute to Hugh Patton. He has served in this country's highest office for thirteen years with commitment and dignity. I respect him for that. Shelly and I wish Hugh, Miranda and family well.

'Friends, we're here today because a disgruntled minister grew tired of waiting for her turn in the hot seat. So she toppled a popularly elected prime minister.

'She says she did this because Australians want change.' He paused. 'That's a complete load of bull. She did it to serve herself—not you. This was an act of gross ambition. Now our nation is without stable leadership. Australia deserves better.

'My team and I are ready to govern. We're going to spend the next few weeks travelling from beach to bush, city to country, boardroom to backyard. We want to tell you about our plan and why we think we can do a better job.

'And we're going to listen. I want to ask the nation a favour: think about what kind of country you want Australia to be. Come up with one thing you love about our country and one thing you'd want to change. When you see me or a member of my team out on the campaign trail, tell us those two things. We will listen.

'Now, I'm happy to take as many questions as you have.'

A barrage of 'Mr Masters' came at him from the floor.

I turned to Beryl. 'What time is that flight to Sydney?'

Jackie oh no

Standing with the nation's media outside the CPO, I tried to hail a cab with flailing arms.

My head was on fire. *Look at that lovely wine bar over there. See the two ladies with shopping bags beneath their bar stools? I bet there are shoes in those bags...*

'Shut up and help me concentrate.'

I cursed myself for failing to complete the day's To Do list when I'd had the time. Now, I had to call my aunt.

'Aunt Daphne?' I slid into a cab and handed the driver the address.

'Ruby, dear, goodness me, I've just seen the news—was your meeting cancelled?'

'Listen, I don't have time to explain, but it would appear that I'm catching a plane to Sydney tonight to discuss "my role"—whatever that is—and right now I'm on my way to your apartment to pick up my bags.' I paused to catch my breath.

'Sydney? Are you sure this is a good idea?'

'No,' I said, 'but I'm sure I want to do it—if that makes sense.'

'Good for you, darling. So long as you're safe.'

'About the apartment?'

'Oh, yes, well, it's a little tricky. You'll need the fat key to unlock the garage and then the eighth key to unlock the first lock, the sixth key to unlock the second lock and—'

I stopped her. 'Are these instructions written anywhere on the map Debs gave me?'

'No.'

'I'll call you when I get there.'

I examined the key ring Debs had given me. There were nineteen keys on the Snoopy ring, and an attached subsidiary ring, distinguished by a fetching Artisan Baker Association tag, held an additional eleven.

We pulled up outside an old warehouse. I paid the driver and hit redial on my phone. 'I'm here, I think.'

'Walk towards the far-right end of the warehouse and you'll see a largish, rusty, industrial garage.'

I followed her instructions. 'Largish' was an understatement. The red, corrugated garage door was three times my height.

'Now use the fat key to unlock the garage.'

I looked at the key ring. 'There are three relatively obese keys. Which one is it?'

'The one with the bit of old gum stuck on the end.'

A sticky, heavy key unlocked the door. I turned the handle.

'Don't turn the handle.'

'Help!' I yelped. The door jolted upwards and rolled inwards, taking me with it. Dangling precariously close to the top, I let go of everything and fell to the ground with a thud. My phone was now on top of the garage door four metres in the air.

'AUNT DAPHNE,' I screamed, 'IF YOU'RE STILL ON THE PHONE, I'M NOT VERY HURT, BUT MY PHONE IS ON TOP OF THE GARAGE AND THE KEYS ARE IN THE HANDLE. I WILL CALL YOU BACK WHEN I'VE FIGURED OUT A SOLUTION.

'Cock,' I said, looking down at my freshly waxed knees to find them gashed and bruised. They now matched my toe. I picked myself up, and dusted the leaves and twigs from my frock.

First, I tried jumping on the spot. A short piece of rope dangled from the door but no amount of self-generated bounce would propel me three metres off the ground. I am not the tallest person, even in my elongating Miu Mius.

Next, I turned to nature, grabbing a branch to hook onto the rope. MacGyver would be proud, I thought, leaping into the air and splitting the lining of my already sullied shift dress. My days as a truant of athletics class had come back to bite me. 'It was your idea,' I yelled back at my laughing head.

With silk lining trailing tail-like behind me, I slumped against the garage wall, where I bumped into a button. 'No,' I whispered, disbelievingly. I pushed it. Sure enough, in a smooth motorised motion, down came the door. I pushed it again to halt the door halfway, hobbled out of the garage, retrieved my phone and keys and redialled my aunt.

She answered immediately. 'Are you all right?'

'Stephen King would have nightmares about that door.'

'Did you hurt yourself?'

'No, I didn't hurt *myself*,' I said. 'Your evil beast of a door hurt me—I haven't had grazed knees since I was six!'

'I'm so very sorry, darling.'

'Just talk me through the rest of it.'

'Get the eighth key—'

'They're unnumbered.'

'I know, sweetheart. Count clockwise from the green key.'

I fumbled through them.

'That one's for the top lock on the door inside the garage.'

'Next?'

'The key two back from the eighth key goes in the lock below and then the green key works with the third lock.'

So far, so good.

'Are you in?'

'Yes, thank you.'

'You're so much like your mother when you're angry.'

If I hadn't been so furious, I'd have been able to appreciate the place. It was a striking old warehouse converted into a large loft with high ceilings and graffitied walls. The kitchen was the centrepiece, with an enormous wood-fired stove between two electric ovens.

I tended to my knees using the plasters in my Toolkit, and called Debs.

Her PA answered. 'She's in a meeting,' he said. 'Is there something I can help you with?'

I explained about my luggage.

'I'm sorry, Ruby. She hasn't been able to get there yet. She should be there by sixish.'

I looked at my watch. It was 4.30 p.m. 'I need you to get an urgent message to her,' I said. 'I'm flying with the Leader of the Opposition to Sydney at half six, so I'll need it within the hour.'

'That's not possible,' he said. 'Even if she leaves now, which she can't, with peak-hour traffic she won't be at your aunt's in time.'

'Cock.' I was dishevelled, dusty, bruised and bloodied. I had nothing to change into except the spare bra and pants in my Toolkit.

'Ruby?' he said. 'You need to get to the airport pronto if you're going to make that flight. I'll arrange a cab. In the meantime—and this didn't come from me—Debs keeps an overnight bag in Daphne's closet.'

Close to despair, I limped into the vast, main bedroom and rummaged through the rainbow of Irish linen in Daphne's wardrobe for something structured. Nada. But there, at the end, was the pot of gold: an ostrich-leather overnight bag embossed with Debs' initials. I grabbed it along with my handbag and ran down the stairs and out the door, locking it behind me. I sent up a quick prayer to the Goddess of Garages, pressed the button and jumped into the waiting taxi.

'Tullamarine. Fast.' In the back seat, I dug through the overnight bag. 'Hallelujah!'

The cabby shot me a quizzical look as I held up a stunning pair of black Scanlan & Theodore cigarette-leg trousers. Size eight and clearly intended for giraffes, judging by the length of them. Underneath was a folded white-collared shirt. It would be a squeeze, but one worth making. The pièce de résistance was the cosmetics bag containing a range of travel-sized La Prairie products.

Out the window, everything about Melbourne appeared artistic; from buildings to overpasses, there was an eye for the aesthetic. Beneath a phallic yellow sculpture arching over the airport expressway, my driver asked which terminal I was going to. I showed him the instructions Beryl had given me.

'That's for charter jets, mate.'

Until that moment, it hadn't occurred to me that I would not be boarding a commercial flight. My plan to occupy the disabled cubicle at the airport and force my body mass into the hopelessly skinny trousers had to be scrapped. There was no way in hell that I would board a private plane in torn couture. I needed to be Jackie Onassis, not Jackie Oh-no-sis.

'Pull over.'

'We're in the middle of the bloody Tullamarine Freeway, love.'

'I need to change.'

'Change what?'

'Clothes.'

'I can't pull over, mate. It's not safe.'

'I'll have to do it here then. Now, if you wouldn't mind keeping your eyes on the road...'

'Don't flatter yourself,' he said, turning up the radio.

I took a deep breath and held it, hitched my dress up over my hips and wriggled into the beautifully tailored trousers, hoping the recent higher-than-average carb intake hadn't added critical centimetres to my circumference.

Grunting and panting, I thrust my pelvis skywards, untangled my underpants from the knot they'd formed between my buttocks and gave the trousers one last tug before zipping the fly. I was in. The hard part was over. I pulled my dress over my head and slipped into the crisp, clean shirt, buttoning it from the top down.

'That was quite a show,' said the cabby while I folded the trouser legs under with the help of a little double-sided tape from my Toolkit.

'You were *supposed* to be watching the road.'

'I bloody did!' He pointed out the window. 'It's those guys that got the show—isn't that the Masters bloke?'

I ducked. 'As in *Max* Masters?'

'I'm pretty sure that's him.' He waved excitedly at the car next to him.

'Stop waving!'

'It's my taxi; I'll wave if I want to.'

I moaned. 'Is he waving back?' My head was firmly between my knees.

'Yeah, he seems real nice.' The car slowed to a stop. 'Hey, I reckon he's going to the same place you are—what a fluke!'

I kept my head down.

'He's coming over to talk to us. I can't wait to tell my wife about this.' He jumped out of his cab to greet Max.

Reaching forwards to put fifty dollars on his seat, I shuffled to the passenger side in a bid to escape unnoticed. There was a tap on my window.

'G'day, Roo,' Max said, grinning down at me. Di giggled; Luke blushed; Flack the Cop couldn't stifle his smile. Clutching at scraps of dignity, I slung my bags over my shoulder, lowered my sunglasses and walked towards the terminal, my head held high. 'Don't we have a plane to catch?'

Luke's phone rang, cutting short the second awkward moment in as many days.

Di ran to catch up with me. 'We didn't have a chance to meet properly before,' she said, chivalrously overlooking the fact that she had just seen my pelvic floor muscles at work. 'I'm Dianna Freya—I handle Max's media.'

'Ruby Stanhope,' I said, my face still hot with humiliation. 'I do complimentary mobile peep shows with a bit of financial policy advice on the side.'

She laughed. 'We've all done it,' she said. 'I love your shoes, by the way.'

'Thanks. I was admiring your red ones earlier.'

'They're my arse-kicking shoes,' she said, 'which come in handy on a day like this. Anyway, we've got *Sunset* coming for a prerecord in ten, so I'd better find somewhere quiet to do it—do you mind helping me out?'

'Sure.' I added a handful of new items to Google to my list.

'Just give my bags to the RAAF lady over there. This is our first trip on the BBJ, but I'm told they just put our luggage in the hull.' She gestured towards a uniformed officer who stood at the foot of a small white jet marked ROYAL AUSTRALIAN AIR FORCE.

Before I could ask her for a quick translation, she'd already taken a call on one phone and was texting from another while running towards an approaching satellite truck.

The uniformed lady came across the tarmac to help with the two handbags, overnight bag, suit bag and Di's dilapidated briefcase.

'Hello,' I said, not knowing whether I should be addressing her by title. 'I'm Ruby Stanhope. These belong to Dianna Freya and me.'

She crossed our names off the list on her clipboard as if she was front of house for the opening of a club. 'Would you like to come aboard?'

'Is anyone else there?'

'Mr Harley is taking a phone call.'

I followed her up the flip-down stairs. The last time I'd been on a private jet was when I flew to an oil project in western Kazakhstan in a 'revamped' Soviet plane that had all the interior charm of a Soho dustbin on a Saturday night. Now I walked down a narrow corridor with shiny wood panelling on my left and silk-covered walls on my right. It opened onto a small room. Twenty or so large leather lounges sat on either side of glossy coffee tables, which displayed a spread of newspapers and magazines.

'Can I get you a drink?' asked the flight attendant.

'I'd love some water,' I said, taking a seat.

She returned shortly with a bottle and a selection of biscuits. 'Mr Harley asked if you would join him when you're free.' She showed me to a small meeting room at the front of the plane, which contained four seats and a large table. Luke, who stood in the corner staring out the window, was on the phone. He turned to usher me in.

'How awesome is this?' he said when he finished his call.

'Quite. Who owns it?'

'The people,' he said. 'This will be our maiden voyage—the Opposition doesn't get to use them until we're in campaign mode.' When he finished the sentence, it seemed to dawn on him that he was now running a spontaneous election campaign. He closed his eyes and pressed his index fingers to his temples.

'What am I doing here?' I asked.

'Well, I'm glad you asked.' Luke opened his eyes and removed the lid from a takeaway cappuccino with pathetic froth. 'We need help.'

'Okay...'

'None of us saw this coming: we haven't started fundraising properly; the party is completely drained of dosh thanks to two recent state campaigns; we're polling terribly on the economy because people lean on the incumbent to take them through these sorts of global cluster fucks; and now we're up against the first female PM, who is bound to have a bit of a honeymoon between now and polling day.'

We watched people scurry around the tarmac, juggling phones and luggage.

Luke continued: 'Somehow, we've got to get our shit together and get the message out that we know what we're doing and that we're better than they are—but that's a pretty big ask with virtually nothing in the coffers, only a handful of fully developed policy platforms and a shitload of semi-marginal seats without preselected candidates.' He stopped to draw breath.

'How, pray tell, can I, an unemployed Brit with not an iota of political background, help you do that?'

Luke slurped the froth from his cappuccino. 'I'm so sick of these hacks who've done nothing else with their lives but politics. Sure, they're useful because they understand the process, but we need a few new ideas if we're going to make it through.'

'I don't have a working visa,' I blurted out.

'We'll sort something out.'

I imagined what Bruce at Immigration would say to that.

'But,' he continued, 'this is going to be a miscellaneous gig—not quite the straight financial stuff I had in mind for you when we first met.'

'How so?'

'It might mean that you need to donate the occasional hair-removal tool and salad-scented paraphernalia in the middle of writing a policy speech for the Business Council of Australia conference. Or provide adult entertainment for weary colleagues en route to the airport...' He stopped to laugh at his own joke then cleared his throat.

'Very funny.'

He changed tenor. 'The LOO's on *Sunset* so we'd better get someone down there with a dictaphone. Do you mind?'

For a second, I contemplated his proposition before realising I barely understood it. 'Sure,' I bluffed. 'Where's this loo?'

He pulled a dictaphone from a crusty old Law Institute of Victoria knapsack and handed it to me. 'L-O-O. Leader of the Opposition.'

The mother of all To Do lists

Over a glass of merlot on the way to Sydney, I reflected on the day. Nothing that had happened resembled, even remotely, the life I'd planned.

I recalled tete-a-tetes with my foppish Oxford ex. Smitten with each other and the life we would share, post-coital future-planning had been almost as electric as the act itself. Propped up on pillows in bed, sharing tea from a thermos, we would fantasise.

'There should be at least two children by the time I'm thirty and you're twenty-seven,' he'd say, 'which will give *me* time to make partner at Preston & Fiddle and *you* a chance to establish yourself at the bank before you take a few years off with our first child until he goes to school.'

Thanks to his presumptuousness, these conversations would escalate into full-blown arguments climaxing in pre-emptive custody negotiations. Make-up sex ensued and so the dysfunctional cycle continued until my final year, when he fell head over heels for his father's secretary, married her and moved to Lexington, Kentucky.

Naivety aside, I had always thought my life would meet basic deadlines as set out in the mother of all To Do lists:

Early twenties: Get graduate position with bank, and boyfriend

Mid-twenties: Get promotion and engaged

Late twenties: Get promotion, married and Holland Park house

Early thirties: Get promotion, first child and holiday villa in Umbria

Mid-thirties: Get promotion, second child and interior decorator for holiday villa

Late thirties: Get promotion, third child and country house

Early forties: Get promotion with transfer to New York office and chichi house in the Hamptons

Mid-forties: TBC.

To date, the only items I could tick off the list were job-related—that part was relatively on track until last Wednesday, when I was made redundant, got trollied on a tremendous bottle or three of red, booked a ticket abroad and took an unexpected career detour via an Australian federal election campaign.

The cabin was now full of fellow campaigners, all bewildered by the day's events. Di, who sat beside me, dwarfed by oversized noise-cancelling headphones, unfurled fish and chip paper on the coffee table and drew six columns with a red marker. Luke and Max were holding a strategy meeting in the office with the party director, Mirabelle Halifax—a voluptuous lady with a thick mane of purplish hair fastened high with nothing but a gravity-defying pencil.

Di removed her headphones. 'Did that cow on *Sunset* really ask him whether the term "bull" was appropriate?'

I nodded.

I'd never realised what a satellite interview is like. It takes skill to stare down the barrel of a camera with the voice of your interviewer echoing through a flesh-coloured earpiece, knowing that people eating their dinner around the country are watching your every move.

Di had briefed Max while doing his make-up. They ran through a couple of lines before the cameraman counted Max in with his fingers. I recorded the interview from a makeshift green room in the terminal. Nothing of note happened until Max was asked 'Mr Masters, do you really think it's appropriate for the alternative prime minister of this country to be using expressions like "load of bull" in a press conference?'

Max hadn't flinched. 'Sure, Stacey—this is Australia. I think most people would be pretty comfortable with that sort of language.'

'Actually, Mr Masters,' said Stacey, 'a Sydney radio program did a quick poll this afternoon and sixty-seven per cent of listeners thought it was inappropriate. Are you suggesting these people are *un*Australian?'

'Absolutely not. Stacey, I haven't seen the poll you're referring to, but if I've offended anyone I apologise—I guess it's just my navy background coming out.'

When the interview ended, Max had muttered crossly to Di about having been blindsided. She now scrawled 'bull' in the first column, along with the words 'team', 'national service' and 'SMEs'.

Then, a frazzled fat man with a pile of papers distributed a stapled booklet to everyone on the plane.

'What's this?' I asked Di.

'Today's coverage and tomorrow's schedule, which is likely to change a trillion times.'

The schedule read like an extreme Choose Your Own Adventure. Unless I was mistaken, we would be doing a media round-up at 4 a.m., three radio and two TV interviews before 7 a.m., a breakfast team-meeting at party HQ before 8 a.m., a school visit in the western suburbs at 9 a.m., and a travelling media briefing at 11 a.m. At midday we'd be flying to Brisbane with media, going to a fundraising lunch, a small-to-medium-enterprise policy launch, a meeting with pollsters and an *After Dark* pre-record, before attending a fundraising dinner and then a strategy meeting.

'This can't be right,' I said to Di. 'It isn't humanly possible.'

'I was thinking it looked a bit light on,' she said. 'I've got forty journos, snappers and crews joining us tomorrow and they're going to want to know what the next week holds.' She swigged at a neat whisky. 'And the truth is, I've got no fucking idea.'

'You mean, the media will travel *with* us?'

'Sort of,' she said. 'We've got a spare plane and bus for them at every location. It's my job to look after them and make sure they've got enough of a story by the end of the day so we get some decent coverage. And I'll be working closely with our advance team—that's assuming we get another couple of advancers; right now it's just Maddy—to make sure each event runs smoothly. Otherwise all the coverage will be about gaffes and cock-ups rather than the LOO and his policy agenda.'

'And what exactly *is* his policy agenda?'

'Good question, mate.' She stared blankly out the window. 'All I know is that this week we're doing something on national service to focus people on the LOO's military background; something on "the team" to let everyone know we've got one and they don't; and tomorrow we're going to say something about small business because this election is going to be fought on the economy.'

Luke surfaced from the office, his sleeves pushed up and tie askew. 'Di, do you mind joining us?'

She rolled up her fish and chip paper and followed him in, whisky in hand.

I went to the back of the plane to introduce myself to the others. I found a vacant seat next to an older man with lenses as thick as Di's whisky glass. 'Hi, I'm Ruby.' He didn't look up from his papers, so I extended my hand to grab his attention. 'I'm Ruby.'

He held out his index finger as if to silence me. 'Theo,' he said, and then went back to his book.

Rejected, I returned to my original seat and merlot. Minutes later, I was joined by a middle-aged man in distressed jeans and a white V-neck T-shirt sprouting tufts of chest hair.

'Don't pay any attention to him,' he said.

'Who?'

'Theo.' He sat down in Di's seat. 'He was told about half an hour ago that we need an SME policy by first thing tomorrow morning. The Shadow Minister and his staff are on their way back from Israel and have no idea the election has even been called, let alone that there's going to be a major policy announcement in their port-folio tomorrow.'

'So why Theo?'

'He's the policy guru. I'm Archie, by the way.'

'Ruby.'

'You're the banker, right?'

'I was. What about you?'

'I've just finished up as press secretary to the Queens-land Premier. Now I'm here to help Di shepherd her flock.'

The pilot announced we would soon be landing. Coffee tables were lowered, seats moved upright and merlot confiscated. No great loss.

'Archie, you don't happen to know if there's going to be accommodation provided for us tonight, do you?'

He laughed. 'Beryl sorts those logistics. You'll be right.'

As soon as we landed, people reached frantically for their phones and switched them on, triggering a trill of ring tones.

Archie took a call. 'Gary, how're you travelling? You're what? Are we off the record, Gary? Good, then I'll speak plainly. You can't seriously be running with a story about the word "bull" when one of the country's longest serving prime ministers has been unceremoniously replaced by his once-loyal minister and we've been plunged into an early election to "reassure" her that she made the right decision?'

Archie winked at me and scribbled the name 'Spin-naker' on a piece of paper. He held it up to show Di, who was on a call with another journalist about the same issue. She rolled her eyes and made a wanking gesture.

'See you, mate. Hope you'll be joining us on the trail—we should grab a beer.' Archie pretended to stick his fingers down his throat.

Di finished her call just after Archie. 'Spinnaker's such a—'

'Princess,' Archie cut in.

They appeared to be getting on famously, but I suspected that Di wasn't overly comfortable with sharing her 'flock'.

She clasped her hands around her mouth to form a megaphone. 'Listen up, kids. We've got snappers downstairs looking for a few action shots of the LOO using the BBJ for the first time—a bit of colour for tomorrow's papers. The coppers and Max will walk downstairs first. Luke and I will go next. Give us about three minutes before you follow. Don't look forlorn, please. Don't smile, but don't look depressed—we need to look in control and businesslike.'

She turned to the party director. 'Do you mind staying put for a bit? I don't think your being here sends the right message.'

'Of course.' Mirabelle stepped back into the office.

'Showtime,' said Max, disembarking to a flurry of flashes. Luke and Di waited a minute before leaving.

Then, to our astonishment, Archie went to the door. I coughed to grab his attention. *Shoosh, Ruby,* ordered my head. He turned and caught my gaze.

'Aren't we waiting here for a few minutes?' I asked casually.

'No need, Roo.' He winked. 'They've already got what they came for.' He proceeded down the stairs. Flash, flash.

Those of us remaining exchanged disapproving glances. 'Di is *not* going to be happy with that,' said Theo.

A few minutes later, we piled into a coach waiting on the tarmac. Di and Archie were sitting in diagonally opposite seats, on separate calls. The ensuing break from conversation, however awkward, provided an opportunity to call Fran.

'Hewwo, this is Cwementine speaking.'

'Clem, it's Aunty Ruby. How are you?'

'Tewwible, Aunty Wooby. Da dentith said thumb childwen take a wong time to wooz teef, so I fought I might make it go a wittle bit more quickwy.'

Fran picked up the extension. 'Hang up, please, Clementine.'

Clunk.

'She saw a cartoon about connecting your tooth to a door and slamming it to make it fall out.'

'You mean that really works?'

'No,' Fran said. 'But she fell flat on her face in the process and almost bit through her tongue.'

I tried not to laugh.

'I have a self-harming four-year-old, Ruby. If this is how she is over the Tooth Fairy, can you imagine the lengths she'll go to when she hears what people pay for organs in the Far East?'

Now I had to laugh. 'At least she's entrepreneurial.'

'I suppose,' she sighed. 'How's the Yarra Valley?'

'I'm in Sydney.' While we'd been talking, the bus had left the airport. I peered out the window at the brightly lit billboards.

'Sydney! Good grief, you haven't married some hideous surfer dude, have you, Ruby?'

'I *have not* and *will not* marry a surfer dude,' I said sternly. Several of my new colleagues turned to stare at me. I smiled awkwardly and lowered my voice to a whisper. 'A snap election has been called by the new Australian Prime Minister. She got rid of her predecessor this morning.

'I met the Leader of the Opposition's Chief of Staff at that party I went to on the weekend. Luke offered me a job on the campaign. I accepted. Sort of.' Saying it excited me. 'I've just flown on a government jet from Melbourne to Sydney, where I'm hoping someone has looked into organising a visa for me so I can do this lawfully. Now, you may speak.'

'Ruby! How long is the campaign?'

'The election is on the third of April.'

'Clementine really misses you, Ruby,' she said, in a neat transfer of emotion.

'I really want to do this, Fran.'

'Well,' she said, then paused to prevent herself from telling me to come home at once, 'Clementine will understand—she'll be happy for you, darling.'

'Thank you,' I said sincerely. 'Must go.'

We had arrived at a hotel outside which Beryl stood with a clipboard. As we got off the bus, she handed us each a room key and our luggage.

At my turn, she said, 'Roo, I have a laptop and log-in details for you, a phone and number, and an employment contract from the party. And someone there is sorting your visa. I've sent an email about this to your new address. Next!'

I ran for the lift and hit the button for the twelfth floor. As the doors closed a manicured hand reached in and stopped them. It was Di. She was still livid. The elevator began to move.

'Archie shouldn't have done that,' I said.

'Too fuckin' right.' The doors opened to the twelfth floor and she breathed slowly out. 'Brekky tomorrow?'

'Love to. What time?'

'Half four, at the office.'

I remembered the sobering schedule. 'Sure,' I said, regretting it already.

I entered my room and opened the curtains at the end of my third day in Australia. There was Sydney in all its twilit glory. The bridge arched gracefully over a busy, sprawling harbour. The herringbone-patterned tiles of the famous white-sailed opera house reminded me of the collars on my father's business shirts. Lights still on in nearby office buildings revealed lonely professionals dining at their desks. Sated couples left restaurants hand in hand.

I was too tired to be hungry. A hot shower and La Prairie face mask later, I wrapped myself in a towelling robe and curled up on the expansive bed. I set my alarm and a wake-up call for 4 a.m., slipped under the brushed-cotton covers and into a deep, unshakable slumber.

Oscar nomination

My alarm howled. I ripped the duvet from my body and switched on the radio. Unleashing my spare bra and pants, I got back into yesterday's clothes, varying the outfit by adding the Stella belt and tucking the shirt.

I found the office: room 1209—three adjoining suites were littered with photocopiers, printers, computers, fax machines and phones.

Di was sitting on a couch in sweat pants and a T-shirt, reading through a pile of newspapers and eating toast. Archie was listening to two radio stations between phone calls.

'G'day.' Di looked up. 'Coffee?'

'Yes, please.' I helped myself and took a spare copy of the *Herald*.

'In a nutshell,' she told me, 'all the papers are as pissed off with Brennan as they are excited by her manoeuvre. This has never happened before. The media have been caught off guard as much as we have, so the coverage is all over the place.'

The *Herald*, a Victorian paper, was headlined MELBOURNE VS MELBOURNE, and focused on both candidates being locals. The front page was split down the middle with a photograph of Brennan at her press conference and the LOO at his. Inside was an eight-page special on the campaign, with stories about Patton's legacy, the historic nature of Brennan's move and readers' comments on Max's use of the word 'bull'. On page six was a photograph of the LOO disembarking the BBJ, with Luke, Di and Archie on the steps behind him. The caption read:

> Maiden Voyage: Opposition Leader Max Masters
> arrives on the BBJ in Sydney last night, followed by
> core campaign team—Luke Harley (Chief of Staff),
> Dianna Freya (Advisor) and Archibald Andersen (Media
> Consultant).

Di caught me looking at it. 'Prick,' she whispered. She handed me page one of a Brisbane paper, which had printed a zoomed grab of the photo, picturing only Di and Archie.

> PREMIER'S SPIN DOCTOR JOINS MASTERS
> The Premier has been abandoned by his Chief Media
> Advisor, Archibald Andersen (pictured), who quit his
> George Street job to help Max Masters win top office.
> Andersen might be just what the doctor ordered for
> Masters, who, until now, has relied on new kid on the
> block Dianna Freya.

I leaned back in my chair to see Archie, oblivious to Di's fury, singing along to a toilet paper jingle on the radio.

The door opened and Luke walked in. Today's tie was a smattering of four-leaf clovers. He caught me staring and looked down as if to check he hadn't spilled anything on it. *Not unless he had luck for breakfast,* my head laughed.

'Where are we at?' he asked.

Di opened her mouth, but Archie was already talking. 'Here's the line-up so far for today's TVs,' he said. Di clenched her fists. 'Our guy's on *Brekky* and *Mornings*. Brennan's announcing her deputy and other cabinet changes today. She did a pretty full interview for *Nightcap* last night. We'll get some but not much coverage for our SMEs announcement.'

'I'm reasonably happy with that,' said Luke 'At least it'll take some of the heat out of the "bull" story.'

'We don't really have an SME policy unless Theo's come up with something genius overnight.' Di pulled a skirt on over the top of her sweat pants. 'We'll get some credit for coming out with something on Day One, but it won't be overly scrutinised.'

'How are we with the travelling media list?'

'Good.' Di yanked off the sweat pants. 'We've got a really hot line-up. Pretty Boy is joining us for at least the first fortnight, maybe the whole campaign.' Luke and Archie groaned. 'On the downside, we've got Gary Spinnaker.'

'Who's Pretty Boy?' I asked.

'Oscar Franklin,' she said.

The moniker suited him. Two weeks of eye candy could be sweet.

I thought you were looking forward to two weeks of wine, said my head. *You've quite the fickle palate.*

Luke scrolled through his BlackBerry. 'The LOO's on his way down. Are we ready to prep him?'

'Yep,' said Archie and Di simultaneously.

'Ruby.' Luke turned to me. 'We need you on the road with us today.'

'Sure,' I said, harbouring anxiety that I would be wearing the same outfit again tomorrow. My head mocked me for my vanity.

The LOO walked in with a bowl of cereal. 'Right, what's happening, kids?'

'We've done pretty well this morning,' said Di. 'The focus is on the brutality of Patton's removal, his legacy, and Brennan as the first female PM. It's a saturated news day, but we've punched through by praising Patton and being critical of Brennan. There's a lot of speculation but not much substance as to how Brennan managed to get rid of Patton so quietly.' Di paused. 'The problem for us today is the "bull" story.'

Max looked up from his Weetabix and rolled his eyes.

'Don't freak out,' said Di. 'I reckon it's worked in our favour. We'd be fighting for airspace if there was nothing controversial about what you said yesterday. Instead, we've kicked off a national debate about swearing.'

Luke took the floor. 'Everyone wants to talk to you today because they think you have a foul mouth. We're due to get some party polling stats tonight so we'll see how it's playing out. My gut tells me it's positive.'

'My dad disagrees with your gut,' said Max. 'He called to tell me Phyllis at bowls reckons I should watch my mouth.'

We all laughed. He was in good spirits. Di and Archie briefed him on the interviews as I ran to my room to pack. Within ten minutes, we were on our way to the television studios.

From the green rooms, I should have been paying

attention to the interviews, but I was distracted by all the beautiful people. I sat on a couch outnumbered by uber-chic fashionistas, rockers and soap stars, their shiny-toothed agents all arguing with producers. In comparison, the radio studios were dully lit hovels full of caffeine addicts in dirty denim and grungy T-shirts.

By eight o'clock I felt ready for lunch, but it was time for a breakfast meeting at party HQ. I had expected the party to be housed in a large, gleaming office building, but we pulled up at a blond-brick block with flickering fluorescent bulbs.

Mirabelle greeted Max and showed us to a meeting room with a laminated oval table and electric whiteboard. The air-conditioner hummed. 'Help yourselves to pastries, people,' she said.

Two croissants later, Mirabelle was running through an outline of the campaign strategy when Di tapped me on the shoulder and beckoned me into the hallway.

'Roo, I need your help. We're doing a school visit in the western suburbs in an hour, and Maddy, who is the advancer, just told me their cricket team is called the Burwood Bulls.'

'Great.'

'No, not great—the Burwood *Bulls*.'

'Bollocks.' I followed her out the door into a waiting car.

'Yeah, mate, more like bullocks.' The car pulled away. 'We can't cancel it because Archie sent a fucking media alert out, so they're all on their way up there.'

'Can't we plan it so Max isn't around any reference to the word?'

'They've got a massive sign out front saying WELCOME MAX MASTERS—GO THE BULLS.'

'Can Max play cricket?' I asked. 'Maybe he could join the cricket team on the oval with a bat and ball?'

'Good,' she said. 'Do it.'

'What do you mean by "do it"?'

'Make it happen.' She took a call.

'But...'

She pointed to my phone. I picked up my new Black-Berry and scrolled through the calendar. There was a number for Maddy. I called it.

'Hello,' said a broad Australian accent.

'Maddy, it's Roo,' I said, puzzled by my own introduction. 'I work on the campaign and Di's asked me to give you a call about this Bulls issue.'

'Thank God,' said Maddy. 'The crews are already getting shots of the sign—we can't ignore it.'

'We don't want to ignore it,' I said. 'We've decided to embrace it. Is anyone from the cricket team around?'

'Yeah, they were told to cancel practice today because the LOO's coming.'

'Tell them that practice is back on and ask if they would mind if Max joins in. What's the atmosphere like at the school?'

'Everyone's really excited.'

'Great. We're nearly there.'

As we pulled up at the school, Di called Luke to explain the situation. Almost instantly, my BlackBerry buzzed. It was Luke.

Good job, L

Di nudged me. 'That's Maddy.'

We got out of the car.

A tiny, toned woman about my age came bouncing

towards us through the car park. Her cropped, sunbleached hair stood out like a halo.

'G'day,' Maddy said. 'You must be Roo. Hi, Di. Let me show you both around.' We began walking.

Maddy could easily have been a school student, bar the well-worn riding boots and BlackBerry. Her tanned face was clean and fresh, not a jot of make-up.

'He's going to serve morning tea here at the tuck shop and then hit the oval for cricket practice.' She pointed to the sprawling green field.

'That was quick—I only called five minutes ago.'

She grinned. 'That's my job—I do everything the LOO does before he even knows he's doing it.'

Di went over to welcome the media assembled at the school gate waiting for the LOO. Max pulled up shortly after, looking relaxed, and greeted everyone before following Maddy through to the school hall. She was like a tour guide with an umbrella at the Spanish Steps.

We then followed the principal to the tuck shop, where Max rolled up his sleeves and joined the ladies serving morning tea.

'The Anzac bickies look great,' he said to one of the students. She broke her biscuit in half and shared it with him. Cameras clicked.

We wandered past classrooms to the oval, where the Burwood Bulls were practising.

'Here we go,' whispered Di. One of the kids threw Max the ball, which he caught effortlessly.

Afterwards, with cricket in the background, Max stood on the oval surrounded by journalists.

'Mr Masters,' said Oscar Franklin, who was even dishier in the flesh, particularly from behind. 'Is it just an unfortunate coincidence that you're here playing cricket with the Bulls on the very day you're trying to run away from the word?'

'I wish the Bulls luck with their game on Saturday,' said Max. 'And there's no need for me to do a bull-run away from anyone today except my old man. He rang to tell me his bowls club wants me to wash my mouth out with soap.'

Everyone smiled.

'Smiles are forgiveness in this game,' Di whispered into my ear. 'Good work.'

The cricket team stayed behind to watch the press conference and have their photos taken with Max. 'Excuse me, miss,' said a sweaty kid, 'can you take a photo of Max and me with my phone?'

'Sure,' I said, holding the space-aged, two-dimensional gadget on its side. I looked into the lens. 'Smile!' Click.

'Um, miss, you took a photo of your eye.'

'Did I? Sorry. That must be why they call it an iPhone.'

No one laughed. Max was flagging—it was the last of twelve photographs in the hot sun.

Oscar Franklin walked towards me and got down on one knee. 'Here, let me.' He took the phone from my hands. 'Say cheese, guys.'

Click.

'Thanks,' I said. 'I'm more of a BlackBerry girl. Those fandangled thingies are clearly designed for James Bond and teenage boys.'

'Franklin,' he said, holding up his own fandangled thingy. 'Oscar Franklin.'

'Oh. Ruby Stanhope.'

'Are you new to the team?'

'I am, actually.'

You're blushing, said my head. *Stop staring at his chest, you pervert.*

'Roo!' Di gestured for me to join her at the big blue bus that had pulled up at the front of the school.

'Bye, Oscar.'

'Lovely to meet you, Roo,' he said with an adorable, dimpled smile.

'Watch out for him,' Di warned when I reached her, then she clasped her megaphone hands around her mouth and morphed into a tour guide. 'Can all travelling media please board the bus now.'

I handed her a bottle of water. A few of the journalists, camera crews and photographers boarded the bus while others stood around to file stories. It was almost eleven o'clock and I'd been up for seven hours. I was starting to flag.

My BlackBerry beeped.

That worked well. Maddy

I wrote back.

Great event, Maddy. Let's grab a drink at the next stop. R

When everyone was on the bus, Di stood up. 'Welcome, everyone, to our campaign. Roo and I want you to know that we're here for you.'

Look what you've got yourself into, said my head.

'Like us, not many of you will have planned to be on the road for thirty-three days. You've all got editors and producers and deadlines. Roo and I are determined to make sure that you always have somewhere to write copy and file stories. If you need information about scheduling, come to Roo or me and we'll tell you what we know.

'First up, we're off to Brisbane, where Max will be giving a speech on small and medium enterprises. We'll circulate a release shortly and answer any questions you might have. Roo will come and meet you all now.'

I obliged. It wasn't even midday, but it looked as though Debs' shirt and trousers would see another day of wear after all.

Fast food, fast policy

I wanted to nap in the air but the journalists were anxious to see our press release. Although it was lunchtime, the media jet could offer only a selection of biscuits. Grumpiness spread like small pox through the passengers.

Di grabbed me by the shoulder and pulled me into the toilet, shutting the door.

'Look, I'm flattered, but I'm not into ladies.'

She didn't laugh. 'We're up the creek,' she said, breathless. 'They're going to eat me alive.'

'Snakes on a plane?'

Still no laugh. 'Luke vetoed the policy Theo's been working on because it was shit, and is rewriting it himself. The LOO's supposed to be giving a speech about a policy that hasn't been written and I've got jack-all to give this lot until it's sent to me.'

'Sit,' I said.

She hyperventilated and shook her head.

'Do as you're told,' I commanded, channelling my mother. She sank onto the toilet seat. I handed her a sick-bag from the dispenser. 'Put your head between your legs and breathe slowly into this.'

She looked up at me like Clem does when she's in trouble. 'Do it,' I said. The world slowed down for a minute. 'Now I'm going to go out there and talk to them and you're going to stay in here and splash water on your face.'

Di nodded, breathing deeply.

I may have sounded cool and confident, but in truth I had a serious case of nerves. I made my way to the front of the cabin and cleared my throat. 'Ladies and gentlemen.' I exaggerated my accent for effect. 'Due to the rushed circumstances of arranging this flight, we were unable to organise lunch for you.' This was met with a collective grumble.

'But when we land, I'll be going through a drive-through,' I improvised, 'so if you could put some thought into whether you're a burger or a nuggets person, I'll take your orders just prior to landing.' Most of them laughed.

'What about the release?' asked a bald grouch in row four.

'We will give you copies of the release half an hour before Max is due to speak. I know this is a pain, but we're having a few technology problems. We're confident these will be resolved by the end of Day One.'

'Day *Two*, you mean,' corrected the grouch.

'Give the girl a break, Gary,' yelled Oscar from the back.

'Thanks, everyone,' I said. It felt like a career highlight even if I would be taking drive-through orders.

Oscar stopped me as I passed him en route to the loo. 'Don't mind Spinnaker, Roo,' he said. 'He's more of a nugget, if you know what I mean.'

I smiled and returned to Di, who was applying concealer to her dark circles.

'You're a life-saver.'

'Hardly,' I said, attempting to be modest.

'Don't tell anyone I had a meltdown,' she pleaded, 'especially Archie.'

'What meltdown?'

We rejoined the cabin. Di fielded a volley of questions regarding a policy she knew nothing about. I worked my way through each row taking orders. I disembarked first in Brisbane. The humidity was so thick that even the palm trees were sweating. I hailed a taxi.

'Is there a McDonald's between here and the convention centre?' I asked the driver.

'There's one at the Gabba. You got a craving?'

'Isn't the Gabba the cricket ground?'

'It's also a suburb.'

I Googled the number and dialled.

'McDonald's Woolloongabba, Codie speaking. How can I help you?' said a breaking voice.

'Hi, my name is Ruby and I need to place a very big order.' I drew breath. 'Twelve Quarter Pounder meals, eight Big Mac meals, six Cheeseburger meals and eleven Filet-O-Fish meals. Half with Coke, half with Diet Coke. I need it all in half an hour.'

'Is this a prank?'

'No,' I said, 'I work for the Leader of the Opposition and there's a plane full of hungry journalists waiting to be fed.'

'We'll do our best.'

I emailed Di.

D, McDonald's at the Gabba is processing thirty-seven
burgers and fries. Done in thirty. Try stalling them with
the release for fifteen. R

R, Stalling not an issue. Still no release from the boys. Shit
a brick. Di

When I arrived at McDonald's, Codie was frenetic,
filling cups of Coke. 'I was praying you'd turn up,' he
said when I introduced myself. 'My manager's on her
lunch break and she'd freak out if I'd fallen for a hoax.'

Ten minutes later, I boarded the bus, laden with greasy
paper bags. By the time the burgers had been distributed
and demolished, we'd arrived at the convention centre.
Di and I joined Luke and the LOO in a backstage room
with a tense vibe.

'Mate, I read the policy doc,' said Di. 'I think it's a
winner.'

Luke's policy, which I'd read on the bus over a Diet
Coke, seemed to be a series of motherhood statements
about the plight of small business. The only real commitment was the introduction of a government mediation
centre to resolve default disputes between banks and business. It was uninspiring and unworkable.

The LOO sat at a desk in the corner of the room
reading through his speech. We sat in silence and waited
for the verdict.

'This is a bogus attempt to make us look like we're ahead
of the game, and what it does is make us seem desperate
to catch up.' Max stabbed his pen into the pile of paper.

Luke fiddled with the lid of his pen.

'The gallery will rightly write this up as policy on the run. It does *nothing* of substance. What happened to our Business Bonus?'

'We couldn't get it costed in time and we can't afford to go out with un-costed policies in this climate,' said Luke.

'You're being melodramatic, Max,' said Di. 'This is just the start of our SME policy. And it's an important start because we're showing everyone that we're in touch with the problems SMEs face and we're prioritising them.'

'She's right,' said Luke.

'What do you think, Roo?' asked the LOO.

Don't fuck this up, Ruby, said my helpful head. *Tell them what you think.*

But this was one of those awkward moments in life when you know that the truth won't help. There was no point in telling Max the policy was meaningless and impracticable—the media already had a copy so Max would have to sell it regardless. Luke looked up at me with anxious eyes.

'My father started his career as a bank manager and used to recount harrowing stories of having to break the news of default and repossession to his clients when they couldn't make their loan payments. It was dreadful for everyone.

'The mediation centre is a good move for bankers and business owners alike. It tells them that you appreciate what they're going through and that while it will not fix the problem it's a start.'

We waited for judgment. Finally, Max sighed. 'I guess so. Who's doing my make-up?'

'I am,' said Di, giving me a pat on the back.

I could hear my own heartbeat, but my head was louder. *First day on the job and you're already a yes-man. Well done, Ruby.*

But Luke was down on his luck, I told my head, despite having the best of intentions and an infestation of four-leaf clovers around his neck. Blame Theo, head.

'Can you track down Archie and tell him that's how we're positioning this?' Luke pulled me out of the room.

'But I just made that up.'

'That's what we all do.'

I dialled Archie's number. Luke took a step closer to me. 'Thanks, Roo.'

I waved his thanks away. 'Archie, it's Roo. Where are you?'

'In the auditorium.'

'Luke wanted you to know that we're positioning this as the first of a raft of announcements for business to demonstrate that this is a priority for the LOO.' I said it so definitively that I surprised myself and immediately wanted to take it back.

'Understood,' said Archie.

I went back into the room, where Max was now amending parts of his speech while Di did his make-up. A shattered Theo was lying on the couch, looking even older than he had yesterday.

'Showtime,' said Max. Luke followed him out.

'Wait here for me, Roo,' said Di. 'I'm going to give Archie a hand.'

Delighted with the opportunity to stop, I sat down and watched the LOO's speech on the screen set up for us.

'I'm Theo,' said Theo, still prostrate.

'I know.'

'How?'

'Because we met yesterday.'

'You must look different today.'

'Actually, I'm wearing exactly the same thing as yesterday, minus the belt and knickers.'

He stared at my crotch.

'I am *wearing* knickers today, just not the same ones as yesterday.'

'Good to know.' He yawned.

'Give me your glasses,' I demanded. They were so greasy they were opaque. He obliged. I pulled a cleaning cloth from my Toolkit and polished them for him.

We listened to Max. He delivered the lacklustre policy with panache and received a standing ovation at the end. I gave Theo his glasses.

'How did you do that?'

'Magic.'

Ten minutes later, Max, Luke and Di came back into the room and slumped on the couch.

'What's next?' Max picked up an apple and began to munch.

'A meeting with the pollsters,' said Luke. 'Your next interview has been canned so it's just the fundraiser and then a strategy meeting.'

'And where are we tomorrow?'

'Somewhere in Australia,' said Di.

'Get the pollsters to meet us here if they can,' Max requested. 'I don't want to get in the car again and I need to call Shelly and Abba.'

We all left the room to let him speak with his wife and daughter in peace.

This is ridiculous, I thought, lying in the hallway

outside, sharing a BlackBerry charger with Di. Was it this manic all the time? 'Any chance I could have half an hour to buy some clothes?' I asked Di. 'I don't really want to wear this for a third consecutive day.'

'Sure,' she smiled. 'I've run out of undies and I don't have time to wash them so I might tag along. Let's go in an hour or two.'

I used the quiet time to read my employment contract, but I probably shouldn't have because it just upset me. The party had offered me a forty-day contract, paying the equivalent of about £8 an hour if I kept working at this pace.

This isn't worth it, Ruby, advised my head. *You're supposed to be on holiday and instead you're fatigued and being paid tuppence for your trouble.*

I went to the bathroom and dialled. 'Aunt Daphne, it's me.'

'Hold on a second, Ruby.' I held for half a minute. 'Sorry about that. One of the pups gets excited when he sees us. I've named him The Widdler.'

'Apt,' I said. 'And the other two?'

'The little girl, Champagne, is bright and bubbly, and JFK's the howler.'

'You named a dog after a president?'

'He was a great orator,' she said. 'How's Sydney?'

'Brisbane, actually.'

'Oh, dear. Debs put your luggage in internal post so it's probably in Sydney by now.'

'Crap. Does her firm have an office in Brisbane?'

'I'll check,' she said. 'How are you finding it?'

'Exhilarating but exhausting.'

'Like all of life's great pleasures,' she said wryly.

'The pay is shit.'

'You're getting paid?'

'Yes, I'm on a contract with the party. It's worse pay than I was getting as a graduate.'

'You were a *banker*, Ruby. And you didn't like it very much. Anyway, darling, you're supposed to be on holiday so you weren't expecting to make any money this month. You should see this as a bonus.'

My head rolled its eyes.

'Sorry, darling, got to go. The Widdler's living up to his name.'

Back in the hallway, Di leaped to her feet. 'Brennan's doing her presser about the cabinet line-up!'

We ran to the convention centre cafe, where, like a mirage in the Sahara, there was a wall-mounted television showing *The Bold and the Beautiful*. Brooke and Ridge were smooching.

'Do you have Sun?' Di puffed.

'You can switch in the ad break,' said the drowsy waitress. 'You haven't even ordered anything.'

Di looked homicidal. I stepped in. 'Two of your largest lattes, please,' I said apologetically as the Commercial Gods showed Di a little mercy.

'Thank fuck,' muttered Di, standing on a chair to operate the thing. Over on the Sun network, Brennan was finishing her press conference flanked by two sharp-suited men: one tall, one short.

'Who are those guys?'

'The short one's Stein, the Minister for Finance,' she said. 'Brennan hates him, but he's the only one who could feasibly step up into the Treasury role. Mayne's the tall one. He's Leader of the House, and Communities Minister.

She must be making Mayne her deputy.'

'Does this mean Stein and Mayne were part of the plot to bring down Patton?'

'Possibly, but not necessarily.'

The waitress handed us what looked like vats of coffee. 'That's $11.90, and you can put it back on *The Bold* now.'

'I've got to go to this polling meeting,' Di said outside.

Clearly I wasn't invited. 'Call me when you're ready to shop.'

With my luggage and litre of flat white, I went outside to get a bit of air. My sunglasses fogged up in the stinking heat. Reaching to defog my lenses, I upended the coffee all over my shirt and trousers. 'Pants!' I screamed, rescuing a Miu from irreversible staining, whereupon I lost my footing and fell. The contents of my hand and overnight bags were strewn across the steps of Brisbane's convention centre.

'Are you all right?' called a man from below. I recognised the resonant voice instantly. Oscar.

'Absolutely,' I lied. 'Minor mishap.' I reached for my arse, hoping that the seam of Debs' trousers was still intact. Oscar, who had been doing a piece to camera at the foot of the steps, climbed towards me. Yesterday's underpants were inside out on a nearby step—I shoved them into my pocket.

'Nice trip?' asked Oscar, lending me a strong arm.

Back on my feet, I thanked him and gave up on covering my latte-drenched flat chest. 'I'd better go and change,' I said, not that there was anything to change into. We collected my scattered possessions, some more embarrassing than others, and I hailed a cab.

Oscar waved as we pulled away from the curb.

'I need to buy some clothes,' I said to my eighty-in-the-shade driver.

'I can see that.'

He deposited me at a large pedestrian mall and said, 'David Jones is just in there. It's a bit pricey, but there's quite the collection of fashions.'

Inside the air-conditioned building I slumped at the nearest counter, behind which stood a woman with a cantaloupe-sized grey bun.

She looked at me. 'Oh, sweet pea.'

I had found the Fairy Godmother.

'Take a seat and I'll bring you a few things. You probably shouldn't try anything on because you're a bit...'

'Damp,' I said. Despite being marinated in caffeine, I was dog-tired and couldn't be bothered with shopping: an altogether unfamiliar sensation.

'Sweet pea,' said the Fairy Godmother a few minutes later. I glanced up at a chic dove-grey pencil skirt, a capped-sleeve, silk indigo top and a cotton, charcoal cardigan.

'You're a ten, yes?'

'I am.' I stood to touch the fabrics.

'I brought you something else,' she said, 'but I don't know if you'll like it.'

It was the kind of little black dress women spend their lives searching for. Scooped in neck and back, it was sleeveless and fitted to the knee with a short slit in the back. I did a mental raid of my shoe cupboard in London for the perfect match.

'I'll take it all,' I said, 'and I'll need three bras, three pairs of pants, another top, jeans and a pair of not-too-high pointed black pumps.'

I emailed Di.

D, doused myself in coffee so I'm at a place called David Jones. I realise we've only just met, but if you want me to buy your pants, I can. R

Thanks Roo. Hipster. Size twelve. Black. D

Houndstooth shopping bags in hand, I cabbed it to the hotel.

'Today was the first complete day of this bizarre election campaign and it was a cracker, with new Prime Minister Gabrielle Brennan promoting her arch nemesis, Bart Stein, to the coveted Treasury position.'

Oscar's six o'clock report cut to a shot of the Burwood High School sign and then footage of Max on the cricket field. 'But in the western suburbs of Sydney, Opposition Leader Max Masters was busy making amends for his bull-in-a-china-shop gaffe with high school cricket team the Burwood Bulls.

'It's been a busy day in the Masters camp,' said Oscar, 'where in Brisbane this afternoon the Opposition Leader announced plans to establish a national mediation centre for banks and small businesses, in what the business community is calling a "positive step forwards". But banks used the opportunity to take a swipe at the Opposition's inexperience.' The coverage switched to footage of a groomed woman with tattooed-on eyebrows.

'This shows a degree of naivety on the part of the Opposition,' she said. 'When businesses default, banks often have no option but to move in and seize assets. It's not personal—it's business. Mr Masters would do well to understand the distinction.'

Di dimmed the volume and the LOO left in a funk,

followed closely by Luke, who was using his debacle of a tie to stretch his arms behind him.

'I thought it was good,' I said.

'It was,' said Di. 'He's just too tired and close to it to know. Anyway, for now we need to finalise an event for tomorrow, tell the cops so they can advance it, watch the rest of today's coverage and figure out what radios we're doing in the morning.'

'Now?'

'Well, yes,' laughed Di, 'but there's nothing to say this can't be done over room service and a glass of wine.'

Theo staggered past us, stretching his arms above his head. 'Two days down,' he said, 'only thirty-one to go.'

'I'll get the wine,' I said.

Bankers anonymous

Having crawled into bed at 2 a.m., I wasn't particularly impressed to find myself back on the BBJ waiting to take off for Perth at half six. The knowledge that I had myself to blame made the experience considerably less enjoyable.

The night before, Maddy had called from Perth to complain about an event she was advancing for later in the week. It was supposed to be the launch of a policy to get unemployed school-leavers to do two months of community service before starting further education, a gap year or a job. Max called it 'Serve the Nation'.

Serve the Nation was to be the perfect Sunday papers story, full of colour and controversy to get people talking about us rather than them.

'I got to the refugee centre in Perth where we were supposed to be launching the thing and found a hand-written "back in five" sign on the door,' Maddy told me. 'Forty minutes later, a dude with six eyebrow rings turned up and asked if I could come back later because he had an Indonesian lesson. I asked whether he was learning Bahasa as part of his work with the refugee centre. He goes, "Nah, man, I met the hottest chick surfing in Bali."'

So that's how Maddy came to be desperate and event-less in Perth.

Meanwhile in Brisbane, Gewurztraminers in our grip, Di and I had decided Day Three was going to be about our cohesive leadership team in contrast with the 'bunch of back-stabbers' on the other side. The problem was that shadow ministers were now scattered across the country. There was no way we could have sixteen of them in Sydney in a matter of hours, so we scrapped that.

Plan B was Ballarat. Our advancer on the ground had checked into his hotel only to be asked by the concierge when the Prime Minister would be arriving.

'I work for Max Masters,' he said, 'the Leader of the Opposition.'

'A thousand apologies,' said the concierge. 'I assumed you were with the Prime Minister's office because they're due to check in tomorrow morning.'

'What's wrong with that?' I'd asked Di.

'Ballarat's a big town,' she said, 'but *way* too small for two prime ministerial candidates at once.'

Crestfallen, she had returned to her caesar salad deep in thought about Plan C. My BlackBerry buzzed.

Good news—found venue. Children's hospital radio program. Lovely, enthusiastic young team entertains sick kids. Will keep you posted. Maddy

I showed it to Di to cheer her up. She lit up like a bride at the altar. 'Gold,' she said, almost knocking me off my chair with an impassioned high five. 'Ask Maddy to have it ready for tomorrow. I'll call Luke, and have Beryl get the planes ready.'

'You can praise me later,' Maddy said when I called. 'I've got to keep sorting through the logistics if we're going to make this happen by Thursday.'

'What about tomorrow?'

Maddy lowered her voice a few octaves. 'What *about* tomorrow?'

'I was so excited that I told Di, who was overwhelmed by the idea and is intent on doing it.'

'Shit, Roo, I'm on my own out here; I can't pull this off for tomorrow night.'

'Afternoon.'

'Fuck a duck. I'll call you back.'

Within an hour, we had an event to match the planned and costed Serve the Nation policy. Patch Radio, a children's community radio program for inpatients at the WA kids' hospital, would show us work being done by its volunteers. It was a perfect match for our policy launch. Di, Luke and the LOO had been ecstatic, but my new friendship with Maddy was on shaky ground.

Now, back on the BBJ, Archie was ready to brief us on the morning's coverage over a few slices of toast.

'I reckon we won yesterday,' he said.

Max looked pleased with himself, but it could just have been that Shelly had joined us for the Perth trip. He took her hand in his.

'This morning's biggest news is the fallout from Patton's demise, with a whole bunch of Brennan's moles coming out of the woodwork claiming credit for getting rid of Patton. They're being called "Brennan's Brutus Brigade", and the *Herald* reckons her honeymoon is the shortest in history. Spinnaker gave us a good run on our SME policy.'

'Roo must've laced his Big Mac with an upper,' said Di on speakerphone. She was at the airport waiting to board the media jet.

'I want you all to be prepared for tomorrow's South-poll,' said Luke. Today's tie looked like metallic seeded mustard. 'Who knows how it'll pan out, but it could be dire. Our own pollsters are telling us that things aren't as rosy as they should be for a new PM, but her novelty will definitely count for something. We stand to lose a few points and we'll need to get to the end of Week One looking relaxed and steady but ready to govern.'

As he talked, I drafted a new To Do list on my Black-Berry.

1. Ask Di about how polls work
2. Put coffee-stained clothes in hotel laundry bag
3. Ask Di who pays for Item 2
4. Confirm visa
5. Sign contract for negligible remuneration
6. Confirm details of Perth event with Maddy
7. Call parents.

The best and worst thing about Perth was that it was so far away from the east coast. Best because it gave Maddy an additional six hours to arrange the event; worst because I was rendered useless for the entire duration of the flight. My BlackBerry sat on my lap like a temptress, tantalising but totally untouchable thanks to the strict 'flight mode only' policy on board the BBJ. The only productive thing I could do was to work with Theo on Max's speaking notes to add a little colour about Patch Radio.

I asked him for a copy.

'I don't have one,' said Theo.

'Do you know who does?'

'No, but if you find one can you let me know so I can stop writing it?'

It was too early to be messed with. 'Are you saying you haven't even written a first draft?' I demanded, surprised by my own tone.

Theo rubbed his greasy glasses on his tie. 'I'll tell you what: how about I show you what I've written so far and if you've got any feedback just let me know.'

He unbuckled himself and stood up, leaving me with the Word document open on his screen. I handed him my cleaning cloth. 'Which document is it?' I scrolled up and down the page to find the text, but there was none. 'This is quite an elaborate joke to play for someone who has an entire speech to write in five hours.'

'Thanks.' He handed back my cloth. 'Now, will you leave me alone so I can get some work done?'

He might have had the appearance of a golf-loving retiree from Bournemouth who considers Burger King in Ibiza an exotic dining experience, but Theo was as big an oddball as I'd ever come across.

I returned to my seat, rested my eyes for a minute and opened them four hours later.

'You snore,' said Theo.

'You're rude,' I said, mopping up the crusted drool in the corner of my mouth.

'Can you have a read of this speech? It needs a bit of...I don't know. Just read it.' He thrust his laptop onto my tray table, took the newspaper on my lap and went to the toilet. I tried not to think about it.

As I read the speech, I could hear Max giving it. The rhythm matched his style of delivery. It captured the spirit of Patch Radio, the policy's purpose and Max's belief in community service. Annoyingly, there was nothing for me to add but praise.

The toilet flushed and Theo returned to his seat, handing me my newspaper.

'Keep it,' I said.

'Thank you. See what I mean about the speech?'

'I think it reads beautifully.'

'Surely you've got *something* to say about it.'

I shook my head. He snatched back his laptop and stomped off.

As I searched my mind for something worthwhile to contribute to the speech, Shelly came to sit with me. She looked far more energetic than the rest of us—this was her first day on the campaign trail.

'So you were an investment banker,' she said. 'So was I.'

Until then, I had been labouring under the misapprehension that the Leader of the Opposition's wife probably didn't do much else. Not once had I thought she might have an independent career, and I hated myself for it.

Talk shop, Ruby, said my head.

'Corporate finance?'

'Securities. Commodities, mainly.'

'Why did you stop?'

'Max became Shadow Minister for Resources and Energy, so I took a break. It's good to be around while Abigail is at school.'

'Do you miss it?'

Don't pry, Ruby, said my head.

Shelly nodded. 'I loved it. It made me tick.' She fiddled

with her gold wedding band and extended her slender, manicured fingers to examine it. 'If you were a journo I'd tell you I didn't and that I'm honoured to be supporting Max in this very important role. But in truth, it shits me to tears that I can't do both.'

'Why can't you?' I backtracked. 'Sorry, you don't have to talk about this, of course. I'm just interested in how it works.'

She smiled. 'There are no hard and fast rules, but if there's a public perception of conflict, we err on the safe side. In reality, as a shadow minister or even as LOO, Max never made any decisions that would affect my work or vice versa, but because the perception could have been used against us both, we decided to choose between careers.'

She leaned in so close I could smell her shampoo. 'Great email, by the way,' she whispered.

'Which email?'

'One of my old banking buddies forwarded it to me. You should be proud.'

Don't encourage her, my head begged.

I flushed red and buckled for landing. 'Does anyone else—'

'I haven't told a soul.'

That's when it occurred to me. 'Theo,' I called. He couldn't hear me. 'Theo!'

'What?' he asked, still annoyed.

'You didn't say why this policy makes us different.'

He stared at the ceiling, then pulled out his laptop, which was supposed to have been stowed for landing, and tapped furiously at his keyboard until the flight attendant confiscated it.

∞

That afternoon at the hospital in Perth, one of the radio hosts led Max, Shelly and a cohort of cameras through a brightly coloured ward. Maddy was in her element. She had spoken beforehand to the Health Department and a group of patients' parents to seek their permission to film. Everyone was thrilled to be meeting Max and Shelly.

Genevieve, a little girl not much older than Clem, showed Shelly how the radio worked. 'You see, Shelly'— her big brown eyes gleamed from beneath an electric-blue bandana—'I have my own headphones so I can hear Patch. Sometimes they have music and sometimes they read stories to us. If I call them I can request a song.'

'What's your favourite song?' asked Shelly, sitting on the hospital bed, next to Genevieve's dad.

Genevieve pulled Shelly in close, whispering something into her ear. Shelly smiled. The sound technicians leaned in with their boom mikes.

'What did she say, Shelly?' asked one of the journalists, notepad at the ready.

'Can I tell them?' she asked the little girl, who nodded coyly.

'Genevieve loves Chris Isaak's "Baby Did a Bad, Bad Thing".'

Genevieve buried her head in Shelly's arm to hide from the laughing journalists. Max was standing at the end of Genevieve's bed. 'Max loves that song too,' said Shelly. 'It's on his iPod.'

'I can request it for you, if you'd like,' offered Genevieve.

'I'd like that very much,' said Max.

Julius, one of the volunteers, showed Max into the tiny studio and handed him a pair of headphones. 'Hi, everyone,' said Julius. 'I'd like to introduce a friend of ours, Max Masters. He's the Leader of the Opposition.'

'Hi, kids,' said Max. 'I want to say a special hello to Genevieve in ward sixteen, who said you would play me "Baby Did a Bad, Bad Thing"—we both love that song.' Julius obliged and Max bopped embarrassingly to the music. From outside, I saw a beautiful shot of Max, Shelly and Genevieve on the preview screen of a snapper's camera.

The scrum pushed through to the press conference room to set up, while Max collected his thoughts.

'Can you do his make-up?' asked Di, shoving a toiletries bag into my hand before running into the conference room.

From Subprime to Primer, joked my head. *Ruby Stanhope's bestselling memoir.*

I unzipped the bag, pulling out a latex sponge and powder pack, and edged towards Max.

'Have I got BO or something?' he teased. 'Believe me, I'd do it myself, but Di says I'm crap at it.'

He closed his eyes. This wasn't like doing my own make-up. The sponge rasped against the stubble on his chin and I couldn't figure out how to highlight a man's cheekbones or whether I was even supposed to.

'How long have these guys at Patch been going for?' Max asked.

'Ten years,' I said, dabbing at his nose. 'They've had the volunteer program in place for about eighteen months and take senior school kids and university students on six-month rotations.' I started on Max's forehead. 'You've met Julius already and you'll meet Ying and Praneeta. They're all school-leavers. Julius is about to start medicine at UWA. Ying's little brother is a patient here in the oncology ward and she's taking a gap year next year. Praneeta is starting a newspaper cadetship in six months.'

Di exploded into the room with Shelly. 'Okay, ready when you...Christ! He looks like a bloody inpatient!'

I stood back as if I'd been caught at the scene of a crime. Max looked like a geisha.

'I see you found the powder,' Di said.

'Sorry, I've never done this before.' I dug through my handbag for the wet tissues in my Toolkit.

'You're like Mary Poppins,' said Max, wiping at his face.

'I'll fix this,' said Di. 'You go and tell them he's on his way in.'

I raced into the conference room next door where everyone was staring at the wall clock. 'Sorry people,' I said, 'two minutes max.'

Oscar laughed at my unintended pun.

Shortly afterwards, a less creamy Max paced into the room and stood beside the Patch Radio volunteers.

'Julius, Ying and Praneeta have chosen to end their childhood by bringing laughter and fun to kids not that much younger than they are—and these are kids who could really do with a laugh. The great work these guys do will have lasting effects. Their well-spent summer will shape them for years to come.

'I can tell you this because when I left school I spent the same summer break volunteering for the local RSL, where I met some incredible old blokes who shared their war stories—stories that were harrowing and inspirational. That summer experience led me to a career in the armed services, and now this gig, and possibly an even bigger one if you decide to give it to me on the third of April.

'Prime Minister Brennan says that there's not much the government can do for the charity sector in tough economic times. I disagree. There's plenty government can and should be doing for the not-for-profit sector because our nation wouldn't function without organisations like Patch Radio.

'If we are elected, I hope the next round of school-leavers will take advantage of the opportunity to participate in our Serve the Nation program. It will pay dividends for us all.'

Leaning on my shoulder at the back of the room was a spent Maddy.

'Well done,' I whispered.

'Thanks, mate,' she said. '*This* is why we do it.'

Fish out of water

Serve the Nation landed us with the most popular story on every news website in the country for two days. Lines were loaded at the nation's talkback radio stations, and TV bulletins ran polls asking viewers whether they supported the initiative. Brennan was on the backfoot, forced to either denounce the policy or back it. She chose the former, resulting in headlines like BRENNAN DID A BAD, BAD THING.

Better still, Luke was given a sneak preview of the Southpoll results, which had us only two points behind Brennan on a two-party-preferred basis, whatever that was. According to Luke, this gave us underdog status without making us losers.

By far the biggest news of the day was the *Nightcap* revelation that a senior government backbencher had masterminded the plot to get rid of Patton on the proviso that he would become Minister for Foreign Affairs, but a callous last-minute manoeuvre had left him stranded on the backbench with the mere promise of a position in the outer ministry if the party retained government.

We fantasised about the conversations they'd be having over at Camp Brennan. The Prime Minister must have thought she'd made the cleverest move in political history, only to have it all blow up in her face by Day Four of the campaign.

Maddy and I had been asked to advance an event for Felix Winks, a human rights lawyer and promising young candidate in the Adelaide seat of Watson. Maddy fancied Felix and was determined to leave a lasting impression.

'Felix and I have history,' she said from the driver's seat of a hire car on the way to the electorate in question. 'National Conference 2001. He moved a motion. I seconded it...' She sighed. 'We're going to do a shopping-centre walk.'

I imagined Max and Shelly in hiking boots on a browsing expedition. 'I'm new to this, Maddy,' I said, unwrapping a white mint-flavoured sweet. 'You're going to have to explain.'

'You chart a path for the candidate through a shopping centre or pedestrian mall so they can stop and talk to people on the way.' She held out her hand for a Mintie. 'For a politician to be able to have normal conversations in normal places with normal people is good,' she said through stuck-together teeth. 'And anything can happen in a shopping centre. You name it: protesters with flaming effigies, old people yelling abuse, kids calling you names, babies crying or spewing or both, and security can kick you out if it gets really bad. It's great.'

'Why not just go somewhere safe then?' I couldn't follow her logic.

'Because when a politician can handle an effigy or a spewing baby without losing the plot, it buys a lot of goodwill. On the other hand, if a baby cries and the polly freaks out and hands the kid back to its mum, that'll make the six o'clock news and everyone will talk about it.'

We parked outside a small strip of shops and offices. 'This is it.' She pointed to a caravan plastered with yellow FELIX WINKS FOR WATSON signs. According to the dashboard, the temperature outside was thirty-two degrees. 'How's my hair?' She sprayed herself with perfume.

'Lovely,' I coughed.

We went inside to find a cluster of campaign workers folding letters. Envelopes stuck to their forearms on account of the lack of air-conditioning. In what looked like a stationery cupboard, we found Felix Winks on the phone. He wore a big NO WHALING badge, which made his lapel sag.

He finished his call, stood up and smiled at us. 'Great to see you, Maddy.'

'Hi,' said Maddy, as if she was auditioning for a porno.

'Roo.' I shook his hand.

'I'd offer you both a seat but I've only got two,' he said. 'Let's go out for coffee.'

He led us down the street to a quaint little coffee shop where everyone knew his name. 'What can I get you?' he asked.

Maddy froze.

'I'd like a latte,' I said. 'And you, Maddy?'

'Same,' she swooned. 'But make it skinny. I only drink skinny.'

Save that poor girl from herself, Ruby.

'So,' Felix said, 'how do you want to do this?'

Maddy reddened. I stepped in. 'Max and Shelly will be here at half four, leaving us enough time for a quick half-hour walk-through.'

Maddy's hand trembled so much she struggled to pick up her teaspoon. I thought I had better continue. 'I understand you've been talking to Maddy about a shopping-centre walk.'

'Yes,' he said. 'The local Westfield works well for me because it's a Friday so we'll get the after-school mums and kids.' His brick of a phone started to vibrate violently on the table. 'This will be centre management—I'd better take it.' He took the call outside.

I turned to Maddy and whispered, 'I have no idea what I'm doing. You need to take over.'

She tore open a packet of sugar and emptied it every-where but in her coffee. 'I'm cool,' she said, 'just a little jumpy—too much caffeine.'

Felix returned. 'We can go for a run-through now if we like. Does that work for you?'

'Yes,' said Maddy, 'we can come together—go together.'

We piled into the car and hit the road, stopping a hundred yards away at a set of lights near a busy intersection. Outside, in the scorching heat, a man was smoothing an adhesive sign onto a billboard. It was a colossal photograph of the LOO.

'What does it say?' Felix squinted in the sunlight.

'MAX MASTERS: STEADY HANDS, READY TO GOVERN.' I scanned the photograph. The silvery tie was perfect with his skin tone. His smile was friendly, his eyes serious. 'Oh no.' I groaned.

'What?' They both turned to me.

I pointed to the adjacent billboard.

EXPERIENCING ERECTILE PROBLEMS? TRY READY, STEADY, GO! CALL 1300 GET IT UP.

'That's just great,' said Felix. 'On the same street as my bloody campaign office.'

I took a photograph of the billboards and emailed it to Luke.

Hi Luke. Postcard from Adelaide. Regrettable slogan coincidence. R

Maddy found a parking space at the shopping centre and we were inside the blissfully cool air-conditioned building when my phone rang. It was Luke.

'Tell me you're kidding.' His voice was low.

'Sorry, Luke, photos don't lie.'

'There's not much we can do about it now, I guess. How big is it?'

'Long and stiff as a board.'

'Shhhh,' he said, 'don't make me laugh—Max is doing live radio. See you in Adelaide.'

I turned to Felix, who was busy chatting with Russell from centre management. Maddy stood behind Felix, shamelessly scoping out his arse.

We were shown the entrance Max and Shelly would use and walked past a number of shops, including a green grocer, bakery, butcher, shoe repair, cafe and pet shop.

'All of these tenants are happy to have Mr and Mrs Masters in their shops,' Russell said, 'except the pet shop owner, because she's worried the flashes will spook the kittens.'

'Thanks for your time, Russell.' Felix shook his hand.

'No worries, Felix,' said Russell. 'My wife and I'll be

voting for you. Will your girlfriend be joining us this afternoon?'

'Girlfriend?' hissed Maddy.

'Nonie's at work,' said Felix, 'but she'll come if she can—she's dying to meet Max and Shelly.'

'Terrific,' I said, to distract him from the sound of Maddy's heart shattering into a billion pieces.

Maddy excused herself. I took the opportunity to check my BlackBerry. I had about eighty unread emails, which seemed impossible because I didn't know that many people in this country let alone people with my four-day-old email address. There was one from Luke.

R

Please find a way to get the media bus to the shopping centre without passing the newly erected billboard.

Couldn't resist.

L

PS Let's chat about your role at some point. Keep up the good work.

I went to find Maddy in the loos.

'Where are you?' My voice echoed through the stalls. 'Anyway, what kind of a name is Nonie?'

I heard a giggle. 'A dumb one,' Maddy said, opening the door. 'He's just so spunky.'

'That means something entirely different where I come from,' I said. 'There are better candidates for you, I'm sure of it.'

'Doubt it.' She reapplied gloss in the mirror. 'There's no time to find a bloke in this job—it's all pollies, staff and journos, all of whom are off limits.'

'All of them?'

'All of them. Why?'

Yes, Ruby, why? asked my head.

'Come on,' I said, 'we need to find a way to get the media bus here without passing the billboard.'

'I'll do that. You wait for the cops and buy me some chocolate.'

I went outside to Felix. 'What are you wearing this afternoon?'

'This.'

My head shook itself.

'Felix, you're about to be on national television and these will become your new file photographs with all the local papers.'

He looked down at his front-pleated chinos and the stripy shirt under his droopy jacket.

'I've watched enough Trinny and Susannah to know that shirt will strobe on telly, the jacket and chinos are too similar to look contrasting and too different to look matched. The LOO will probably be wearing a suit because he's coming straight from the plane.'

He looked wounded.

'Sorry.'

'No worries,' said Felix, perking up a bit. 'I'll go home and change. I've got a really gangster pinstripe—'

I shook my head. 'Anything plain?'

'Nonie knows my wardrobe better than I do. I'll get her on the phone.' He dialled and gave me his handset.

'Nonie, my name's Roo and I work for Max Masters. I need your help. Has Felix got any block-colour suits?'

'I am *so* glad you asked. I bought one for him, but he never wears it because he thinks it's too flash. It's just a two-button black suit I got in the sales last year from Hugo Boss. It fits him like a glove. He has a white shirt and textured red tie to go with it.'

'Gorgeous,' I said. 'Is it clean?'

'It's still got the tags on. Listen, while I've got you on the phone I was thinking of wearing a little royal-blue summer dress and white cardigan—does that sound okay?'

'How little?'

She laughed. 'Below the knee.'

'Shoes?'

'White sandals, low-heeled.'

'Lovely,' I said, 'I look forward to meeting you.' I handed Felix his phone. 'Go home. Nonie knows what to do.'

When the cops had arrived and were satisfied with the venue, I went in search of chocolate and called Debs to track down my suitcase.

'Young Ruby,' she said, 'you'll be pleased to know I sent your bag to Perth with my colleague.'

'Actually, I'm in Adelaide.'

'Bugger. Are you going to be there overnight?'

'I have no idea.'

'Well, when you know, tell me and I'll have it couriered to you. Are you still wearing your pink frock?'

'No,' I said. 'I bought myself some new gear and I sort of borrowed your overnight bag from Daphne's cupboard in Melbourne.'

'Did you now?' She laughed. 'And all this time I've been self-flagellating for my poor wardrobe-challenged niece, only to discover she has stolen my favourite pants.'

'I didn't steal any of your pants. That's disgusting.'

'Trousers are pants in this country, dear girl,' she said.

'The only people who wear trousers are old men and, in any case, they usually refer to them as slacks. Flip-flops are thongs, thongs are g-strings, sweets are lollies and a lay-by is a purchasing method—not a lorry stop. And we don't say lorry. It sounds like a girl's name, not a truck. Rhymes with fuck—far more appropriate. Daph has the list.'

'Whatever,' I said. 'Anyway, Aunty Debs, I'm very impressed that you referred to me as your niece. And there I was thinking you were a puppy-hating commitmentphobe.'

'I did *not* call you my niece. Anyway, I've got to go, champ. Super busy.' She hung up.

Then I remembered the trousers. I had left them and Debs' shirt in the Perth hotel laundry. I emailed Beryl.

Beryl

Could you please track down the number for housekeeping at the hotel in Perth? I need to do some urgent trousers recovery.

Roo

For the life of me, I couldn't remember the name of the hotel. I did recall that the bed had been comfortable and I hadn't spent enough time in it.

Armed with three bags of something called Fantales, I got a text message from Maddy.

In manager's office with Felix who looks seriously hot. Nonie looks like Cate bloody Blanchett with Angelina Jolie's lips. Come quickly—Luke on way from airport. M

She wasn't wrong. Felix looked like he'd stepped off a red carpet and Nonie was a vision in a bias-cut, cobalt silk dress.

'You two look the part.'

'You must be Roo,' said Nonie, rushing to embrace me. Maddy shot me a murderous look.

We made our way to the designated entrance to wait with the media scrum for Max and Shelly, Luke and the rest of the campaign team.

'Welcome back to Watson, Max,' said Felix when the LOO arrived. They began the walk.

I hung back at a safe distance with the journalists. 'Where have you been?' Oscar breathed in my ear.

'Here and there,' I said. 'And you?' Maddy, who was walking with Luke, turned around. I tried to ignore her stare.

'I just came in from Perth. We missed you on the media plane.'

'Who's we?'

'Me.'

'I'd better stick with Max,' I said, quickening my pace to join Luke and Maddy at the front of the scrum.

'Don't think we didn't see that flush of colour, missy,' said Maddy. 'Am I right, Harley?' But Luke was charging ahead, pea-green tie flapping behind him.

Max, Felix, Shelly and Nonie were at the bakery sampling hot cross buns when they were approached by a woman and her young son who had obviously just been to the pet shop. Max got down on his haunches. 'Hi there,' he said to the boy. 'I'm Max. What's your name?'

'Steve.'

'And who's this, Steve?' Max pointed at the lone goldfish Steve was holding in a water-filled plastic bag.

'Nemo 2.'

'After Nemo the movie?' asked Felix, chuffed that he knew the reference.

'No,' said Steve, 'after Nemo 1—Jaws ate him.'

Felix and Max rose to talk to Steve's mum, Nancy—it was safer up there.

'Mummy,' said Steve, tugging on Nancy's skirt.

'Don't interrupt, darling,' she said sternly and kept talking to Max. 'My husband runs a small business and it's really tough at the moment.'

Max and Felix nodded.

'BUT MUM!' A small puddle had formed at Steve's feet. 'Nemo 2's home is leaking,' he cried. 'A lot.'

Felix grabbed the bag and ran, chased by Max, carrying Steve, followed by Nancy, Flack the Cop and a squadron of snappers. Felix burst into the pet shop. 'I'm Felix Winks,' he said, competing with meowing kittens, 'and this is Nemo 2 and he needs a top-up.'

'I told management you people weren't welcome in here,' said the pet shop owner, double-bagging Nemo 2. Journalists scribbled furiously. 'You'll scare the animals!'

Max joined the fold. 'I'm sorry about all the commotion,' he explained, 'it's just that we were chatting with Steve's mum, Nonie here, and—'

'Nancy,' corrected Felix. 'Nonie's my girlfriend.'

The confused cameramen switched their attention to Nonie, who was with Shelly outside the shop.

'Hi,' she grinned and waved. The moment was awkward enough without the poor girl slipping in Nemo 2's puddle, and thudding onto the ground, dress well above the knee.

'Code red,' Maddy said.

Luke hung his head.

Cameras zoomed.

'The billboards look like paradise now,' I said.

In the can

It was the middle of the night, or at least I thought it was. I knew I was in a hotel room because the sheets were tucked in too tightly and my skin smelled unfamiliar from the citrus-scented soap. I couldn't find my BlackBerry, so I hit 0 on the bedside-table phone, in search of answers.

'Good morning, Guest Relations, this is Michelle.'

'Would you mind telling me what time it is?'

'Certainly, ma'am. It's 3 a.m.'

'Thank God it's Friday.'

'Saturday. Will that be all, ma'am?'

'Actually, Michelle, I was wondering whether you could tell me which hotel I'm in.'

'The InterContinental, ma'am.'

There was no way to ask the next question without sounding stoned. 'And which InterContinental is that?'

'Collins Street, ma'am—there's only one InterContinental in Melbourne.'

'Of course,' I said. 'Very kind of you.'

If nothing else, our encounter might have given Michelle something to talk about with her graveyard-shift colleagues. 'You'll never believe this,' she would say to the porter. 'Some hussy on the fifth floor has no idea where she is, let alone whose bed she's in.'

Go back to sleep, Ruby, said my head.

'I can't,' I replied. 'I'm wide awake now.'

Well, do some exercise or something. Don't just lie there. Your body and I are fed up with these sleepless nights, so you may as well do something productive with them.

'Sorry,' I said. Clearly, I was well on my way to Barking.

I opted for a swim. A plain black bra and pants would have to suffice. I threw the fluffy white robe over the top of my makeshift ensemble, grabbed a towel and headed for the fitness centre.

It was quiet. The plopping sound my feet made as they entered the water ricocheted off the walls. I went in up to my torso. The temperature change triggered an outbreak of goose pimples. With one deep breath, I immersed myself.

Underwater, the blue lights turned my skin the colour of powdery snow. My hair pulsed out in front of me like a blonde jellyfish and tiny baubles of air escaped my lips, shattering when they hit the surface.

I came up for air, heard the filter whirr and plunged back under, soaking up the silence. My head had stopped hectoring me; my body was grateful for the stretch. The peace was intoxicating. Not because I was distressed, but because I knew no one could hear me, I opened my mouth to scream. The sound was muted; bubbles scurried.

When we were kids, during long summer holidays in

Bellagio, Fran and I held underwater screaming competitions. We would pretend we were mermaids jostling for the position of Mer Queen, which was usually determined by the loudest scream or highest number of consecutive underwater somersaults. As there were but two contestants for Mer Queen, both of whom were the competition's only adjudicators, they were summers fraught with fights. We would jet up and down the pool for hours until our hair turned green and our eyes pink from the chlorine.

After about an hour of mermaid jetting, I was ready for a shower. I towelled off, re-robed and headed for the lift. It reached me with a ping and opened to reveal a sleepy Oscar Franklin. He was deliciously rumpled, with messy hair, faded shorts and a moth-eaten T-shirt. Gone was his usual pristine TV state; this was far sexier. His face was still creased from the bedsheets.

'Hi,' I said, trying to normalise near-nudity with small talk. 'Why are you up so early?' I tightened the belt around my robe.

'I could ask the same of you.' He stopped the lift doors from closing with an outstretched arm, the kind of limb I thought belonged only to plastic action-hero figurines.

'I woke up and couldn't get back to sleep, so I decided to go for a swim.'

He scanned my face. 'I can see that.'

I dabbed at lingering water droplets with the collar of my robe. 'Well, I'd better go.' My heart beat a little faster for seeing him, but it was easy enough to tell myself that it was nothing more than swim-related breathlessness.

'Why? What's there to do at 4 a.m.?'

'You're a political journalist. You should know the day starts in half an hour.'

'I was going to hit the gym,' he said, swinging his iPhone headphones around his finger, 'but if breakfast with you was on the table, I'd ditch the treadmill in a heartbeat.'

'Sorry,' I said, 'I've got to get showered and read the papers.' I stepped into the lift. He didn't leave it.

'See you, Roo,' he said after a moment. 'Let's grab a drink sometime.'

The air-conditioning was freezing on my wet skin.

'That would be nice,' I said, fumbling with the key card. My eyes wouldn't stop looking at his until the doors closed between us.

Descending, I exhaled in a bid to regain control of my erratic heart beat. I examined myself for stray bra straps in the mirrored walls of the lift.

Ruby, pooh-poohed my head, *he's a journalist.*

'I know,' I whispered.

After a hot shower, I decided that today was the day to break out the little black dress. I'd heard from Di that Saturday night was drinks night, and I wanted to be a little bit gorgeous for it. I dressed, repacked my bag just in case I had to leave again, then went to the temporary office, where Archie was leafing through the fat weekend papers over tea and toast.

'Morning, Roo.'

'Morning, Archie. Need a hand?'

He frisbeed a copy of the *Saturday Herald*. 'Go for your life.'

A campaign diary piece from Gary Spinnaker on the front page read like a time-lapse video of my week. 'Spinnaker says we won the week.'

Archie nodded, brushing crumbs from his jeans.

I read aloud. 'Masters gets kudos for transforming the

rude shock of this early election into a golden opportunity. In contrast, our new Prime Minister started her week as patriot and strategist but ended it rather on the nose.'

'We're copping it on other fronts, though,' said Archie. 'The *Weekender* has homed in on the preselection situation—there's a feature on the quality of candidates—and in Adelaide, they've cottoned on to the billboard situation. On the bright side, yet another member of Brennan's Bruterati has come out to play today.' He gleefully handed me a copy of the *Queenslander*.

A leaked voicemail message from a disgruntled back-bencher had made its way into the inbox of a senior journalist. The transcript was delectably detailed.

> Mate, it's Gabby. Listen, we can't do this without you and, as I said, you'll be rewarded for your support. I need to be able to count on you [inaudible] the transition as smooth as possible if we're going to do this at all. Give me a call when you've decided.

'That's just careless,' I said.

'Yeah, well, today's mould can be tomorrow's blue cheese in this game.'

The LOO burst into the room dressed in a grotesque pair of sweat pants and a T-shirt, followed closely by Di and Luke. 'Okay, girls and boys,' Max said, 'where are we?'

'Melbourne,' I said, thinking he might have felt as bamboozled as I had at 3 a.m.

He laughed.

Luke, who was wearing a tie that resembled spaghetti bolognaise, gave a more businesslike answer. 'We might have won Week One, but there's a dangerous perception out there that we're a shoe-in because Brennan's honeymoon was over before it began. We have thirteen seats to win in twenty-seven days, and that's if we hold on to the ones we've got.'

'Way to poop the party, Luke,' joked Max.

'The fact is,' Luke continued, 'they haven't even begun to probe our policies because they've been so distracted by our opponents. The Sunday papers are working on something for tomorrow. I got a call this morning to ask if I would be around early this afternoon if they needed comment. I reckon it's going to be the preselection angle.'

'Me too,' said Di. 'I got wind of it last night on the plane—one of the guys knew off the top of his head how many outstanding preselection battles there were. We've only got three days before the nominations close.'

'But they're not winnable seats,' said Archie. 'They're all safe government seats.'

Max dropped the spoon in his cereal bowl with a clunk and stared at Archie. 'There's no such thing as an unwinnable seat, mate. We need to be running great local candidates in every seat. It's our fucking duty. People need choice.'

'I was just saying—'

Max cut him off. It was the first time I'd seen him angry. 'You were just saying that some seats aren't worth fighting for. Let me tell you something: every seat matters to me. Luke's right. The party's inability to organise itself reflects poorly on us, and there's no way we're going to take any of this week's coverage for granted. Understood?'

'Sure,' said Archie, 'I didn't mean to—'

Max shook his head dismissively and resumed eating his cereal. 'When's this ad shoot?'

'We leave in ten minutes,' said Luke. 'Milly has all

your gear—she'll meet us there. You can change when we get to the studio.'

'Roo,' said Max, 'can I see you for a minute?'

Now what have you done?

I gulped. 'Sure.' Had I overstepped the line with Shelly? Had he seen me in the lift with Oscar? Shit, shit, shit.

'Mate,' he said quietly.

I leaned in.

'Would you mind getting me some shaving cream?'

Relief. 'Any particular brand?'

'Well,' he said, his voice even quieter, 'I don't mind that stuff you gave me.'

'The avocado one?'

'Shhh. Yes. I've run out.'

'I'll find out if they sell it in Australia and get back to you.'

'Good job, Roo.'

Di was packing her briefcase. 'What was that about?'

'Top secret,' I said, and wrote 'avocado' into my scrappy-looking To Do list.

We made our way out to the waiting cars. It was a baking day in Melbourne. My shoes felt like hot water bottles as we stepped onto the steaming bitumen.

Suddenly, a man emerged from the bushes, yelling 'Max!' The LOO, on his mobile, turned around just in time to be snapped. He smiled tensely to mask his surprise and got into the car, the smile plastered on his face.

Di was red with anger. 'I scanned the exits earlier for snappers and there was no one here—not even the cops saw him. Stealthy bugger.' One of her phones beeped. It was the LOO from the car in front.

The cops said he's tailing us. Very A-list. Imagine
his disappointment when he realises I'm not George
Clooney—just a politician in his tracky dacks! MM

The photographer was on a motorbike behind us. Di
asked our driver to stop. 'I'm going to find out what he
wants. You keep going. Find a way for us to lose him.'

On my BlackBerry, I found a number for the staff
member at the scene. Her name was Millicent.

'It's Ruby Stanhope calling. I'm in the car with Di
behind the LOO en route to the shoot.'

'Hello there, how far away are you?' asked a posh
voice as Di leaped out of the car and accosted the biked
crusader.

'Listen, Milly, we're being followed by a snapper on a
bike. He's already got a shot of Max in sweat pants and
he wants more.'

'That's awful, darling—not the ghastly grey ones with
the yellow speed stripes?'

'The very same.'

'Quelle catastrophe!'

'Which is precisely why I called. Is there any way we
can get him in underground somewhere?'

'There's a basement car park around the side of the
building. I'll be waiting there to open the garage door.' I
could hear the clip-clop of high heels on concrete.

The photographer came zooming around the corner in
time to see us disappear into the basement. An efferves-
cent woman with raspberry-red fingernails cantered along
behind the car in a pair of the tallest possible studded
Jimmy Choos. I recognised them instantly from various
online shopping sessions.

Max and Luke tumbled out of the other car.

'Do we know who that was?' asked Luke.

'Di's trying to find out.' I averted my gaze from the perfect Jimmy's as they caught up with us.

Millicent doubled over to catch her breath. 'Hold this.' She thrust the most delicious-smelling Balenciaga tote into my hands so that she could yank up her jeans. 'I'm Milly, by the way.'

'Roo,' I said, breathing in its leathery goodness, 'but you mightn't get this back.'

'Millicent the Magnificent,' bellowed the LOO, his voice echoing around the car park.

'Maximilian.' She kissed him on either cheek. 'You told me you donated that heinous ensemble to charity—not that there's anything remotely charitable about grey marle.'

'I did,' he said, pulling at the drawstrings of his elastic waistband. 'These are new.'

'Remind me to talk to you about appropriate workout gear.' She linked arms with him and led him to the studio. 'Today we're shooting two thirty-second ads and something longer for YouTube. I have three outfits for you. Let's get you into make-up.'

We entered a brightly lit, white-walled studio where about forty people were waiting for us, all in spray-on skinny jeans, canvas sneakers and Buddy Holly glasses. In the centre of the room was a contemporary desk beside an Australian flag and an array of personal items from Max's Melbourne office.

A stumpy man in a black cowboy hat strode towards Max in the make-up chair.

'That's Marc Tully,' whispered Milly in my ear. 'He runs the ad agency.'

'Max,' swooned the Napoleonic ad man, his ample

belly spilling out over strangulating acid-wash jeans, 'glad you could make it.'

'G'day, Tully,' said Max. 'How long's this going to take?'

'Shouldn't be longer than three hours.' He handed Max a script and tapped his foot.

'I'm going to need a biro,' said Max, flipping through the script. I grabbed one from my Toolkit.

'Luckily for you and me, I picked up this month's *Vogue* this morning,' said Milly. 'It looks like we're going to be here all day.'

No self-respecting clotheshorse could support her habits on a staffer's salary. 'So, Milly, what's your role on the campaign?'

'I'm an advisor.'

'What kind?'

'General,' she said cryptically, pulling a pile of glossy magazines from her bag.

'Are you with the LOO's office?'

'No.'

'The party?'

'No.'

'How many questions do I have left?'

She shut her magazine and looked me dead in the eye. 'I'm Max's sister.'

Google before you speak, Ruby. Balls. 'Oh,' I said. 'I'm sorry, I didn't know.'

'Not at all,' she smiled. 'I'm a fashion-buyer but in my spare time I try to rescue my kid brother from stylicide.'

'So you do this on a voluntary basis?'

'Precisely. It's more selfish than it sounds—in my line of work, I can't have him swanning around looking like a dag.'

'What's a dag?'

She pointed at Luke, his spilt-spaghetti tie glistening beneath the studio lights.

'Do you choose Max's ties?'

She nodded.

'He's lucky to have you. Maybe you could consider giving Luke a bit of pro bono guidance.'

Di charged into the room, returned from the stalker confrontation. 'I'm fucking irate,' she yelled. 'Where's Luke?'

I pointed to a coffee machine in the corner where he was expertly frothing milk in the middle of an animated phone call. Di approached him and whispered something in his ear. I saw him turn pale.

'We need a minute with Max,' Luke said to the make-up artist, who was grooming Max's eyebrows with a tooth-brush.

'Almost finished,' she said perkily, oblivious to the mounting tension.

'A minute,' Luke repeated, but she ignored the cue.

I stepped in. 'Amanda, isn't it?'

'Armada,' she corrected. 'Like the Spanish one.'

Max bit his lip to squash amusement.

'What a lovely name.' I imagined a flotilla of her clones making their way across the Pacific Ocean. 'Armada, before you do anything else, we need your advice on ties.'

'Of course,' said Armada, liberating Max, who went with Luke and Di into what looked like a storage room.

A minute later Max came tearing out, gasping at air. 'I think I'm going to be sick,' he said, scanning the perimeter for a bathroom.

'Come on, darling,' said Milly, 'come with me.'

'Did he eat the California rolls?' asked Armada, patting

her stomach, 'cos I'm feeling a bit funky too.'

I found Di prostrate on the floor of the storage room.

'What on earth is going on?'

'Remember the story for the Sundays?'

'Yes...'

She sat up and ran her fingers through her hair, letting her forehead rest on the heels of her hands. 'It's not about the preselection. It's far worse. When Max was serving in the Persian Gulf, one of his subordinates assaulted an unarmed civilian. The victim suffered serious head injuries.

'Max was the officer in charge of reporting the incident and disciplining the perpetrator, but he never did anything about it. The man has given an interview to the *Sunday*, saying that he can no longer live with himself and feels duty-bound to talk about it. He has post-traumatic stress syndrome. They also have interviews with the family of the victim, who has since died.'

She handed me her BlackBerry. There was an email from a journalist outlining a series of allegations against Max. He had already dubbed the scandal Slaughtergate. We had until 4 p.m. to comment. My palms grew clammy. 'Cock,' I said. 'How can I help?'

'Work through the allegations and develop an exhaustive list of questions that Max might be asked at a press conference. We're going to prep him in half an hour. We need to deal with this head-on. I'm working up some messaging for him and Luke's trying to work through the facts with Max.'

'Does he deny it?'

Di shook her head.

Outside the storage room, Armada sailed towards me.

'Um, I need to like finish his make-up now.'

Tully joined us, imperiously clapping his hands. 'So, where's Max? We'll do a run-through in five.'

'Sorry, I don't think that's going to happen. You'll need to talk to Luke.' I looked around the studio for somewhere to sit and think.

'Babe,' Tully said, 'you're not suggesting we won't be filming today, are you? We've got a cast of thousands here. Unless we get the three ads in the can by this afternoon we'll forfeit our prime-time slots.'

The babe bit made me wince. 'I understand your frustration,' I said politely as my hands formed fists, 'but I don't have any answers for you. Could you or your staff find us some desks to work at and give us a bit of privacy? We're attending to an urgent matter.'

'Me too, sweetheart. It's called an *election campaign*.' He etched inverted commas in the air with four puny digits. The veins in his neck looked like an embossed road map. 'Right now, all we've got are a couple of billboards and a fucking website.'

His face was so close to mine that the brim of his hat touched my forehead and I could make out the borders of his porcelain veneers. Scanning the room for potential weapons, I fixed my eyes on Milly's shoes and wondered if she'd let me borrow one for a little bludgeoning.

'Back off, mate,' said Luke behind him, tapping him on the shoulder. 'Nobody speaks to my staff like that.' There was molten fury in his eyes.

'Look, Harley, this bird doesn't seem to appreciate what we've got to achieve here today.'

'Ruby is not a bird, Tully. She's a policy advisor and has a far greater appreciation of the complexities of this campaign than you will ever have, as was all too evident from the script you wrote.'

'Settle down, Luke. We're all on the same side here, mate,' Tully tried.

'Don't tell me to settle, you numbskull. I'm your client, not your underling—you'd do well to remember that.'

I fantasised about spitting in Tully's ridiculous hat and putting it back on his head, but he'd already left.

'You okay, Roo?' Luke put his hand on my shoulder. His tie was all higgledy piggledy. It *was* spaghetti bolognaise: a photograph of the stuff printed on the cheapest satin.

'No, actually, I'm not okay,' I said, straightening his tie. 'I'm bitterly disappointed to have missed the opportunity for a bit of good old-fashioned Australian dispute resolution.'

'You could've taken him.'

'Definitely.'

I didn't feel up to the task of preparing my boss, the Leader of the Opposition, for a press conference on a scandal big enough to derail his campaign. But there wasn't time to be spooked. Under the hot studio lights, I got to work.

Catch Twenty-Loo

It wasn't until halfway through Max's opening statement that I first understood the physical endurance it takes to be a journalist. With scarce surface area on the speaker's lectern, one must hold one's recording device close enough to capture speech, but distant enough to avoid obscuring the shot.

That afternoon, it was my job to record my boss's explanation of what had or hadn't happened in the first Gulf War. All I could think about were the pins and needles in my outstretched arm. And my swelling bladder. Oscar held his iPhone next to the boring digital dictaphone Luke had lent me.

Max finished his statement. 'I'll take any questions you might have.'

I had one. 'Mr Masters,' I saw myself saying in a dead-arm-induced hallucination. 'Why is it that all our limbs must suffer in order to take multiple recordings of the same words? Surely there's enough camaraderie between us to share one?' I swapped arms and felt sensation return sharply to my right elbow.

'Mr Masters,' said Gary Spinnaker behind me. 'This represents a clear and intentional breach of duty. Why should voters trust that you won't breach duties associated with the higher office you now seek?'

We'd rehearsed that question in the car. I looked up at Max. A bead of sweat in the centre of his hairline threatened to drip onto his forehead.

'I made the wrong call,' he said, 'and I will cop the consequences that come with that. All I can do is hope the Australian people understand that I wasn't aware of the incident until some months after it happened. When I was informed of it by the officer responsible, who was clearly suffering stress, I made enquiries. There were no witnesses, no reports of injury and no complaints from the victim or his family. I was advised that the officer's condition had become debilitating and that he was experiencing vivid hallucinations and nightmares. He then requested an honourable discharge. Notes from his debrief led us to believe that the incident he referred to was a figment of his imagination. I haven't heard from him since—either in an official capacity or otherwise.'

'What would you say to the victim's family?' asked a woman at the back of the room. We'd prepared for that one too. Against the advice of the Defence Department, Max had insisted on calling the victim's mother that afternoon.

'That's not a hypothetical question,' said Max. 'Today I called the family of the victim. I expressed my sympathy to them for what they have suffered.'

'But Mr Masters, this is not just about your subordinate, is it? It's about you. You're responsible for this cover-up and you're only talking about it now because you know it will be in tomorrow's papers.' This came from the investigative freelancer who had researched the story for months and was incensed that his blockbuster exclusive had now become an all-you-can-eat buffet for his competitors.

Max paused and looked down at his shoes. There was a rat-a-tat-tat as photographers clicked, eager to capture the image of his remorse. When he looked up, the sweat bead had migrated to the tip of his nose, and even though those present knew it wasn't one they would do nothing to stop it being portrayed as a single tear. A millisecond passed and he wiped it away.

I found myself assessing whether a teardrop would be good or bad for the campaign instead of listening to his response. Good, I concluded, because there weren't words that could convey Max's anguish. I had spent the afternoon watching the man relive his inaction.

A few hours earlier, he had been physically ill at the thought of having overlooked the man's wrongdoing. 'I didn't think he was capable of violence,' he kept saying, his eyes somewhere off in the distance. 'I thought he just wasn't coping with the stress. Usually there would be reports and complaints coming in if something like that had happened—we'd hear it from the community—but there was nothing.'

Sitting on the floor behind him, Milly cradled her little brother as Fran would me. 'I know, darling.' She rocked him gently.

We were trying to prepare him for the press conference, but he didn't give a damn. 'Fuck the presser,' he said.

'Get me his mum's number and an interpreter right now.'
So we did. It was a harrowing call to witness. When she forgave him, he wept. This was a good man.

Now, when my left arm died and the sound technician behind me groaned under the weight of his boom mike, I willed my bladder to hold out just that little bit longer, promising to treat it better in future. I could hear my father's voice when we went for Sunday drives long ago: 'You should've gone before we left the house, Rubles!' I'd had the opportunity back at the studio, but instead went in search of Almighty Avocado at the nearby chemist's to cheer up Max. Thankfully, it was a successful mission.

'Last question,' called Di, to my relief. Oscar took it, catching me examining his hands; he flexed his fingers. 'Do you anticipate this incident will be investigated, Mr Masters, and, if so, isn't it possible you will face charges over it?'

'That's a matter for the department,' said Max. 'I informed them this afternoon that I offer my full cooperation with any of their processes. Thanks, everyone.' He gathered his papers and stepped away from the lectern. I made a quick exit, avoiding Oscar's gaze for fear that I might wet myself.

The marbled bathroom down the corridor was empty so I slammed open the door to the first cubicle, hitched up my LBD and sat down on the perfectly clean seat. 'Ahh,' I said, but I'd ahhed too soon.

It was the splosh in place of the usual trickle that first alarmed me. Second, the absence of the dictaphone that had been resting on my lap. Third, the trickle that followed. And last, but by no means least, the realisation that I was on one of those evil, hyper-sensitive auto-flushing loos, designed by some cruel person to become a surprise bidet to anyone prone to flinching mid-stream.

On the upside, I hadn't yet moved a muscle. Well and truly on the downside, I had emptied my bladder on Luke's dictaphone and was stuck with my dress hitched up to my waist and knickers around my ankles until I could find a way of fishing it out. The slightest movement might flush it entirely.

It was quite the dilemma. I turned my head to the wall, ever so slowly, to gauge the sensor's position. AUTOFLUSH TECHNOLOGY—HYGIENE IS OUR PRIORITY, said a green sticker. 'Hygiene my arse!' I growled. What could be less hygienic than having one's region splashed with toilet water?

With the tip of my pointed shoe, I dragged my handbag towards me then into the air. I held my breath and reached to grab it, my torso still as a statue so as not to ignite the sensor's wrath. In full MacGyver mode, I rifled in search of fishing implements. Hairbrush? Too bristly. Handkerchief? Possible fishing net. Lipstick? Prone to mush. Sewing kit? Potential line. And then I saw my saviour: a solitary sanitary pad. Sticky as hell, it would lure the all-seeing, all-knowing sensor into thinking I was still seated, giving me enough time to fish out the dictaphone.

I peeled the pad from its plastic liner, turned gently and stuck it over the sensor. Success. 'Cop that, sensor!' I squealed. Dismounting my porcelain horse, I grabbed a Sanitary Items Disposal Bag from the wall-mounted dispenser beside me. It was fishing time. On my knees, I looped pink thread from my sewing kit through the handles of the plastic pouch and bent over the bowl, ready to scoop me a dictaphone. It bobbed merrily on the surface. There was still hope. But before I knew what was happening, the pad lost its grip and swung from the wall by a single adhesive strip.

You should have used double-sided tape, my head contributed.

The sensor flashed a red light at me as if to poke out its tongue as I watched the great white monster effortlessly swallow Luke's dictaphone whole, with no thanks but a gurgle and a burp.

Damp and defeated, I dabbed at my forehead with squares of toilet tissue. My phone vibrated on the cubicle floor.

Where'd you rush off to? I was going to ask if you were up for a drink tomorrow night. Oscar

My luck had changed.

I'll gladly have a drink with you in exchange for a sound file of Max's presser. R

Deal. I've emailed it to you. What happened to yours? Oscar

Diluted sound quality. R

'Where are you?' asked Di in a harsh whisper down the phone line.

'In my room. Wardrobe malfunction.' I tried not to let the soggy bits of my dress touch me as I pulled it over my head. 'I'll be down in a second.' It was too soon for my new couture to be consigned to the laundry bag, but there's nothing sexy about wee water.

'Grab your bag and meet me downstairs in two—we're off to the airport.'

'No.' I stomped my foot like Clem in a tantrum. 'I don't want to.'

'Suck it up, Roo.'

'Where are we going?'

'Cloncurry.'

'What curry?'

She laughed and hung up. It was a serious question. It sounded like something from the takeaway menu at Bombay Bicycle Club back home.

Maddy was in a cab with Di outside the hotel. Bob Marley's 'Stir It Up' poured out of the subwoofer.

'Hi, Roo,' mouthed Maddy, waving at me as I leaped into the back seat beside her. In the front seat Di was in the middle of an animated call.

'Hi,' I said, 'where have you been?'

'When was the last time I saw you?'

I considered her question. 'Adelaide.'

Di glared at us from the front seat, so Maddy reached into her handbag for a pile of boarding passes fastened with a bulldog clip. It looked like a deck of tarot cards. She flicked through them, holding them open at the previous Thursday's date so that I could read on. Adelaide to Sydney, Sydney to Cairns, Cairns to Darwin, Darwin to Melbourne—all in forty-eight hours. I wrote her a message on the back of a receipt that had been roaming in my handbag. *How are you even awake?*

She lowered her sunglasses and wrote back: *I adore my job.*

I raised an eyebrow at her.

Campaigns are like love affairs, Maddy wrote. *The adrenaline keeps you going. You sleep when it's over.*

This was precisely the way I felt about the experience except that for Maddy I expected the affair was motivated by her love of the party. Mine was more of a rebound fling, the kind you have with someone simply because he's not the man who broke your heart. I met him on holiday in the tropics. He was unpredictable, exotic even. With him I did things I'd never have dreamed of. I needed superhuman energy levels to match his stamina. We didn't even speak the same language, though out of necessity I had learned the basics.

'Excuse me, sir,' Di said to the driver, 'can we turn on the radio?'

Reluctantly, he switched off Bob Marley. Di commandeered the dial.

'In breaking news, former prime minister Hugh Patton has commented on Slaughtergate from his family home in Sydney,' said the announcer. We could hear seagulls over the harbour in the background.

'Ladies and gentleman,' said Patton, 'I've brought you here today to tell a story. In my first term as prime minister, I recall the chief of the defence forces bringing a proposal to my attention that had been initiated by a naval captain stationed in the Persian Gulf.

'The captain's proposal was for post-traumatic stress specialists to be available to service personnel for up to six months after each tour of duty. Cabinet rejected it for funding reasons, but we were all touched by its sincerity. It was the action of a captain deeply concerned for the wellbeing of one of his subordinates. That captain was Max Masters, Leader of the Opposition.'

Di threw an air punch.

The announcer continued, 'Mr Patton refused to answer any questions, but when asked whether this meant that he supported the Opposition over his own party, he said simply that the story speaks for itself.'

'Holy shit!' said Maddy. 'Did the former prime minister just bitch-slap his successor?'

'Brennan will be spewing blood,' said Di with a grin. Apparently this was a good thing.

'You done?' asked the cab driver. He cranked up the volume on 'No Woman, No Cry', which carried us all the way to Tullamarine—my fourth time there in eight days.

In the Qantas Club, over more than our fair share of a passionfruity sauvignon blanc, Di explained why we were on the road again.

'Essentially, our candidate for Rafter in western Queensland is a bit nuts. The party's been in such a rush to preselect candidates that due diligence has been a little less diligent than we would have liked.' Di chowed down on a stash of over-sauced party pies. 'This lady's a blogger. She blogs under a nom de plume so a Google search won't bring it up, but it would appear that'— she paused and lowered her voice—'it would appear that she plots the landing patterns of extraterrestrials from Saturn.'

'That's more than a bit nuts,' said Maddy. 'That's about eight Iced VoVos short of a packet.'

'Two questions,' I said. 'One, isn't Saturn a gaseous planet? And two, what on earth is an Iced Volvo?'

'VoVo,' howled Maddy, 'not Volvo.'

I was still blank.

'It's a biscuit—pale pink icing with a landing strip of jam sprinkled with desiccated coconut.'

'Sounds foul.'

'Don't knock it 'til you try it,' said Di through a mouthful of pie.

'I did find some delicious sweets in a supermarket the

other day,' I offered. 'They're like English toffees covered in chocolate and wrapped in blue paper printed with tidbits of trivia on film stars. I got Brad Pitt. Very chewy and quite more-ish.'

Maddy and Di looked at each other as they laughed, their eyes watering. It was a sort of contagious hysteria.

'You mean Fantales?' Maddy clutched her sides as fat tears rolled down her face.

'Yes.' I was somewhat bewildered. 'You know them?' I found the half-eaten packet in my overnight bag and put it on the table.

We giggled like teenagers at a sleepover and the lounge staff frowned as we polished off the Fantales, the mini pies and every last drop of the sauvignon blanc.

When they called our flight, I was still under the impression we were headed for Australia's Brick Lane.

Felicia Lunardi

I opened the vertical blinds in my room at the motor inn to the hum of an over-exerted air-conditioner.

Perhaps that's why it's called Cloncurry, I thought, peering through the window at garam masala–coloured dust outside. Trying to ignore my spectacular white wine hangover, I stepped into my pencil skirt for the third time that week, threw on my cleanest top and went outside to find the girls.

It was then that I discovered the etymology of the name: it's called Cloncurry because it's scaldingly hot. Not Melbourne-hot or even Brisbane-hot; Cloncurry brings something unique to heat. Discarded gum trodden into the footpath formed a gooey puddle rather than the usual sticky clump. A squashed marsupial on the road was steaming as if in a tagine. Each of my thighs had suction-cupped the other and my shoes gripped the concrete like velcro. It was a rancid heat. I wondered whether the

Cloncurry Embroiderers' Guild met in the morgue for an environment more conducive to fine needlework.

'Shut it!' commanded Di as I slid open the glass door to an icy shed marked AIR-CONDITIONED DINING ROOM. She was leaning on the water cooler, gulping from a pint glass, reading the Sunday papers. Maddy sat at a laminex table tucking into what looked like, but couldn't possibly have been, a bowl of porridge.

'Morning, Roo,' she chirped. 'Grab some breakfast. It's delicious with banana and brown sugar.'

Di and I exchanged glances. 'Maddy, sweetheart,' I implored, 'it's about two hundred degrees outside; why in God's name are you eating hot porridge?'

'I'm from Mount Isa,' said Maddy, pointing near the westernmost point on the map of Queensland hand-stitched into her placemat.

'So, what's on the agenda?' I asked.

Di poured some water onto her chest and fanned it dry with a newspaper. 'We have to go to the candidate's place for a chat.'

'Can't she come here?' I asked, standing directly beneath the air-conditioning vent.

Di shook her head. 'Today's her campaign launch and a gaggle of journos are arriving later this arvo because Mick O'Donoghue is launching it.'

'Who's that?'

'He was the most recent PM on our side—Patton defeated him over a decade ago, but he was hugely popular and people still love him. He's from this part of the world.'

'How are the papers?'

'Reasonable,' said Di, throwing me a copy of the *Sunday*. 'We managed to take the sting out of Slaughtergate and the Patton thing has helped us, but they've still got shots of the victim's family, the officer involved and Max in his tracky dacks.'

'I'll bring the car around front for you two wusses—we'll leave at a quarter to ten.' Maddy scraped at oats cemented to the bottom of her bowl.

'Wusses?'

'People who don't enjoy being microwaved,' explained Di.

There's a word for everything in this country.

'Oh, and Roo, you might want to get changed.'

She was right. I was already drenched and had walked all of eight feet between my room and the dining shed. There was nothing else clean in my overnight bag, so I battled across the road—which was like walking against the flow of a giant hair dryer—to Carl's Camping Gear.

'G'day,' said a leathery man in his mid-sixties. 'What can I do you for?'

'Hello,' I said, wishing I could say 'g'day' without it sounding so much like 'giddy'. 'Listen, I need something a bit cooler.'

He looked me up and down. 'Thongs.' He disappeared behind his counter.

'I beg your pardon?' I steeled myself to slap him before he popped up with a pair of flip-flops bearing the Australian flag. 'They're magnificent,' I said, stepping out of my melting pumps onto the union jack and southern cross.

'Now, we don't have much by way of ladies wear, but I do have some shirts.' He presented me with a pile of plastic-wrapped T-shirts, including a canary-yellow vest with XXXX QUEENSLAND AUSTRALIA emblazoned on it in red block letters.

'Is this supposed to be some sort of pornographic reference?'

'That's Fourex,' he belly laughed.

I was still blank.

'Beer. You tourists crack me up.'

I emerged from his shop wearing a billowing yellow XXXX vest as a belted mini dress, aviator sunglasses and by far the most comfortable pair of shoes I'd ever owned. It wasn't my most flattering ensemble, particularly as the yellow didn't do much for my deathly pale skin tone, but I couldn't have cared less. As I approached the hire car, Maddy honked the horn and Di managed to wolf-whistle through her raucous laughter as she photographed me with her BlackBerry.

'Oh yes,' I said, 'mock the tourist.'

'You spaz,' said Maddy. 'There's a clothes shop just around the corner!'

Spaz?

She connected her iPod to the car and put on some Dixie Chicks.

'So, how far away is this property?' I asked Maddy once we were on the road.

'About ninety minutes south of here, give or take a few.'

'Won't we be in New South Wales by then?'

'Not even close, sweet girl. This great state has almost two million square kilometres.'

'In miles?'

'Dunno,' said Di, holding her phone to the sky to find a signal, 'but the UK is about a quarter of a million.'

'The seat of Rafter alone is bigger than the UK,' said Maddy.

It was unfathomable. 'What's this candidate's name?'

'Felicia Lunardi,' said a straight-faced Di. 'I shit you not.'

An unfortunate name for someone about to face national ridicule for spotting aliens in western Queensland, I thought, before allowing the highway to rock me to sleep.

'Roo,' said Maddy, stirring me, 'we're almost there.'

It was just past eleven, and even with the air-conditioning at sixteen degrees, the car windows were hot to the touch. We pulled over at a large homestead where a tall, muscular woman in a long denim skirt and collared shirt came to welcome us with a sideways wave which I later realised was not a local greeting but a routine fly-clearing motion.

'You're from Max Masters' office?'

'That's us,' said Di, with two tiny flies above her lip. 'I'm Di, and these are my colleagues Maddy and Roo.'

I'd already danced the dirt drive towards her shaded verandah to escape the heat and hundreds of flies that seemed to be using my back as an insect airport.

'Don't mind Roo,' said Maddy, 'she's a Brit.'

'Very pleased to meet you all,' she said, staring at my mini-dress. 'I'm Felicia, but everyone calls me Flick. Con's just made some pikelets and a jug of cordial, so why don't you come inside and have some morning tea.'

We followed her into a huge country kitchen where a mustachioed man in an apron was spooning jam and cream onto perfectly formed drop scones. 'My husband, Con,' said Flick. 'Con, meet Di, Maddy and Roo.'

'Sit down and tuck in while the pikelets are still warm,' he said. The table was cluttered with piles of FLICK LUNARDI FOR RAFTER paraphernalia.

'Sorry for the mess,' said Con. 'We're in the middle of folding and stuffing postal vote information.'

'Now,' said Flick, pouring us each a glass of orange squash, 'what are you all doing here?'

Di took the floor. 'The thing is, the party found your blog.'

'So what?' said Flick. Con hung his head.

'Well, it's a little...unconventional,' Di said gently. 'The other side knows about it so it's only a matter of time before it's public knowledge.'

'Let me get this straight,' said Flick, raising her voice. 'You guys came all the way out here because you've seen a blog linked to my campaign office IP address about other life out there. You think I'm a fruitloop.'

That's it in a nutshell, said my head.

'Yes,' said Di.

Flick rocked back on a sturdy chair. 'I'm the first proper local candidate the party has had out here for years. We're working our bums off trying to improve this margin, with little or no help from you lot, and now you come up here to tell me I mightn't be good enough for this seat?'

Di appeared unfazed.

'Let me tell you something, flossy,' thundered Flick. 'The people who will go to the ballot box in this electorate know who I am. They don't give a shit about Max Masters and Gabrielle Brennan—they want to send a local to Canberra. I've worked too bloody hard on this campaign, driving and sometimes flying tens of thousands of kilometres for a cup of tea, waiting weeks for a new photocopier, running a federal election campaign from a bloody dial-up modem—'

'Tell 'em, darl,' interrupted Con.

She looked at him intently.

'It's okay,' he said. 'You tell 'em or I will.'

She shook her head.

'It's my blog,' said Con.

'Don't, love,' said Flick. 'You don't have to do this.'

'Yes, I do, sweetheart.' He turned to us. 'It's my blog—Flick's covering for me.'

Di sighed, relieved.

'I've taken long service leave from the mine to work on the campaign,' Con explained. 'Sometimes when we're at the campaign office I use the internet there. Rings of Love is my username.'

'Would you be willing to say that on the record?'

'No, he would not,' said Flick.

'Sure,' said Con.

I took the last bite of my third delicious drop scone.

'Why don't we meet you at the launch,' said Di. 'Call me when you've made a decision about how you want to handle this.'

The function room at the weatherboard pub smelled like beer, salt, chalk and air-conditioning, with a hint of nicotine still lingering from before the ban. Three coin-operated billiards tables had been pushed aside to make room for the campaign launch. Maddy and I unstacked a tower of plastic orange chairs and tested the microphone while Di briefed Mick O'Donoghue. He had arrived half an hour before the launch. 'It's been an absolute bloody stinker today, hasn't it?' said the tanned octogenarian in an almost indecipherable Australian accent. 'Dry as a dead dingo's donger.'

'Donger?' I whispered to Maddy. She laughed.

'Silly bugger,' said Mick, when Di told him about Con's sightings. 'Imagine if I'd gone blurting out all my thoughts on a public noticeboard in my day. So, what's the game plan?'

'There's a whole bunch of gallery who have turned up to hear you speak,' said Di. 'The sitting member has been backgrounding on the blog, which for all they know is Flick's. I've drawn up a few lines for you to look over in case you're asked about it.'

He spotted his reflection in a framed photograph of Her Majesty circa 1976 and licked three wrinkly brown fingers to smooth down his remaining silver hair. *If I hadn't seen him do that, I'd have let him borrow the comb in my Toolkit.*

'Which journos are coming?'

'All the local press,' said Di. 'The *Queenslander*, a junior bloke from the *Herald* and one of the TV guys who's been travelling with the national campaign.'

'Who?'

'I don't know if you'll know him,' said Di. 'His name's Oscar Franklin.'

My tower of chairs toppled and crashed.

The former prime minister stared at me. 'Oscar,' he said, 'the looker.'

'I need to go to the motel and change before the launch,' I told Maddy.

'They're about to arrive. There's no time.'

'I can't let anyone see me like this. It'd be unprofessional.'

My head threatened to disown me. *You look like a tattooed banana.*

'You look fine,' lied Maddy. 'Anyway, you and I have to distribute the press release for Di. She doesn't want the gallery to know she's micromanaging this; otherwise, they'll sense we're anticipating disaster.'

I ducked into the loo behind the lectern and tipped my Toolkit into the sink.

Nothing in there is going to disguise the fact that you're wearing a promotional beer vest and flip-flops to a press conference.

'Nobody likes a naysayer,' I snapped, digging through my stash for instant remedies. My right hand spritzed my pits with perfumed antiperspirant. My left attacked my knotty hair with a comb. I gargled mouthwash, blotted greasy skin, added lashings of mascara to the existing coat and plastered nude gloss to my lips.

Ten minutes later, I burst out of the bathroom. 'Ta da!' I twirled on the spot.

Maddy's eyebrows were so raised they had almost crossed her hairline. The empty function room I had only just left was still quiet but now full. Most of the thirty-five orange seats had bottoms in them, including Oscar's very cute one in the front row. Cameras rolled. Sound technicians smirked. I glanced sideways to see Flick and Mick at the lectern in front of Her Majesty and the Australian flag. Mick cleared his throat. The microphone screeched.

Ruby, if I could self-decapitate right now, roll out the door of this ghastly hellhole and hitchhike back to Melbourne Airport at the mercy of a 25-stone lorry driver called Kev, I would—even if Kev was a yodeller.

'Terribly sorry.' I shrunk into the stifling silence.

Oscar patted the empty seat beside him. I sank onto it and hung my head. 'Nice wife-beater,' he whispered.

Wife-beater?

My BlackBerry buzzed.

'This isn't live, is it?' I whispered to Oscar at the end of Mick's speech.

He nodded.

'Why? It's a teeny-tiny campaign launch in the middle of nowhere.'

He handed me a breaking news story. PM SLAMS OPPOSITION FOR 'ET' CANDIDATE.

'Balls.'

Photographers and cameramen moved towards the lectern where Mick was shaking Flick's hand. There was applause from campaign supporters as Flick moved to centre stage.

'I'm happy to take a few questions now,' she said.

'Mrs Lunardi,' said Oscar, 'there are reports of an internet blog called Rings of Love originating from your campaign office. The blog appears to be about crop circles and extraterrestrial life in western Queensland. Is it yours?'

'No, it's not.'

'Well, whose is it?'

She paused. 'I am lucky enough to have a huge number of volunteer staff who work hard to see our party elected nationally and, of course, in the seat of Rafter. They tell me they want to put a local back in Canberra for Rafter.

I was born and raised in western Queensland and have lived here all my life. My husband, Con, has worked in Isa as a mining engineer for twenty years. Since I was twenty I've been a nurse for the Royal Flying Doctor Service from Normanton to Longreach and everywhere in between—'

'Do you think crop circles are messages from life on Saturn?'

'No, I don't. Now if you don't mind, I've got work to do. Thank you all for coming.' She took Con by the hand and walked out. The cameras and questions followed.

I went to the verandah, where a man wearing the same vest as me was having a smoke.

'What the fuck, Roo?' said Luke when I dialled his number.

'I'm truly sorry, Luke. I left an empty room to go to the bathroom and came back ten minutes later to find it full of people.'

'Felicia's launch was due to start at four. So, at four, when you'd finished in the bathroom, did you happen to think to yourself, "Hmmm, maybe I shouldn't burst through the doors and scream 'ta da' like a bloody stripper jumping out of a dirty old man's birthday cake"?'

No, you didn't.

'And what were you doing in the loo for ten minutes anyway?'

'That's no question to ask a lady.'

'You're not a lady; you're a policy advisor.'

'No, I'm not: you haven't given me a single piece of policy work since I joined.'

'Diddums.'

His sarcasm was unattractive.

'Why the hell are you wearing a wife-beater to work? It's fucking unprofessional.'

'I had to improvise. It's exceptionally hot here. My flip-flops are melting. You've no idea...'

'So why did every member of the national press gallery manage to come in appropriate attire? And Maddy?'

'Maddy must be reptilian because she ate hot porridge for breakfast in three-hundred-degree heat! She's the kind of person who'd order bread and butter pudding in Bora Bora!' My voice bounced off the corrugated-iron awning. 'In any case, I'm rather surprised to be receiving fashion advice from a man with a tie collection resembling land-fill!'

Silence.

'Luke?'

'I expected more from you, Roo. Much more.'

'Well, I'm sorry to have been such a disappointment.' The lump in my throat made my voice waver.

'Di is livid. You'll be in the papers tomorrow and on the TVs tonight.'

'Terrific. I'm going to make my television debut wearing promotional beer gear.'

The smoker took offence, stubbed his cigarette and walked back inside.

'Jesus, Ruby, did you stop for a second to think about how this might impact on Felicia Lunardi? Her campaign already looks like a fucking freak show.'

I bit my lip and lowered my Aviators.

'By the way, where's my dictaphone?'

'I believe the LOO has it.' Technically true.

'What?'

He cut out. I kicked an empty beer can at my feet.

It's not too late to join yodelling Kev, you know, said my head.

'Fuck off.'

'Sorry,' said a voice behind me, 'I just thought you could use some company.'

I turned to see Oscar unbuttoning his collar and rolling up his sleeves.

'Sorry, I was talking to myself.'

'Do you always tell yourself to fuck off?'

'Only when I'm very cross with me.'

'For what it's worth, Channel Eleven viewers will miss out on seeing Fourex Roo.'

I looked up at his strong jaw and warm smile. 'That's very kind of you.'

'There's a caveat.'

'And what's that?'

'That we get off this barbeque of a balcony and rejoin the sane people in the air-conditioning. You did promise to have a drink with me.'

Lord knows how many rum and Cokes later, I was dancing on the pool table singing 'Land Down Under' into a cue, to an audience of miners and journalists. It was safer up there; Di was barely speaking to me, though Maddy had assured me it would blow over. Cyclone warnings in Townsville meant that our planes were grounded until morning.

Halfway through 'True Blue', Maddy, Di and the journalists headed for the door.

'What's with the mass exodus?' I said into my pool cue.

'It's getting late, Roo,' said Maddy. 'We're on an early flight.'

Oscar was at the bar, buying me another.

'It's only ten, Maddy. Stay for one more round!'

She shook her head and ran to catch up with Di.

At midnight, the publican called last drinks, and I tried to get down off the pool table.

'Let's get you some air,' said Oscar, lifting me. He took me by the hand and led me up a narrow staircase to what looked like an attic.

'I don't need air,' I giggled. 'I'm not as think as you drunk I am.'

Oscar opened a window and climbed outside. 'Come on, Roo.'

I stepped out onto the sloping tin roof, still warm from the sun, and looked up. 'Stars are very shiny.'

'Astrologists in western Queensland tonight confirmed stars are, quote, very shiny,' he said in his newsreader voice.

'Astronomers,' I corrected.

'Whatever.' He kissed my eyelids closed.

'It's quite an important distinction,' I said. 'Astrologists wear purple velvet in the middle of the day and like crystals.'

'Also shiny.' He kissed my mouth.

Oscar Franklin is kissing you.

Well spotted, head.

'Oscar?'

'Hmm?'

'You taste like a pirate.' I pulled away from his delectable lips.

'It's the rum.'

'Yes, I suppose it is the rum.'

We continued.

'Oscar?'

'Hmm?'

'It's important to point out at this juncture that I haven't had much experience with pirates, so I'm not really sure how they taste. Probably a bit salty, with a touch of parrot'—he opened his left eye—'not that I'm a parrot-eater.'

Now you're kissing Oscar Franklin. This one's a bit more intense. I'm no expert, but perhaps it's best not to talk about parrots and pirates when you're being kissed.

Wise counsel, head.

'All right, you two.' The publican clapped her hands behind us. 'Pub's closed. I'm locking up now.'

Oscar pulled me to my feet and swivelled me towards the publican. 'Thanks for a splendid evening. This is a lovely pub.'

She laughed. 'No worries, love. Hoo roo!'

'I am.'

Territorial

Di marched me to the tiny WC on the media plane.

'*Tell* me you didn't pash Oscar Franklin,' she demanded in a hoarse whisper.

'Pash?'

'Yes, Roo, pash,' she said, before morphing into a thesaurus. 'Neck, snog, tongue, suck face, make out with...'

Admittedly, I was familiar with the verb, but had hoped to buy myself some time to formulate an appropriate response. 'Firstly, I wasn't so much a pasher as a co-pashee'—at least for the first one—'and secondly, definitionally, it wasn't a pash, just a quick kiss.'

She smashed her head rhythmically against the wall. 'At the pub, I take it.'

'Kind of *on* the pub.'

'I'm not going to ask what that means.'

'How did you find out?'

'It's Clon-fucking-curry, Roo. It's not every day that

famous journalists are in town with former prime ministers. People talk.'

'Does anyone else know?'

'No,' she said. 'Just me, the publican and presumably Oscar, unless you spiked his drink. What happened?'

I told her the story, skipping over some of the detail, like the part where it took us an hour to cross the road from pub to motel or when he said my lips were so red and swollen that I looked like I'd just eaten a Redskin, which he assured me was an Australian delicacy.

'There's nothing to be concerned about,' I reassured her. 'It's not as if I fancy him.'

I hurt, throbbed my head, playing a particularly graphic montage of the incident in question. *How do you expect me to do my job properly if you poison me with liquor? I could have prevented all of this.*

Di leaned in close. 'Let me give you a piece of well-trodden advice, Roo: don't shit where you eat.' She slid the latch to release the bifurcating door. 'By the way, you're in shot but not mentioned on page eleven of the *Queenslander* and two of the *Herald* with a little caption: "Advisor Roo Stanhope copes with the heat." I had to work hard to bury it like that. I know Luke's already spoken to you about it. Don't let it happen again.' With that, she rejoined the cabin.

I was knackered, brutally hungover and had a To Do list the length of the Trans-Siberian Railway. With the FASTEN SEATBELT sign on for our descent into Darwin, I returned to my seat, which was a safe distance from Oscar's—we hadn't yet spoken—pulled a worn scrap of paper from my handbag and tried to prioritise some items.

1. Confirm visa (LIFE/DEATH URGENT)
2. Sign contract for negligible remuneration (FINANCIALLY URGENT)
3. Track down luggage (STYLISTICALLY URGENT)
4. Track down coffee-stained trousers from hotel laundry in Perth (SEE ABOVE)
5. Call Fran, Clem, parents, Daphne, Debs, etc. (LONG OVERDUE)
6. Arrange birthday present for Clem (MUST DO BEFORE MONDAY).

'Balls.' I saw MONDAY at the top of the day's media brief. Counting back the hours in my head to allow for the time difference, I discovered a small window of opportunity in which I might save myself from the ferociousness of an almost five-year-old.

As soon as the wheels hit the tarmac, I Googled 'same day gift delivery London'. Of seventy-two thousand results, including fruit baskets, champagne and edible underwear, I came across Balloons on a Bike, which boasted 'tasteful balloon bouquets hand-delivered across western London'. I placed an online order for two dozen fuchsia helium balloons (some pearlescent, some with polka dots) and a big silver 5 to be delivered by noon in London. Hurrah.

Darwin is vastly underrated, I concluded as we made our way on the media bus to the seat of Forster, where we were due to visit a market. Avoiding Oscar's knowing gaze, I distributed bottles of water and spread the good news that we'd be spending at least a day in the Top End. As we waited for Max and Fred Smythe—the local member—to arrive for a photo opportunity, I lost myself for a moment in the exquisite aromas emanating from each stall. It was as if the myriad of flavours from the tropical East were being pounded by a pestle in a massive mortar: lemongrass, ginger, lime, garlic, chilli, star anise, fish sauce and coconut, fused with the smell of onions caramelising on a barbeque at the nearby burger hut.

Max pulled up with Shelly and Luke, followed closely by Fred. A relaxed posse formed around them to capture a few shots.

Luke came over, straightening his solar system tie. I wondered if it glowed in the dark. 'Hi,' he said.

I stared at my shoes and then straight at his chest. 'Nice tie,' I fibbed, 'but potentially risky given Rings of Love.'

'Good point.' He removed it.

'I need to get back to the hotel,' said Luke. 'Think you can manage this photo op?'

'Absolutely.' He didn't seem angry anymore, which was fortuitous because I couldn't have coped with that in addition to everything else.

We made our way through the market, Max and Fred shaking hands and tasting local produce, Shelly complimenting handicrafts.

Under the cover of my dark glasses, I hadn't been able to gauge whether Oscar saw the night before as a slip of the tongue, so I was relieved when he approached me with a cup of home-brewed ginger beer. 'It's supposed to be excellent for hangovers.'

'Thanks.' I took a quick sip and checked my periphery for onlookers.

'I had fun last night, Roo.' It was barely audible, but resonated.

'I did—'

Flack the Cop startled me with a tap on my shoulder. 'A word, Roo?'

'Excuse me, Oscar,' I said in my most professional voice and followed Flack to a quiet spot behind a Malaysian laksa stall.

'Territory Police have informed us there's a small group of protesters approaching the market.' He removed his curly earpiece. 'They're demanding to speak with Max.'

'What are they protesting?'

'Apparently they're unhappy with the Opposition's immigration policy. We think they're possibly dangerous—they're linked to a white supremacist group and have a history of violence. We're getting Max and Shelly out of here in two minutes.'

'Maybe he should confront them,' I suggested. 'I mean, it wouldn't do us any harm to be tough on these arseholes.'

'With respect, I'm not asking your opinion, Roo.'

'Thanks for the heads up,' I said. 'Let's keep this low key—let me tell Max and Shelly what we're doing.' He nodded.

I pushed through the friendly crowd. Max was sampling chicken satay when I reached him. 'We've got to head to the cars now,' I said calmly, smiling. 'Violent white supremacists are on their way. We need to get out of here for everyone's safety. Follow Flack the Cop.'

As he posed for a camera phone with a local supporter, I could see the curiosity in Max's eyes as he weighed risk against political opportunity, then Shelly gave him the sort of look that only a spouse is entitled to give, a look he reluctantly obeyed.

'Thanks for showing me around, Fred.' Max shook his hand.

'There's plenty more to see,' said Fred, confused.

But Max had already veered off the agreed course and

was making his way, smiling and waving, surrounded by cops, towards the cars. They sped off into the sunset as soon as he and Shelly were safely inside.

It was obvious to the media contingent that something was up.

'What's going on, gorgeous?' asked Oscar.

'Do you mind holding this for me?' I handed him my ginger beer. 'Duty calls.'

I found Fred and whispered in his ear. 'I'm Ruby Stanhope from Max's office. On advice from the police, I need you to head back to your office.'

'These are my constituents, mate,' he declared, raising his voice a little. 'They're expecting me to walk the length of this market, so that's what I'm going to do—with or without Max and his missus.'

We were surrounded by cameramen and hungry boom mikes. Oscar moved closer, his eyes pleading for an explanation. I was stuck. I couldn't tell the world the LOO skedaddled because we got a tip-off that a squadron of skinheads was on its way. I couldn't try to get the media back onto the bus because it would look like a cover-up. It was a case of waiting for the inevitable.

We didn't have to wait for long. Minutes later, a seething mob of crazies marched towards us, surrounded by uniformed police. Carrying vile banners, the protesters chanted maniacally. Cameras lapped up the commotion while journalists emptied their pockets in search of pens and dictaphones.

Too short to see past the onlookers, I watched a sequence of stills on the digital display of a *Herald* photographer's camera in front of me. One man's back was tattooed blue with a white cross in the centre. A middle-aged woman's face was painted with the Australian flag, but the blue and red had combined in the tropical humidity, turning her an unpleasant shade of violet. I'd seen these sorts of demonstrations back home. Seething haters are the same the world over: ugly. The laksa lady pulled down a roller door to shut up shop, and Fred the MP stood paralysed at the sidelines for a moment before fleeing to his car.

Oscar's satellite truck pulled up on the footpath. With the protest as his backdrop, he used the camera to pick his teeth and readied himself for a live cross.

'Thanks, Peter, I'm reporting live from a Darwin street market in the seat of Forster, where anti-immigration activists are protesting the Opposition's new immigration policy, announced yesterday.' He had to yell above the din. 'The policy would see an increase in skilled migration as a means of boosting economic activity if the Opposition was indeed to win...'

The aubergine extremist bounded into shot. 'Masters wants to let 'em take our jobs,' she howled, 'so we'll make sure he won't get the job he wants.'

'I guess that says it all,' said Oscar, who was very pleased with himself for being in the right place at the wrong time. 'Back to you, Peter.'

My BlackBerry buzzed in my bag.

'Hello?' I shouted.

'I just saw your lover boy and his purple friend on telly,' said Di, 'and now my phone's going ballistic.'

I let the lover boy remark slide. 'I know. It's frantic here. Fred fled. What should I do? I can't very well bundle everyone back onto the bus—they're all trying to get as much of this story as possible.'

'Tell them the bus is leaving in five minutes and if they're not on it they'll need to find their own way back to the hotel. And don't answer any questions—not even from your boyfriend. *After Dark* wants an interview with Max.'

I bit my tongue and did as I was told.

My relentless phone rang.

'Wooby Stanhope?' said a little voice.

'Clem?'

'Yes, this is Clementine Genevieve Gardner-Stanhope calling.'

'Happy birthday to you,' I sang, 'happy birthday to you, happy birthday—'

'Please stop singing, Wooby.'

'So now that you're five you don't need to call me Aunty anymore?' I felt the beginnings of a sore throat.

'No,' she said, 'I'm not talking to you, but Mummy made me call you to say thank you for the balloons.'

'Why are you cross? Didn't you like them?'

'No, I did *not* like the balloons you sent me.' A foot stomped. 'I did not like them one little bit.'

I could hear Fran in the background urging her to show some manners.

'Thank you, Wooby. There, Mummy, I've said it, now can I hang up?'

Fran seized the phone. 'Hello, Ruby,' she said, to the sound of a slamming door.

'Isn't it a little early for adolescence?'

'The delivery company came this morning, Ruby. When a five-year-old girl receives a floating mass of inflated buggies, storks and rattles in an array of blues led by a giant helium baby proclaiming IT'S A BOY! this is the kind of reaction you can expect.'

'Bloody Balloons on a Bike. They must have confused

the order or something. Somewhere in western London, proud new parents are welcoming their son to the world with a bunch of pink balloons and a helium number 5. It cost me a small fortune.'

'She's inconsolable, Ruby.'

'Put Clem back on for me,' I pleaded. 'I can explain it to her.'

'I can't; she's refusing to speak with you—she now refers to you as "Mummy's sister".'

'Shit,' I said, 'I don't have time to fix this now—I'm trying to round up the nation's media to distract them from a group of white supremacists.'

'Well, we all have our priorities, don't we, Ruby? I have to go. I have eighty cupcakes to ice, twenty-seven allergy-safe party bags to fill and a piñata to papier-mâché.'

She hung up on me.

It hadn't been the best twenty-four hours, what with the Luke reprimand, uncouth canoodling, lingering hangover, pirate breath, warning from Di, white supremacists, Clem cluster-fuck and the beginnings of man flu. Now, for the finale, Max was about to be interviewed on *After Dark* about the immigration backlash. And it was only Day Eight.

As the bus pulled into the hotel car park, there was a new text on my BlackBerry. Oscar.

> Dramatic afternoon. Can't imagine what this means for your Immi policy? Sorry if the ginger beer was too public. Had fun last night. We must do it again...

But not the worst twenty-four hours either.

Stuffed up

'Rhinosinusitis,' said the doctor, disposing of the foul-tasting ice lolly stick she'd just shoved down my throat.

'Excuse me?' I sprayed.

'You have an acute case of bacterial rhinosinusitis.'

Bloody Oscar. My head was quick to blame.

'You know, there are nicer ways of telling your patients they're be-horned and beastly.' I mopped up the slurry of liquids streaming from my nose. I was proud of my little joke, given my condition, but the doctor seemed unamused.

She passed me another tissue with her left hand while writing a script with her right. 'It just means your sinuses are stuffed.' She ripped a piece of paper from her pad. 'Here, take these three times a day with food—that ought to clear it—and keep taking paracetamol to keep your temperature down.'

Having tested its limits, I jettisoned my newest tissue,

thanked the doctor for her humourless diagnosis and stepped out into the fresh Canberra air.

Yes, Canberra. Two nights earlier in balmy Darwin, Luke had pulled me aside when the LOO finished his gruelling *After Dark* interview, which had focused almost entirely on immigration, a topic now dominating the headlines. 'Can I have a word?'

'Sure.' What I really wanted was to make a run for it, mortified at the thought that Di had broadcast my lip-locking adventures in Cloncurry—soiling my dinner plate, or however she tactfully put it.

Why should you care? asked my head. *It's not as if it's any more unprofessional than, say, interrupting a press conference with a 'ta da' or sending a recording device to its watery grave or allowing a harmless photo opportunity to morph into a race riot.*

'I need you in Canberra, mate,' said Luke.

Relief rushed through my arteries. 'Whatever for?'

'One, you look like death and I don't want any of the travelling party catching whatever *that* is. Rest tomorrow.'

It wasn't exactly a compliment, but understandable given that Maddy had asked me earlier in the evening if I'd mistakenly used a coral lip pencil in place of my usual charcoal eyeliner.

'Two, the debate's on Sunday night and I'd like you to join the prep team.'

Now, that was a compliment. I might not have been in the game for long, but I knew that The Debate was a campaign event trumped only by The Launch and Polling Day itself.

As Luke explained, the politics leading up to it are like those surrounding a mediaeval duel. As soon as there's a whiff of an election date, each candidate races to become the challenger. Once challenged, the opponent must either accept or have very good reason to decline. The debate then becomes focused on timing, venue, format and the like. 'My opponent has expressed a preference for a single moderator—I would prefer a panel of three journalists from the press gallery,' one candidate might say. 'Three journalists?' the other would reply. 'I thought we should invite the audience to adjudicate—they are, after all, the ultimate adjudicators.' And so, the one-upmanship would continue until the minutiae were sorted and the parameters set.

In the present case, the LOO had challenged the Prime Minister to a debate. She had duly accepted, but on the condition that it be held in the Great Hall of Parliament House on the second Sunday of the campaign. The LOO accepted, but pointed out how unusual it was to hold the debate so early in the campaign and requested that his opponent leave open the possibility of a second debate. She had not ruled it out. So if one candidate did badly there could well be another round.

With a pile of reading in my laptop bag, I'd boarded a midnight flight to Canberra. It hadn't been such a good idea to catch the eight-hour flight from Darwin (via Adelaide, where the lounge was closed) to Canberra with nasal passages full of ball bearings and eyes that might pop free of their sockets if I sneezed. Business Class was full, so I had found myself inexorably sandwiched between a man the size of a Smart Car and a woman with a teething baby.

I wasn't just sick; I was homesick and miserable. My niece was fuming, my sister distant and my aunts a faint memory. Cobwebs and a few hundred quid were all that remained of my bank account because I kept forgetting to sign my employment contract. I hadn't slept properly in a fortnight and I'd been cruelly close to the Barossa Valley and Margaret River on several occasions without picking up a brochure, let alone a bottle. To top things off, I'd fallen in lust with the political equivalent of Romeo Montague. As the infant beside me howled through the turbulence, I too had shed a few quiet tears.

It was a glorious Thursday morning in Canberra when I filled my script at the Manuka chemist, a perfect twenty-four degrees. I tilted my head skywards and basked in the gentle sunlight, asking that it warm my face and hair. My prep meeting wasn't until noon, so I had a rare ninety minutes to myself. I probably should have done something productive with them, like find a laundromat or remove the chipped pearl lacquer from my fingernails, but I erred on the side of indulgence. Securing a half-sunned table for one at a tiny cafe, I read only the Food & Wine, Arts and Literature sections of the papers over two lattes, a mushroom risotto and a lightly dusted gelatinous cube of rose and pistachio Turkish delight.

Where in the world is Roo? xxx

Oscar had staged a virtual invasion of my heavenly peace, the second message since Darwin, but his company wasn't unwelcome.

Sick in Maunka. Rhinosinusitis. As ugly as it sounds. R
My initial would suffice. Frankly, there had been enough kisses for now.

Couldn't be ugly on you. I'm a bit stuffy too. Manuka is practically my hood—I live in Kingston. How long are you there for? x

I drafted and redrafted my reply. Charming as he might be, I couldn't very well tell a journalist my purpose for being in Canberra. My head praised me for heeding its warning.

Not sure at this stage. Where are you? R

I knew where he was. In fact, I even knew where he was headed next, which was more than he did.

Arnhem Land. It's amazing—hope you missed this for something important? Your guy has announced he'll fund trips for school students to visit Indigenous communities in their state—I just blogged my support. Looking forward to seeing more of you. x

That was presumptuous. If I hadn't needed to be at Parliament House twenty minutes later, I probably would have spent the next hour wrestling with my aching head about the pros and cons of dating the enemy, but there was a bigger debate to be had.

From newspaper photographs, I'd always thought the Australian parliament had all the architectural grace of a squat hatstand, but as I walked through its main doors into the huge entrance hall, I changed my mind.

Staffers on their BlackBerries traipsed across the vast space. A travel-weary school group clad in crumpled uniforms marvelled at the high ceilings, their nervous young teacher conducting a solemn headcount. Three pairs of high heels went clip-clopping across the floor, the identities of their wearers hidden behind cardboard trays holding dozens of precariously balanced takeaway coffees. An old man stepped out of their way, rapping his knuckles against a marble wall, while his wife browsed the decorative teaspoons in the gift shop. This was the national parliament and there was nothing stuffy about it. The open hall told me a lot about the country I was getting to know.

I approached a staffed desk and said I had a meeting at the Leader of the Opposition's office, giving them Beryl's name.

'She'll be down in a minute to sign you in, love,' said a uniformed man.

'Roo!' bellowed Beryl as she came rushing towards me like an excited child. 'It's great to see you.' She grabbed my hand and squeezed until my fingers fought for their release. 'Come with me,' she said. I attached a flimsy cardboard UNACCOMPANIED VISITOR pass to my jeans and followed her through a maze of indistinguishable corridors with identical wall clocks ticking in unison.

We arrived at an enclave of empty partitioned offices, each desk in total disarray as if everyone had just stepped out for a fire drill.

'Where are all the people?'

'On the campaign, love. We all thought we were headed for another uneventful sitting week, so most of them didn't have time to pack up their desks or kiss their families goodbye.'

I spotted a cluttered desk with a pinky sparkly-framed photograph of Maddy on a horse. It made sense that she rode, being from the country, but then she never spoke about it. We'd never spoken much about anything other than politics and even then only the politics of the day, yet I felt like we were bosom buddies with the kind of kinship it would take years to cultivate in normal circumstances.

'That's Luke's office,' said Beryl, pointing to a room with a door. He too was a mystery.

The phone rang. 'Wait here,' she said, running to get it.

Inside Luke's office, a mahogany-framed legal quali-fication hung on a white wall. Three ties—one a gaggle of yellow smiley faces—dangled from a wire coathanger on the doorknob. A novelty Magic 8 Ball weighed down a pile of paper in his in-tray. Next to the door was a finger-painting of a house, a cat, two big people and one small person. *By Dan Harley. Grade 1A.*

Dan Harley?

Dan Harley?

I went to find Beryl. 'Is that painting by Luke's neph—'

'I'm sorry, he's not in the office at the moment. Can I pass on a message?' She pointed to the microphone on her headset and scribbled me a note. *Debate prep mtg. First door on left.*

I walked into the large, hospital-green room which was full of faces—some familiar, some not. Theo, who stood pen in hand at a whiteboard, came to greet me.

'Roo, you look like shit.'

'Thanks for your honesty, Theo.'

'Let me introduce you to everyone.' He started with an enormously pregnant lady, the kind you want to follow around with a mop and bucket in case she erupts. 'I'd like you to meet Senator Sasha Flight. She's expecting twins.'

'In case Roo couldn't tell,' she said warmly, attempting to fasten a flimsy cardigan around her impressive circum-ference.

Theo moved around the room. 'This is Joel Tobin. Joel is from the Shadow Treasurer's office.' He couldn't have been a day older than eighteen, but I tried not to let this distract me. 'Meadow here works for the Shadow Health

Minister,' Theo said of a severe, matronly lady. 'And you know Archie.'

Archie pulled up a chair for me next to him. I poured myself a cup of tea.

'Roo Stanhope is a financial policy advisor,' said Theo. Not that there's any evidence of it, I thought. 'She's been out on the campaign trail since it began and has her finger on the pulse.'

How are you going to blag your way through this one, Ruby?

'As we know,' said Theo, 'the debate will be broadcast live from the Great Hall at 7.30 p.m. on Channel Eleven, with that mindless, narcissistic himbo as compere.'

'Oscar Franklin?' I asked, praying I was wrong.

'That's the one,' laughed Senator Flight. 'Pretty Boy.'

Shit, shit, shit.

'There will be a coin toss to decide which candidate will speak first. The candidate who loses will make an opening statement of no longer than three minutes, followed by the other candidate. Pretty Boy will then invite the five panel members to ask two questions each. The candidates will have thirty seconds to answer each question and thirty seconds to rebut before the compere silences them. Each candidate will be given two minutes to make a closing statement. In a nearby studio, audience members will rate the candidates contemporaneously, and television audiences will see a smiley face feature at the bottom of their screens, showing the studio audience's response. Franklin will then join the studio audience and facilitate a discussion about the event.'

'Can the candidates see the smiley faces?' asked Meadow.

'No,' said Theo. 'No one in the Great Hall will be

able to see the smiley faces until they watch a playback.'

'Are we having a live audience?' asked the senator.

'Yes, mainly staff members, MPs, family and friends.' Theo removed his mismatched cufflinks and rolled up his sleeves. 'Now I suggest we start brainstorming our opening statement.'

When the delivery boy arrived, it was midnight and we still had a solid four hours ahead of us. It was like rehearsing a university stage production. The senator, who had a knack for cutting questions, took the role of media panel, resting a pizza box on the camel hump that housed her twins. Theo did the LOO with such precision that, from outside the room, Beryl thought we had Max on speakerphone. Meadow played the Prime Minister, and Archie acted as compere. Joel and I finetuned language on the whiteboard.

At dawn, we adjourned for a quick tea break. Curled up on one of the reception sofas, I rolled two joints from tissues—a plug for each leaking nostril—and listened to the army of goose-stepping clocks until I was having a nightmare about the crocodile from *Peter Pan*.

'Rise and shine, Roo,' chirped Beryl to the sadistic flicker and hum of fluorescent bulbs as she switched on the lights and spread the day's newspapers on the coffee table. 'It's almost eight, darl, and you've got a teleconference in five minutes.'

'Bollocks.' I removed the crusty joints from my nose and shielded my burning eyes from the lights. When they'd adjusted, I sat up to glance at the front pages.

IMMIGRATION POLICY HITS MASTERS WHERE IT HURTS, said the *Queenslander*. BRENNAN CLIMBS THE POLLS, said the *Herald*.

'Racist pricks,' said Theo, reading over my shoulder.

'Who?'

'The three per cent of voters who have ditched us since the last poll was taken. You've got dried snot on your face and, no offence, but you look even worse than you did yesterday.'

'Your fly's undone and you're older than my dad.'

He blushed and zipped himself. 'Thanks.' He tucked the *Herald* under his arm and whistled his way to the gents.

I dialled into the teleconference. Di was the only one there.

'How you feeling, Roo?'

'Horrendous.'

'Go into the press office,' she yawned.

I waddled to the end of the corridor and into an open-plan office littered with newspapers and more television screens than the White House Situation Room.

'Go to the desk in the far-left corner with the Special K on it. Open the top drawer and help yourself.'

'Are you some sort of chemist kleptomaniac?' I rummaged through her impressive stash. There were tubs of multivitamins, tampons galore, Lemsip sachets, eyedrops by the bucket load, yards of dental floss, enough whitening strips to make-over a whale, packets of lozenges and every kind of fast-acting analgesic imaginable.

'Now joining...' The recorded teleconference voice interrupted us. 'Luke and Max,' said a raspy Luke from Townsville. Archie joined me on speaker. Theo dialled in from the gents.

'Di, can you kick us off?' asked Luke.

'Sure. The skilled immigration thing has gone down about as well as an impromptu Bar Mitzvah at a mosque in Tehran. We've failed to communicate the need for skilled foreigners when so many Australians are out of work. The government has taken the populist low road by silently siding with the kinds of morons we saw protesting in Darwin.'

'That's just bullshit,' said Theo. 'The core of our policy is to get people out of the driver's seats of taxis and into the specialist jobs they're trained for, like health or IT. This will help fill our skills gap, which will increase our productivity.'

'Di's not suggesting there's anything wrong with the policy, Theo,' said a fatigued Luke. 'She's just saying we fucked up communicating it. We're back down to the two-party-preferred result we had at the beginning of the campaign.'

We didn't need to see the LOO's face to know the demoralising effect the poll was having on him. 'I'm getting calls from every marginal-seat candidate in the country,' Max said. 'Punters are telling them that they're not going to come over to us unless we roll over on the immigration issue.'

'But it's the right thing to do,' said Theo.

'Nobody's arguing with you,' said Max, 'but I need to give them something a bit more persuasive than that if we're going to win this thing.'

It could have been the hit of Ibuprofen or maybe the sleep deprivation. One thing was certain: at that moment, my head allowed me to trust my instincts. 'I'm new to this game,' I said, 'but I think Theo has a point here.' Archie sent discouraging signals which I promptly ignored. 'If you back down on this issue, the gallery will eat you for breakfast. It'll be all flip and flop, no backbone. The issue will probably fizzle out in a week, but won't you lose even more ground from the about-face?'

'Go on,' said Max.

I took a deep breath. 'I think you should stick to your guns because it's the right thing to do. It will serve as a point of differentiation between you and Brennan. Brennan will say and do anything to win this election, just like she said and did anything to topple Patton. You won't lie to the Australian people. You won't compromise on what you know to be right. Be the hero.'

'That's all very nice, Roo,' said Archie, in the tone of a children's television presenter. If my nose hadn't required urgent attention, I would have pointed out that I read History at Oxford while he was cold-calling arts and crafts magazines to sell in his clients' exciting new knitting patterns. 'Problem is, Max,' Archie continued, 'you'll be more martyr than hero when we can't squeeze the complex detail of this policy into a sound byte.'

'Maybe *you* can't, Archie,' skewered Di, 'but I'm willing to give it a shot.'

'The stakes are too high,' said Archie. 'You do this sort of thing when you're *in* government, not when you're trying to win it.'

Max sighed. 'I think the debate's the time to get this message across. I'm going to plough on. Have it ready for me to look at by this afternoon when I'm on the plane to Canberra.'

The Debate

'Is it your birthday, Roo?' asked Beryl, poking her head around the corner of my partitioned nook in the press office. She was all gussied up, even wearing make-up in honour of the debate, which was less than a couple of hours away. I thought hard about her question and checked the date on my BlackBerry. March the fourteenth, two days since the polls had dived.

'No,' I said, 'why's that?'

'There are three deliveries for you at reception.'

This was exactly the distraction I needed from the Pre-Debate Jitters, the name I'd given to the acrobatic troupe using my bladder as a trampoline. Grabbing a pair of scissors, I sat at Beryl's desk, which reeked of her musky perfume, and ripped into the largest of the three packages. 'Hallelujah!' I squealed, giving the senator rather too amorous an embrace as she waddled through the door. 'My suitcase has arrived—he's been on a national tour without me and I've missed him so.'

I cradled the battered and bruised Samsonite like a handsome beau returning from war. There was a little note inside.

Dearest Ruby,

We've taken the liberty of packing all of your things into this suitcase.

All our love, your aunts, Pansy & her pups

With such a happy reunion, the other two packages seemed ancillary, but when I opened the medium-sized one, it was all too good to be true. Inside were Debs' black pants and white shirt, both unblemished. Luckily for the senator, she wasn't within reach. By parcel number three, my eyes glistened with joy. This one was a fat cylindrical shape and came with an elegant cream card.

Get well soon, Roo. Believe in the healing power of Redskins. See you tonight?

Oscar x

Beneath layers of bubble wrap was a curvaceous kitchen canister in thick, warped glass with a shiny silver lid: the kind one might find filled with vanilla sugar in Nigella Lawson's pantry. It was brimming with individually wrapped sweets. 'Roo's Redskins' was handwritten in Tipp-Ex on the lid.

'Yummo,' said Di, helping herself. 'Who gave you these?'
I blushed.

'Christ almighty,' she said. 'Pretty Boy's compering the fucking debate tonight, Roo!'

I couldn't look her in the eye. It wasn't shame that prevented me, just that I hadn't had enough time to make any sensible decision about where things with Oscar might go next. Until I had the answer to that question, defending myself was pointless. I had seen the inside of my eyelids for only eleven of the past seventy-two hours, a violation for which my spinning head was yet to forgive me.

Shelly's arrival with Milly and Abigail saved me from further interrogation. 'Abigail,' said Shelly, 'have you met Roo?' The girl, who had her father's features, shook her head, clearly bored. She was busy listening to her iPod.

'Redskin?' I offered.

'Thanks.' She unwrapped one.

'You look great tonight, Shelly.' She was wearing a shell-pink asymmetric shift dress, nude peep-toe platforms and a wooden necklace which tied with ribbon at the side.

'She does, doesn't she?' said Max, who had pushed through the hinged doors of his office into the reception.

'Dad!' squealed Abigail, taking a running leap into his arms.

The trampolining sprang back into action. Theo was pacing in the corridor outside, chanting to himself like a tone-deaf Gregorian monk. I wheeled my suitcase into the Ladies and pulled out a clean bra and matching pants, diamond studs, knee-length blueberry silk dress, and a pair of vertiginous inky python slingbacks, the first pair of different shoes other than flip-flops I had worn in a fortnight. I washed my face, painted it, spritzed my décolletage and brushed the life back into my hair.

It was time.

Theo stopped dead in his tracks when he saw me. 'You don't look like shit anymore.'

'Thanks, Theo.' I must have looked fabulous. 'We've got to take our seats now.'

He shuddered. 'Not yet.'

'Come on, Theo.' It was like talking a cat out of a tree. 'We've done all we can now—the rest is up to him.'

As we walked through the corridors, we saw the bright lights of a fast-moving media stampede. Sound guys led their cameramen backwards by their belt loops so they didn't fall over. At the epicentre was the Prime Minister. She looked different in person. Taller, somehow. Dressed in a black skirt suit and turquoise top, she appeared calm but determined.

'How are you feeling, PM?' yelled a journalist at the front of his species.

'Terrific. Looking forward to it.'

From a safe distance, we watched the phenomenon move through the doors and onto the parquetry floors of the Great Hall, where rapturous applause broke out.

I knew Luke would be with Max. I called him.

'Luke?'

'Yes,' he whispered.

'The PM's wearing turquoise.'

'What's that?'

'Green.'

'So?'

'Max is wearing green.'

'So?'

'Tell Milly from me that Max needs to change his tie.'

'On it. Thanks, Roo.'

Theo and I took our seats next to a wide-eyed Beryl, behind rows of shadow ministers, MPs and their spouses. On stage, Oscar was chatting with the press panel while make-up artists powdered their faces. The familiar trill of clicking cameras emerged through the doors. The scrum broke, giving way to Max, who sported a red tie. We leaped from our seats and gave him the rockstar entrance he deserved. Shelly and Abigail took their seats in the front row.

'Good evening, ladies and gentlemen,' crooned Oscar. 'Tonight's debate will be broadcast live, and in order to get through it and give each candidate equal time we need to refrain from applause and heckles until the end. We're going live in thirty seconds, so switch off your phones—that includes you, press secretaries—and try to get all the coughs and sneezes out of your systems.'

'He's such a hunk of spunk,' whispered Beryl.

My mind wandered as Max delivered the opening statement I had in large part drafted.

I'm too tired to argue with you about this now, my head pleaded. *You know my views on Oscar, Ruby. Don't make me reiterate them on less than three hours' sleep.*

For once, my heart seized the microphone, demanding equal time. *Darling Ruby, I heave and surge in that man's presence. I'm all aflutter just thinking about his kiss, those sweet messages, that thoughtful gift. Look at him. Feel me. I've been out of action for years thanks to that killjoy on your shoulders. Why not just go with it? Let go. See what happens. And that's just me—you should hear what your poor, forsaken body has to say!*

I shut them out and tuned back in to the rhythm of the other debate.

'Mr Masters and his party say they plan to give Australian jobs to highly skilled foreigners. I have always governed in the national interest, no matter how difficult the circumstances of those abroad. They are not my responsibility. The Australian people are.' The Prime Minister sipped from a tumbler of water.

'The thing is,' said Max. His pause was prolonged and uncomfortable. Theo clutched my leg. 'The thing is...' His voice softened. 'We all know it would be popular for me to bury my party's skilled immigration policy and send it off into the abyss for a prolonged committee review until it's forgotten and covered in dust.

'But I'm not prepared to do that. And the reason is simple: I have been chosen to lead, not follow. This policy, however unpopular, will inject the skills that our economy needs to grow. Growth brings with it more jobs. More jobs will spur more growth; and growth, jobs.' Theo's grip eased.

'Ditching this policy is in my political interest. I was told this week that these sorts of policies are the things you do when you're in government, not when you're trying to win it.

'But I'm not going to lie; I'm going to lead. If people want a follower, a cynic, a clever, calculated tactician, then I guess my opponent will be pouring champagne on the third of April. But I will sleep soundly beside Shelly knowing that I did the right thing.'

We didn't need to see the smiley face graphic. We felt it.

At the end Max and the Prime Minister shook hands and she oozed off the stage.

Back in Max's office, bottle tops were flying off beers. Luke poured me a glass of wine.

'Tasmanian pinot,' he said.

'Thanks.' I sipped. It was good. 'Not wearing a tie?'

'I was. Milly confiscated it.'

We smiled.

'I'm glad you weren't in Darwin this week,' he said.

'Oh.'

'No, I mean I'm glad you were here working with Theo and the team. You should be proud of your contribution, Roo.' He paused for a second. 'I've been meaning to say sorry for being hard on you the other day after your wife-beater incident. I was just trying to—'

My phone rang once.

'Trying to?' I asked.

My phone rang again. Oscar's name flashed up on caller ID.

'Trying to—' Luke said.

My phone rang a third time. 'Sorry, I'd better take this.' I picked up and excused myself from the room.

'Roo, I'm in a commercial break. Are you free later for dinner at my place?'

My heart thumped against my rib cage. 'Text me your address.'

I rejoined the celebration, where Luke was proposing a toast. 'To Max—you've done us proud.'

'To Max,' we chorused.

I grabbed my handbag and made a beeline for the taxi rank.

'Joining us at the pub, Ruby?' Luke picked up his briefcase.

'Not tonight.'

'Come on, Ruby, the house red's a pinot.'

I shook my head. Luke put down his briefcase. Di raised an eyebrow.

'Where are you off to, Roo?' asked Max. 'Hot date?'

'No, I'm having a quiet night in—I'm shagged.'

'Or about to be,' said Di. I shrugged off my colleagues' wolf-whistles and made my way to the cab rank.

∞

I pressed his doorbell. Miles Davis was playing. Footsteps crescendoed towards the door. It opened. My God, he was gorgeous.

'Hi.' He kissed the no-man's-land between my lips and cheek. 'Come on in—I'm making pasta.' He took my hand and led me to his kitchen, which was sectioned off by a wall of wines. 'The last time I saw you, you were definitely a spirits girl.'

'That, I assure you, was an aberration.' I helped myself to a corn chip. 'Wine is my life partner.'

He handed me a glass and clinked it with his. 'Same here.'

I used my remaining energy to lift myself onto his stainless-steel counter.

'You know,' I said, 'this is the first home I've been to in two weeks.' I swirled the wine around my mouth. It was a rosé, a little pink for my liking. The alcohol rebounded off the cavernous pit of my stomach, going straight to my head.

His sauce was burning.

'Do you need any help?' I asked, resisting the Type A urge to stage a kitchen coup.

'I think I'm okay.' He hacked an avocado into inedible chunks. 'I rang my mum from Coles to ask how to do it.'

That didn't sound promising. From the counter beside the stovetop I stirred and turned down the heat, tasting the sauce from the back of a spoon. Ghastly. There was an overpowering smell. Melting plastic, I concluded.

'Oscar,' I said, 'something's on fire.'

'Hmm?' He swivelled from his chopping board to face me.

I lifted the pan from the hob. The Usage Guidance sticker remained on its base.

'Shit,' he said. 'I peeled off all the other ones.'

Before I could say 'Don't, you'll burn...' he reached out to pick at a singed corner of the sticker.

'Ow!'

I turned off the stove and pushed him over to the sink, turning the tap to tepid.

'Ow, ow, ow!'

'Hold it under here until I tell you to remove it.'

He winced, holding his scorched index finger up to the light. 'It hurts.'

I grabbed his wrist and forced it back under the running tap.

'Oooowww!'

I kissed him to shut him up.

'Oowww...'

I kissed him again, this time with gusto.

'Wwww,' he said into my mouth. He seemed to forget about his injured finger and brought his hand to my face. I returned it to the running water.

'This seems a dangerously elaborate ploy to get me to kiss you,' I said.

'It still hurts and I'm hungry.'

'I should have brought my Redskins. Some guy gave them to me.'

'He sounds like a keeper. But while I believe in the healing power of Redskins, I'm in need of something more substantial.'

I took off my cardigan. 'Let me look in your fridge.'

'Voila!' He opened the stainless-steel doors.

'Are you a mad scientist?' I was overwhelmed by pungent furry plates and half-opened takeaway containers.

'I prefer "pioneering" to "mad".' He poured more wine.

'I've always thought it remarkably unfair that some people, like you, are born with newsreader voices, like Guy Smiley, while the rest of us, like me, are stuck with the dulcet tones of Miss Piggy. Everything you say sounds perfectly reasonable even if it's utter rubbish.'

'You mean, if I were to say'—he cleared his throat—'"in breaking news from the twin peaks of Mount Buggery this afternoon, Prime Minister Gabrielle Brennan and Opposition Leader Max Masters have formed a coalition and will job-share the role of Benevolent Dictator so as to enjoy better work–life balance", you would think it totally legit?'

'Perfectly so,' I laughed, holding a plastic packet of cheddar at arm's length to inspect its best-before date. 'Except perhaps for the Mount Buggery bit.'

'Mount Buggery is fair dinkum. Very pretty place— near Mount Beauty in Victoria. I could take you there.'

'How romantic,' I said. '"Dear Mummy and Daddy, I've met a lovely Australian boy. He took me picnicking between the twin peaks of Mount Buggery. Much love, Rubles."'

'I'm sorry, did you say "Rubles"?' he laughed.

'Do you have any more sauce?' I pushed past the moth farm in his pantry to the tin of kidney beans.

'There's more in the fridge, but isn't this stuff salvageable?' He tried to pull the wooden spoon from his taffy-like concoction.

'I'm not sure how to put this delicately,' I said, shaking the sauce bottle. 'It's the sort of thing you might scrape off your shoe with a long, sturdy stick.'

'Geez, tell me what you really think, Rubles.' He braced to taste it. 'Fuck me, that's feral.' He spat into the sink then covered its remains with a tea towel, as one might a corpse. 'I don't cook all that often.'

I suspended my disbelief. 'I need a tray, a cheese grater and an oven.'

'This is incredible,' he said to me later, eyes full of adulation over a simple supper of make-do nachos and guacamole. 'I didn't know that thing still worked—I figured they would have disconnected it years ago.'

'Ovens aren't usually subscription-based services.' It was nearly midnight and the quiet night had grown cooler on the back deck of his cottage, which was surrounded by overgrown lavender and rosemary. A light breeze lifted the scent of his next-door neighbour's climbing rose. There was something pleasantly English about Canberra's gardens which I found comforting and familiar.

'Masters did really well tonight,' said Oscar. 'How do you think it went?'

'It was a good debate.' I helped myself to a stem from the thriving lavender shrub within reach, savouring its perfume. 'Do you always compere these things?'

'Actually, this was my first. It's always our network's gig, but Anastasia, who's one of my more senior colleagues, usually does it. She's on her way out, though. Not rating so well these days. Viewers think she's a bit batty.'

'I thought you did a good job of it. It must be difficult to know how to cut people off when they go over time.'

'That's the challenge,' he said, putting one of his perfect arms around me and smoothing the goose pimples from my chilly shoulder. I nestled into his warm chest. He smelled like cedar. 'Brennan must be kicking herself for missing the opportunity to fight back on the immigration question. It was a brilliant play by your guy. It must be quite fun rehearsing these things; is it?'

My neck stiffened. The guard I had only just dropped resurrected itself. 'Who's asking? Oscar the journalist or Oscar my dinner companion?'

Good question.

He smiled until he caught a glimpse of my expression in the fickle light of the remaining tea candle. 'Hey, what happens on the deck stays on the deck.'

'Do you ever broadcast from the deck?'

'Roo, I swear: anything you say to me is deeply off the record.'

I raised an eyebrow.

'Cross my heart, hope to die, stick a needle in my eye.'

I wanted to believe him; I longed to let go. But my sister always told me that protection is mandatory for sensible girls, so I pulled away and said, 'If it's all right by you, I think we need to establish some rules here to inoculate against any unintended consequences—for now, let's just try to draw the line at talking about work.' I held my breath and made a solemn vow to my head: if he hesitates, I will call Canberra Cabs.

'Of course.' He took my hand. 'Come to think of it, if it's all right by you, I'd prefer not to talk at all.'

When we reached his bedroom door and the zip of my dress snaked down my spine from thoracic to lumbar, I put it to a final vote in the name of parliamentary democracy. All those in favour say 'aye'. *Aye,* said my heart. *Aye, aye,* said my body. Those to the contrary, say 'no'.

Um...said my head.

I think the ayes have it.

Ex-PMS

It was the best three hours' sleep I'd had in weeks. I stretched luxuriously, checked for lingering Tex-Mex breath and rolled counterclockwise. Empty, tangled sheets were disconcerting before the sound of a whistling kettle reassured me. While I'd have preferred a little spooning, Oscar's absence meant there was still time to make myself look like a naturally pretty-in-the-morning person, which I am not.

According to the space-age alarm clock on his bedside table, it was a quarter past four: half an hour until the first phone hook-up. There goes the leisurely breakfast, I thought; but at least I wouldn't be forced to eat anything cooked by Oscar. I tiptoed nude to the bathroom, collecting and donning various items of clothing strewn along the way. Face clean, hair smoothed and mouthwash gargled, I was ready to face the morning.

I went to the kitchen. Oscar was out on the deck looking scrumptiously rumpled in the dewy dawn, scrolling through his BlackBerry and oblivious to my presence. Checking the coverage of last night's debate, I guessed. I needed to do the same.

I found my handbag on the kitchen bench and held it up to the brightest downlight to search for my phone. It wasn't in its usual spot, or in any other likely crevice. I retraced my steps. I had checked it when we were cooking last night. I'd put it in my pocket when I took the nachos out of the oven. Then it had buzzed on the outdoor table with the usual series of alerts at midnight, when the national newspapers published online. After that, I'd abandoned it and most of my other belongings for a more direct form of communication.

Pouring boiling water over a pair of squashed English Breakfast tea bags in the two cleanest-looking mugs, I opted for a proven phone-locating technique: calling it. I dialled my number, nursing Oscar's cordless landline between ear and shoulder while carrying the steaming mugs towards the deck. My phone rang. The decibels of each ring seemed to rally with each step towards the glass doors. With my hands full I knocked gently on the glass with my knobbly knee, keen to avoid a boiling spillage. Oscar turned to see me, then his deck chair appeared to eject him, which in turn launched his phone from his hand like an air-to-surface missile. It landed somewhere in the darkness. Chivalry executed with such urgency should not go unrewarded, I noted.

'I didn't know you were up,' he said, opening the door to relieve me of the mugs. 'I came out early to make you breakfast.' He kissed me fervently. 'So go back to bed and I'll bring it in to you.'

My stomach lurched at the prospect of a breakfast

made by Oscar. 'That's very sweet, but I really must get going, just as soon as I find my BlackBerry.' I hit redial on the cordless. My phone rang again, sounding close.

'I'll find it for you.'

'It sounds like it's coming from under the deck.' I dropped to my knees. 'It must have slipped through the cracks last night.' On all fours, I pressed my ear to the floorboards.

'Well, how about you get some breakfast while I find the phone,' said Oscar, but I was hot on its tail. I crawled along the weatherbeaten deck, tracking the ringtone to a terracotta pot.

'Voila.' I brandished my ringing phone. 'One lavender-scented BlackBerry.'

'Well sleuthed, Nancy Drew,' said Oscar. 'Now, what'll it be, vegemite or jam?'

Vegemite suffers from excess salinity at the best of times. Add the ecosystem in Oscar's pantry to the equation and you could de-ice a 747 with half a jar. 'Jam, please,' I said. 'You get the toast and I'll turn my mind to your phone—I'm on a roll.'

'My phone's in the kitchen.' He helped me to my feet and we went inside.

Oscar was definitely not a morning person. 'Perhaps you've got a bout of campaign brain,' I suggested. 'You were on your BlackBerry when I came to the door, before the poor little thing was catapulted into the garden, remember?'

'Actually, come to think of it, that was probably your phone,' he said sheepishly. 'I thought it was mine.'

That's when it hit me with the force of an articulated lorry. My head span. My body shuddered. My heart squirmed. He lowered four pieces of white bread into a retro-looking, brushed-metal toaster. 'Butter?'

'Yes, please.' I blew the granules of dirt from the trenches around each key on my BlackBerry and entered my password, checking its vitals.

'Oscar,' I said, 'you don't have a BlackBerry.'

'So?' He was defensive. 'One piece or two?'

'Two.'

I called his phone with mine. Within seconds, Nina Simone was singing 'Sinnerman' from the kitchen bench.

'You have an iPhone.' I held his sleek, shiny songstress in my left hand, and my newly perfumed, navy-blue brick in my right. 'They're the apples and oranges of telephonic devices. Your phone has about as much in common with mine as a Transformer has with a Teletubby.'

He laughed, but his smile soon twitched into an awkward grimace. 'I'm not sure what you're getting at.'

'When you believed I was sound asleep in your bed, you thought you might take my phone and plunder it for information.'

'Roo,' he purred, brushing my hair from my eyes, 'don't you think you're being a bit melodramatic?'

'No. I don't.' I disengaged.

'Come on, gorgeous,' he said. 'It's not like I saw anything—the bloody thing's password-protected anyway.'

The toast popped.

'Be a gentleman and call me a cab.' I stepped into my slingbacks and clutched my handbag to my chest.

Standing stupefied on the footpath, I watched the paper boy pedal halfheartedly towards me, scouting out the most inconvenient nooks and crannies in which to wedge his customers' plastic-wrapped news.

'The cab's on its way,' said Oscar, joining me. 'Listen, I get that you're angry, but I don't want you to think this was some sort of calculated manoeuvre on my part.' He smiled apologetically. 'I'm not that clever.'

Still numb, I distracted myself with a quick To Do list while he went on.

1. Sandbag eyelid levees to avert tear overflow (RECURRING ITEM)
2. Get in cab
3. Suppress temptation to use hairbrush as bludgeon
4. Depart with decorum
5. Dial into conference call.

He was still going when the familiar smell of LPG arrived; my trusty steed pulled up with the kind of screeching noise I was learning is universal to Australian taxis.

'It was just sitting there on the table and I guess I fucked up.'

Item 1 had become superfluous and Item 3 imperative.

'I really like you, Roo. I had a great time last night.'

'It's just so'—I rummaged for the right word as I slipped into the back seat—'clichéd.'

He shut the door, pressing his palm against the window and holding it there until we pulled away from the curb. Ticks for Items 2 and 4.

'Where to, love?'

'Parliament House, please.'

I texted Maddy when we paused at a red light. Next to us was a road island being used as a stopover for a congregation of cockatoos flaring their mango mohawks.

Wearing last night's clothes. En route to House. Any chance you could bring my suitcase into the disabled cubicle down the corridor? Will reward you with Redskins. R

The driver turned on the radio. 'Former prime minister Mick O'Donoghue has let loose on his party and its leader today in a highly critical opinion article for the *National*. O'Donoghue, who was succeeded by Hugh Patton almost thirteen years ago, is known for his episodic outbursts, but the timing of his latest damning appraisal, just a fortnight before polling day, will lead many Opposition candidates to despair. Esme Eisteddfod has the story.'

It was shaping up to be an exquisite Monday.

OK but need four Redskins and an explanation. M

I swiped through security and dialled in for Item 5 on my list while making my way to our meeting place. Maddy, also on the call, scurried down the corridor, wheeling my precious travelling wardrobe behind her. She wiggled a suggestive eyebrow up and down which, without warning, rendered Item 1 disastrously overdue. Boiling tears streamed fast and free down either cheek, dripping one by one off my chin like lemmings. Phones to our ears on the same call, Maddy and I sat on the tiled floor, her hand patting my back in time with the ticking clocks.

'If I ever get this job,' said Max, 'can one of you please restrain me from ranting like Mick when I lose it?'

'He seemed fine in Cloncurry,' said Maddy. I cringed at the mention of the place.

'Ex-PMS, or Former Prime Ministers' Syndrome, is a highly debilitating condition,' explained Luke. 'Specialists say there are very few symptoms in the lead-up to an attack, aside from higher than usual phone usage, by which time it's often too late to prevent an outbreak. Triggers can include relevance deprivation, boredom, alcohol, natural light or the good fortune of his successors.' He laughed at his own joke.

'Has anyone read it?' asked Max.

'Yeah, he's taken pot shots at all of us,' said Di. 'He reckons we've got the wrong stance on immigration, which will lose us the election, and apparently we've had to hire hot-shot consultants from the UK because we haven't got a clue how to run a campaign.'

'Roo Stanhope: Political Consultancy,' mocked Archie, distracting me from my misery.

I pulled myself together. 'I'm sorry, I've obviously missed something here so I'd be happy to refund this morning's extortionate consulting fee if I'm mistaken, but isn't O'Donoghue supposed to be on *our* side?'

'Ex-PMS tends to blur vision,' Luke continued with what he must have thought was winning wit. Clearly he'd had a better night that I had.

I never thought I'd say this, but you should've gone to the pub.

'In other news,' Di pressed on, 'Max kicked arse in the debate last night and the PM has ruled out an additional debate, leading everyone to conclude she's chicken. The general feedback from punters is that even if they disagree with us on skilled immigration they think Max is a strong leader, so all in all it's a good result.'

'Thanks for your hard work on that, team,' said Max. 'I just got a call from Mirabelle. Our pollsters are saying we've probably picked up a few points since the debate, so we're pretty much neck and neck again. Do we have an agreed plan for the week ahead?'

Luke took the reins. 'Today you're in the Gold Coast to launch our 2021 High Speed Rail Network, then we're off to the other end of it in Fremantle. Our new ads will be coming out tonight in time for the Southpoll—they criticise the government's dirty tactics. Shelly is a guest host on *Brekky* tomorrow morning and we've got a few big FM interviews lined up for you.'

'Remind me to ask Abigail about what's cool at the moment,' said Max.

Maddy rolled her eyes and smiled.

'We're told Brennan will be making some sort of resources announcement,' said Luke, 'but she'll hammer home her tax cuts all week. On Wednesday night we'll be doing an economic policy announcement in Sydney. Thursday and Friday will be spent in Melbourne, and then country Victoria, reiterating our higher education policy and recycled water proposal. Saturday will be largely dominated by the "one week to go" analysis. At this stage you'll be with Shelly and Abigail in Melbourne for the day—get some rest. Next Thursday is the launch and then we've got Southpoll coming out on Saturday, before the PM's launch on the Tuesday before polling day. Any questions?'

I had some questions. Why did I shag a journalist? What's the maximum penalty for common assault occasioning bodily harm in Australia? Please can I take a duvet day? But there wasn't time. I gave Maddy the rest of my Redskins, took a raincheck on the explanation and had a lightning-speed shower. In convoy to the airport to catch our Coolangatta-bound flight, we listened to O'Donoghue on the airwaves. He used sentences beginning with 'back in my day' and ending with 'not good enough'.

My phone buzzed. It was Luke texting from the car in front.

Missed you at the pub. Sorry for late notice, but I need you to salvage a candidate in Tassie. Get yourself a flight to Launceston. I'll brief you when you get there. L

Excellent, said my head, *exile is exactly what you need.*

Any chance Launceston is a tropical coastal resort with day spa and daiquiris aplenty? R

No. L

When we reached the airport, Maddy bade me farewell with a hug while I reluctantly booked my flight to what she called Woop Woop.

My phone rang again. Fran.

'How are you?' I didn't need to ask. She was terrible; I could hear it in her voice.

'Fine.'

'No, you're not.'

'Yes, I am. Why would you think I'm not fine?'

'You sound very unfine.'

'Unfine isn't even a word, Ruby. I'm completely fine. Clementine's fine. We're all fine. Everything's fine.'

'So you rang to tell me you're fine?'

'No, of course not. I rang to see how you are. You should try it sometime.'

I deserved that. 'Sorry, things have been really hectic here because we only have a fortnight until the election.' I scanned the lounge for intelligence-gatherers from the fourth estate. I lowered my voice just in case. 'I've been in Canberra, we've just had the debate, I was on the prep team for it, and there's a particularly good-looking journalist who turned out to be a—'

'Mark's having an affair.'

'What?' I was flabbergasted.

'I mean Mark Gardner, the man I married. The father of my daughter. Your brother-in-law. He is having an affair.' Her news made my articulated lorry feel more like a unicycle.

'Are you sure?' It seemed a logical question to ask until I got the answer.

'Yes, I'm sure. We woke up yesterday morning and he told me he's been sleeping with the professional indemnity partner.'

'Christ.' I urged my body to get over the shock as quickly as possible. 'What did you say?'

'I think this is the most distressing part. I said, "Hurry up and get dressed; we're going to be late."' She heaved hysterically and slurred, '"Hurry up and get dressed, we're going to be late."'

'Late for what?'

'The church fete.'

'Are you drinking?'

'Yes. Wodka.'

Fran doesn't even like vodka. In fact, she has loathed it since becoming terribly ill on excess flirtinis at a work function, the projectile result of which also put me off the stuff. That and pineapple juice.

'Good lass,' I encouraged. I needed to be there. There was no way I could do this from a chesterfield in the Qantas Club, Canberra.

'I don't know what to do, Ruby. Clementine seems oblivious to it, which is good. I can't bring myself to talk to Mark about it and even if I could he's at a jurisprudence conference in Bangladesh.' She swigged at her drink, ice cubes clinking against the side of the glass.

'This is what you're going to do,' I improvised. 'You're going to get on a plane with Clem and fly to Melbourne. You need time to digest this and you can't very well do that when you're drinking alone and caring for a five-year-old.'

'I can't go to Australia,' she wailed. 'Clementine has school.'

'She's five, Fran. What important life skill will she miss? Advanced Hopscotch? Communal Hamster Care? Colouring Inside the Lines 101? She's obnoxious enough as it is without superior crayon abilities.'

She laughed and hiccoughed. 'Where would we stay? What would we do?'

'Let me call Daphne and Debs. I'll just say Mark is away on business and you're thinking of coming out for a visit. I'm sure they'll put you up at their place in the Yarra Valley. Daphne couldn't be broodier at the moment and Clem will love it—there are puppies.'

'Will you be there, Ruby?' she asked with heart-wrenching desperation.

Now it was my turn to be the grown-up. 'I will be there.'

Sailing blind over Cataract Gorge

Woop Woop had the hottest candidate I'd ever seen. Melissa Hatton, who had the kinds of curves that would make Marilyn Monroe weep with envy, picked me up from the airport in her equally va-va-voom emerald vintage Jaguar. She was on the phone and so was Luke, so he couldn't brief me.

'Thanks, mate, I'll see you at the fundraiser tonight.' Melissa drove under the boom gate at the car park. 'I really appreciate your support. Yep. Yep. See you there. Bye.'

She turned her head slightly. 'I sincerely hope you're Roo Stanhope,' she said, holding the parking receipt between her perfect teeth. 'Otherwise I've just picked up a complete stranger from the airport and someone from Max Masters' office is waiting at the luggage carousel.'

'I am.'

She smiled. 'I like to drive and talk so I figured this would be a good opportunity to fill you in.'

I'd like to drive and talk too if I had wheels like hers. The crème-caramel leather interior was almost edible. I ran my fingers along the smooth, glossy wood panelling.

'She was my dad's pride and joy,' Melissa said, answering my unasked question. 'He bought her brand new from the dealer in 1987, and got in a bit of strife with Mum when he drove home that day. The stock market had just crashed so a lot of people were doing it tough, but Dad loved this car until the day he died.'

At the traffic lights, Melissa twirled her platinum-blonde hair into a flawless chignon fastened with a tortoise-shell clip, and used the rear-view mirror to apply 1950s pin-up red lipstick to her pronounced pout. 'So, you're here because everyone reckons I'm going to fuck up.'

It didn't seem to be a question, so there was little point in denying it.

'The local papers and radios hate me because the current member and even some of the guys on our side are running a shit-sheet campaign against me, saying I only got the gig because of nepotism and sex.

'It's a very tight margin—about 0.1 per cent with redistribution. That makes my campaign a national media issue so the vultures are feeding on my misfortune.' We whizzed around a corner and across a narrow bridge suspended between two vertiginous rocky cliff faces. 'If you've got time for a coffee I'll take you somewhere spectacular that looks out over Cataract Gorge.'

'Sure,' I said, trying not to think about how eerily still the water was below us. 'Have you done anything to dispel the rumours?'

'I took all the editors, radio blokes and even a proprietor out to lunch weeks ago. All of them. I answered every question, addressed every rumour in full; but apparently mine is the story of a vixen political princess and that sells, so they publish it.'

'Where do the rumours come from?' I stuttered, hoping that my question wasn't the Tasmanian equivalent of asking Paris Hilton the secret to her extraordinary internet hit rate. There was something vaguely ironic about sailing blind over Cataract Gorge.

'Well, for one, some party members who didn't like my old man when he was local member have taken a stand against me. Two, the party pushed through my preselection, making it look like I thought I was entitled to the gig and that I don't respect party processes.' She swung into a parking space out the front of a cafe. 'And here's the cherry: I'm a hot blonde. People think hot blondes are airheads. So despite my being one of the state's best legal brains, people compare me to my fat and failed used-car salesman of an opponent and think that he's got a better idea about what's best for Donaldson.'

She sashayed inside, towards a secluded table, with the kind of walk that should always be accompanied by the brass section of a big band. 'Evening, Joyce,' she said to the frost-pink-lipped proprietor.

'G'day, Missy, what can I get you?' Joyce asked, ignoring the sniggering pair of nose-pierced waitresses clearing the adjacent table.

'My usual malted milkshake. And you, Roo?'

'Sounds delicious.'

'Two, then.' She rolled up the sleeves of her chocolate-brown business shirt.

'What shits me to tears,' she said when Joyce was out of earshot, 'is that the party virtually begged me to run in Donaldson. I gave it a lot of thought, of course. I'm a public prosecutor, for fuck's sake—why would I want to throw that in to run for one of the most marginal seats in the country? Frankly, I was holding out for something safe. But I can't very well go and say that on the record, can I?'

I shrugged.

'Add to that an unfortunate photograph from a cocktail party in the early nineties—I had a fling with a prominent businessman when his divorce wasn't finalised—and Bob's your uncle: you've got a scandal.'

My phone rang. 'Do you mind if I take this?'

Melissa nodded and I stepped outside.

'Sorry I couldn't take your call earlier,' Luke said. 'Things have been frantic up here with this rail announcement. How's Donaldson?'

'A bit grim, to be honest. I've just had a chat with Melissa Hatton.' I checked she was still inside and whispered, 'She seems oblivious to the intimidating image she's built for herself.'

'Doesn't surprise me. Our polling is terrible in Donaldson and it's a key seat. She needs to pick up her game. Do you think it's salvageable?'

'I think you're better placed than I am to answer that.'

'Come off it, Roo. Tell me what you think.'

'Okay, in all my weeks in politics I've never met a woman so loathsome to other women. Even in this cafe, the waitresses can't stop whispering about her.'

'So what do you think she should do?'

Don't ask me.

My gut took over. 'She needs an image overhaul, she needs the local party to unite behind her and she needs to give newspapers here something good to say about her.'

'Sounds about right. Why don't you come up with a strategy and we can talk it through on the phone if you like. I reckon you should stay down there for a few days and work with her team. Take as long as you need.'

Her?

'Me?'

'Gotta go. Keep in touch.'

I went back inside just as Joyce arrived with two old-fashioned stainless-steel beakers with frothy heads and curly pink straws. It was grossly unjust that this woman could drink litres of blitzed ice-cream, confected chocolate syrup and full-fat milk and still wind up looking like Rita Hayworth as Gilda.

'Can I be brutally honest, Melissa?' I took an enormous swig of aerated sweetness to give me strength.

'Go ahead.'

'You're in danger of losing this election because you're perfect.'

'Come again?'

'I mean look at you. They think you have it all. You're drop dead gorgeous. You have an incredibly successful career. You drive the sexiest car in Launceston. You're from a privileged background. People simply don't feel they can relate to you.' She took the first few as compliments and the last as a stiletto through the Achilles, but I stuck with it regardless. 'This isn't your fault, but it is your problem. The question is: how do we fix it in two weeks so that you can become the next member for Donaldson?'

The remaining droplets of her milkshake looped the loop of her straw. 'I know what the question is. What's the bloody answer?'

'Off the top of my head, I think it goes something like this. Firstly, we need to counter the perception that you didn't fight for preselection. The party dragged you into this mess; they need to be saying publicly that they approached you to run for Donaldson on your merits.

'Secondly, we need a national figure who will attest to your intelligence. Someone intellectually weighty and preferably ugly. Maybe a retired judge, an academic or some sort of colleague. You probably have scores of case examples where you have put notorious criminals behind bars.

'Thirdly, and this will be our Everest, we need to get women behind you. You need to be approachable, not formidable. Dial down the make-up, stick with suits and help at a school canteen somewhere. Host a function for female small-business owners. Go to a nursing home and play cards with old ladies. Let everyone else paint you as bright and successful while you're busy bringing yourself back down to earth.'

She sighed. 'You seem an intelligent woman and an attractive one at that, Roo. How can you ask me to change the way I look in order to appeal to other women? It's so bloody counterproductive to the cause.'

'Melissa, with respect, they haven't sent me down here to reform the Tasmanian sisterhood; otherwise, I'd agree with you one hundred per cent. They sent me here because you need to win the hearts and minds of Donaldson and you have two and a half weeks in which to do it. You're not going to get there by lecturing your own sex on how they *should* respond to a woman like you. They already despise you, so playing the vampy victim isn't going to cut it. Take a look at those two in the corner.' I gestured over my right shoulder to the whispering waitresses. 'They bitch and they vote.'

She sighed. 'Where do we start?'

The following Saturday, in a demure navy-blue pant suit and low ponytail, Melissa Hatton was asking people at the Donaldson Secondary College fete whether they wanted their burgers with beetroot or without. Since the start of the week she'd had her face painted as Spider-Man at Tazzie Devils Childcare, joined in at the bingo hall for Ladies' Day and lent her green fingers to the rose bushes at the RSL. Best of all, she was having a ball, which was evident in the colourful images published in the local press.

After a bit of string-pulling, I'd arranged for party director Mirabelle Halifax to do a television interview in Hobart. She took full responsibility for having to step over the usual processes in order to install candidates at short notice in a number of seats, but pointed out that the Prime Minister had intended to wrong-foot the Opposition by calling such an early election. Designed to coincide with the launch of our dirty games campaign against Brennan, Mirabelle's message seemed to ease animosity towards Melissa.

Launceston was turning out to be exactly what I needed in order to avoid being mired in self-loathing over the Oscar debacle, not least because I discovered the town was within staggering distance of the Tamar Valley, home to some of the nation's most delectable drops. With Fran and Clem on board a BA flight to Melbourne and a calm couple of days in the Yarra Valley ahead of me, my life didn't appear as disintegrated as it had at the beginning of the week.

Melissa and I were now on our way to a lunch interview with local newspaper editor Bob Roberts, or 'Blobby', as he was affectionately known. Our mission was clear: expose the other side's mud-slinging without making Melissa appear precious.

It hadn't seemed right to have such an important meeting at an ordinary inner-city eatery. So I'd arranged a table à trois at a cellar door restaurant overlooking lines of vines zigzagging their way down to a delightful bend in the Tamar River.

Sadly, Blobby was precisely as I'd imagined him. Rotund with beady eyes framed by the sort of spectacles my gran was partial to. 'Good to see you, Missy,' he said, licking fat fingers to force a few recalcitrant strands back into his over-slicked comb-over. 'Who's your friend?'

'This is Roo Stanhope.'

I felt blessed when the bread arrived and the licked hand that was poised to shake mine found itself irresistibly pulled towards the butter dish. He stuck his hand into the air, revealing a hydroponic armpit.

The hovering waiter cleared his throat. 'Ready to order, Mr Roberts?'

'Yes, and I'd like salted butter, please.'

Melissa tapped her foot under the table as Blobby ordered braised pork belly before snatching the wine list from my hands and choosing something as uninteresting as it was expensive.

'Our readers seem to have enjoyed your bingo prowess, Missy. The oldies loved your dad, God rest him. How are you feeling about the campaign?'

'I think we've had a great week. People are unhappy with a whole range of things and this is the kind of seat your counterparts around the country will be watching closely, so of course your coverage matters.' She declined a glass of wine, which was a good decision—I could smell its acidic pomposity a mile off.

'Are you up the duff or something?' he roared.

'No,' she winked, 'no time for fun and games when you're working as hard as I've been.'

It was my turn. 'Tell me, Bob, I'm quite new to this business in Australia, but I'm interested to know from someone as experienced as you whether malicious rumours are part of the usual argy-bargy of Australian political campaigns.' I brandished a few of the shit-sheets I'd photocopied earlier.

Blobby spat something into a napkin before examining a document entitled DON'T PUT A RICH BITCH IN DONALDSON.

'Well,' he spluttered, dabbing at a droplet of wine on his cuff, 'I guess these are a bit more personal than one might normally expect.'

'Melissa's remarkably thick-skinned about them,' I said, attempting to swirl some life into the overpriced shiraz, 'but I just don't see how this sort of slander has a place in contemporary politics, particularly when Melissa is such an upstanding member of the community. She's single-handedly responsible for throwing some of Tasmania's worst criminals behind bars, whereas her opponent...well, I've said enough.'

He smiled and used his tongue to dislodge a stray piece of stringy meat from his teeth.

'Bob knows me, Roo,' said Melissa, ordering a glass of milk. 'I'm flawed like the rest of 'em, but what sets me apart from the rest is that I don't bother with the gutter

politics, something I had hoped wouldn't go unacknowl-
edged by the town's biggest circulating daily.'

'Come on, Missy,' croaked Blobby, 'the fact that you're
not shit-sheeting the other mob isn't a story, and you've
got no evidence to show that these come from the other
side anyway—they could just as easily be from your own
party.'

'That's where you're mistaken, Bob.' I pulled out an
email from a man claiming to have volunteered on the
sitting member's campaign. He'd quit when he was asked
if he would use his photocopier to produce thousands of
leaflets and tuck them under windscreen wipers in the
local supermarket car park. 'Here's a source. Call him if
you like, or of course I could give it to the *National* if
you're not interested, but Melissa insisted that we show
loyalty to local business.'

'Of course we'd be happy to give him a bell.' He wiped
his hands on the tablecloth. 'I hate those windscreen
wiper flyers.' He pulled out a credit card and declared,
'Lunch is on me.'

He wasn't wrong. It was all over him.

Too late To Do

Before I lost my job, got pickled on peanut noise, switched hemispheres and joined this travelling circus, my life was a relatively straightforward one. Sure, I was a sexless workaholic hermit, but I had a routine, and when my routine let me down I had coping mechanisms that worked.

One such coping mechanism was the To Do list. Its purpose was clear: to prioritise tasks numerically and execute them in that order. For me, the list usually had three benefits. First, to find clarity in the chaos of an overworked mind. Second, to avoid panic-duplication by committing every outstanding task to paper. Third, to self-reward with a super-satisfying tick for each completed item.

I found myself reflecting on the surprise failure of said coping mechanism as I sat on a lime-green plastic chair in the waiting room of the Immigration office at Melbourne Airport. When Beryl had handed me my employment contract and working visa application form on Day One of the campaign, signing and returning them had been at the top of my list.

Now, on Day Twenty-Two, those two items were lost somewhere in the middle of a paper-clipped, eight-page medley comprising three Post-it notes, the back of what I hoped was just a draft media release headed OPPOSITION ANNOUNCES MEDITATION CENTRE FOR SMES, a crinkled chewing gum wrapper, two Qantas boarding passes and a tax receipt for three large flat whites.

Certain coping mechanisms, I concluded after some deliberation, are limited in their reach. People who can depend on a To Do list have desk jobs, ergonomic chairs, stationery, fire drills and dress-down Fridays. To Do lists are unsuited to nomadic insomniacs who are so busy they can scarcely find the time to urinate. For them, a To Do list is less about coping and more about escaping.

'Ah, Miss Stanhope,' said a long-socked man with a familiar voice. It was Bruce, who had stamped my passport all those weeks ago. Flipping flippantly through a clipboard like a hospital intern on his morning rounds, Bruce was more vertically challenged than I remembered, which is the great advantage of a job behind a counter with an adjustable stool.

Until then, the only man I'd seen in the flesh wearing long socks had also worn a sporran and said 'och'. Bruce led me into a little room, sat behind a grey laminex table and gestured for me to take a seat. 'How's your holiday been, Miss Stanhope?' He took a pen from the top of a sock.

'Well, to be frank, it hasn't been much of a holiday,' I yawned. I'd been up since half three that morning to catch the first flight out of Launceston to Melbourne. It was upon my arrival there that I had been greeted by Bruce's colleague who led me to the International terminal. 'My time in Australia has been much like that reality TV show, *The Amazing Race*. Have you seen it?'

'I don't own a television,' said Bruce.

'Essentially, contestants race around the world on a kind of obstacle course and overcome challenges along the way in order to win the grand prize. They get to see some extraordinary sights but spend less than a day in each location. Imagine passing by the Taj Mahal on a public bus or approaching the gate of the Forbidden City but not going in.'

Stop talking, Ruby, hushed my head, but I needed Bruce to understand why I hadn't submitted my working visa application form.

'That's what my time in Australia has been like. I've been to Melbourne, the Yarra Valley, Brisbane, Canberra, Perth, Sydney, Adelaide, Cloncurry, Darwin and Launceston, to name a few, but I've been so busy with work that I haven't really had time to experience any of those places.'

'I'm glad you raise your employment status. I saw a photograph of you in the *Herald*. It listed you as an advisor to the Leader of the Opposition. I see about a thousand new faces a day, but I remembered yours.'

'Thank you, Bruce. You see, I don't like being a drain on society like most tourists, so I got a job. As you might appreciate, things have been a bit hectic so I haven't had time to complete and return this working visa thingy.' I produced the scrunched form from the bottom of my laptop bag. It was in reasonably good nick aside from the coffee mug stain encircling a 'sign here' sticker.

'Miss Stanhope,' said Bruce, with folded arms, 'I clearly

recall warning you that your tourist visa did not permit you to seek employment here.'

'I wouldn't say I sought employment here; it sought me.'

Pipe down, Ruby!

'Miss Stanhope, you have just admitted to violating the terms of your visa.'

'Actually, Bruce, come to think of it, I forgot to sign the employment contract they sent me.'

Bruce put the blue pen back in his sock and pulled out a red one.

I went on. 'Isn't that astonishing? I never thought for a minute I would find myself working for nothing in Australian politics. I came out here for a holiday and thought I'd return to London with a few cases of wine as a souvenir and settle back into something in private equity, perhaps. Then I met Luke, who saw something in me that I didn't see in myself.'

'Miss Stanhope—'

'Hang on, Bruce, this is important. Banking didn't make me happy. I was good at it but I didn't love it. It wasn't my bread. And here I am now with nothing but food and board and an empty bank account, but the work is so fulfilling that I've barely noticed my financial situation. And that, Bruce, is why I don't have the right visa.'

'Do you have access to a solicitor, Miss Stanhope?'

'Ruby, mate,' said Debs when I rang. 'I'm in a meeting right now; can I call you back?'

'I would say yes but I'm in a meeting too. With an Immigration official at Melbourne Airport who has just asked if I have access to a lawyer.'

'Jesus, Mary and Joseph,' she said. 'I'll be there in thirty minutes max. Don't say anything. Not a word. Shut the fuck up.'

Sure enough, thirty minutes later, she marched into the room entirely unflustered, threw her briefcase onto the table and said, 'Deborah Llewellyn, acting for Ruby Stanhope—would you mind giving me a few minutes alone with my client?'

'Please.' He shut the door behind him.

'Thanks for coming at such short notice,' I said as she took Bruce's chair opposite me.

'No worries,' she said, looking under the table. 'Are those my pants?'

'Yes,' I said. There was no point in denying it.

'And shirt?'

'Yes.' After a week in Tasmania, they were the only clean items in my Samsonite other than a bikini and sarong.

'Why are you being questioned by an Immigration officer?'

'I forgot to complete my working visa application form so Bruce says I've violated my conditions of entry.'

'Who's Bruce?'

'The long-socked man outside.'

'What kind of man wears long socks?'

'Bruce and highlanders in kilts with sporrans.'

'Does Bruce wear a sporran?'

'Maybe on weekends. He seems to use his socks to store pens and his glasses case, so he probably doesn't need one. Listen, Debs, can we go back to how I'm going to get out of this situation?'

'I'm no immigration lawyer, kiddo—there's no money in it—but I watch enough *Border Protection* to know that

247

you're probably going to be asked to leave the country.'

'But, you see, I can't leave the country because we have an election in'—I counted my fingers—'exactly twelve days, and Fran and Clem are arriving tomorrow.'

'Bruce doesn't strike me as the kind of public servant who would find either of those arguments compelling.'

'Surely people do this sort of thing all the time. They can't all be deported. Do you think they'll seize my assets? Hopefully they won't touch my shoes. I hardly have a cent to my name, having forgotten to sign my employment contract...'

'Hang on, cupcake.' She stopped rocking on her chair. 'Are you telling me you're not actually employed?'

'Technically, no. That is to say, I tell people I work for Max Masters, I travel around the country on his plane, I keep expense receipts for the party to reimburse me—I must add that to my list—but I've never been paid by them.'

'Let me make a few calls, kiddo. Stay here. Calm down. Don't talk to Bruce.' She left the room.

My BlackBerry vibrated violently across the table, but I couldn't answer it. I could barely breathe. I don't want to go, I thought. I can't leave before the election. I've worked so hard for it. I want to win it and then I want to work for the government. The idea of missing the election because of a stupid administrative oversight was nauseating. I paced the perimeter of the small room.

I barely noticed that Debs was back. 'Ruby, stop pacing and sit down.'

I did.

'At the table, kiddo.'

I got up off the floor and took my seat opposite her.

248

'I have a possible solution. Apparently we can argue you haven't violated the terms of your visa because you were working in a voluntary capacity, but you'll have to forgo remuneration for the period worked until your new visa is valid.'

'Fine.'

'We can then rush your working visa through, but to do that we need two things. Your employer needs to verify that you were never paid and sponsor your new visa application.'

'That's great news,' I squealed, teary-eyed. 'Let's do it!'

'Settle, petal,' she said. 'I've spoken to Bruce about it and he reckons that would be okay by him on the condition that your employer or a representative of your employer comes here to vouch for the sponsorship arrangement.'

'Now?'

'Yes. And I'll need my pants and shirt back, preferably dry-cleaned, by way of legal fees.'

I nodded.

'Get someone over here pretty quickly—I'm due in court in two hours.'

I called Beryl to ask who was in Melbourne. 'Your options are Max or Luke,' she said. 'I don't like your chances.'

It would have to be Luke.

He answered in a harsh whisper. 'Is it urgent, Roo? I'm at the LOO's house discussing logistics for the launch.'

'I'd call it urgent,' I said. 'You see, I'm facing possible deportation unless I can show Immigration that I haven't been paid for my work to date and that my employer will sponsor my working visa application. They need someone in person.'

His voice muffled as he put a hand over the phone. 'I have to go out for an hour—something urgent has come up, but it's nothing to worry about.' I heard footsteps. Louder. 'Where are you?' A car door shut.

'The Immigration office at Melbourne Airport with a long-socked man called Bruce and my lawyer.'

'I'm on my way.'

He wasn't angry per se, just a bit stressed, when he arrived. He looked different in jeans and a T-shirt: better somehow. 'Are you okay?' He grabbed my shoulders.

'I'm fine.' I couldn't look him in the eye, so I focused on his chest. His T-shirt had a tiny label stitched into it. Huge Boss. 'You must regret hiring me sometimes. I'm more trouble than I'm worth.'

'I'm told we got the last three weeks of you for free, so we're about even.'

My head hung.

He squeezed my shoulders tighter. 'I'm kidding, Roo. I can't believe I almost lost...Deborah Lewellyn?'

'Little Lukey Harley,' roared Debs and slapped him on the back.

'Are you doing immigration law now, you big softy?'

'Not a chance, mate. Feet still firmly in the commercial camp. Just helping out my partner's niece.'

Bruce tapped his foot. 'I take it you propose to employ this woman, Lukey?'

'Sorry, yes, Luke Harley's my name—I'm the Chief of Staff to the Leader of the Opposition.' He handed over a card. 'I'm sorry for the confusion here, officer. We were under the impression that Miss Stanhope had all her paperwork in order. We appreciate your vigilance.'

Bruce's chest puffed visibly when Luke addressed him

by his title. 'Just doing my job,' he said. 'And are you in a position to sponsor Miss Stanhope's working visa, which entitles her to work in your employ for a maximum of twelve months in this country?'

'Yes,' said Luke, looking at me, 'I am.'

'Well, *he's* not in a position to sponsor her,' corrected Debs. 'His office is.'

'That's what I meant,' said Luke.

'In that case,' sighed Bruce, licking his index finger to turn the page of a form, 'this is slightly unorthodox but just sign here to say so and I will release Miss Stanhope.'

I embraced Luke. 'Thank you, thank you, thank you.'

'It's my pleasure.'

'Miss Stanhope, I need you to go directly to the Immigration Department in the city and fill out some paperwork. You are not entitled to do anything other than voluntary work until you have your working visa. Am I clear?'

'Understood. Thank you, Officer Bruce.'

Debs picked up her briefcase. 'Right, I'm off. Can you find the Immigration Department without getting detained by other authorities along the way?'

'I'll take her,' said Luke. 'I've got my car here.'

'It's fine,' I said. 'I can take a taxi.'

'Come with me, Roo.'

'Yes, boss.'

Later at the department it became clear that Bruce's socks were standard issue for gentleman bureaucrats. I took a number: 483F to be precise.

'You can go now,' I said to Luke. 'It'll be a long after-noon.'

'Shut up and fill in those forms.' Luke took phone calls

from his lime-green plastic chair in the waiting room while I had a 47-minute discussion with Barry about my eligibility for an F78V43, apparently known in the trade as an 'Effer.' When Barry knew more about me than I did, Luke took me back to Treasury Place.

'I'm glad you're not leaving,' he said between drafting emails in the lift. 'Please try to avoid deportation in future.'

Crossed

Wherever I go in life, I will always have a mental snapshot of my sister pushing her luggage trolley into the arrivals hall at Tullamarine. She had faded and shrunk in the last few weeks. Her usually plump, pink lips were mauve and chapped. The shiny thick mane she so often swept into a loose bun was now a dull tuft. Her rosy skin was as white and thin as paper. She was still beautiful, but Mark's infidelity had aged her and I hated him for it.

Clem on the other hand was exactly as I'd left her, minus two teeth. Her Wiggles knapsack bobbing up and down, she ran to me with a gappy grin, my birthday gift faux pas apparently forgotten. 'Hello, Aunty Wooby. Mummy said it's already tomorrow in Australia and that we've been on fast forward for eleven hours.'

'Mummy's right, Clem.' I cuddled her tiny body. 'I can't tell you how good it is to see you.'

'Why not?' she asked.

'It's an expression,' I explained.

She looked up at the ceiling in confusion. Her mother let go of the trolley, like an old lady letting go of her Zimmer frame, and flopped into my arms.

'I'm so sorry he did this to you,' I said quietly. It seemed insufficient.

'It's good to be held,' she said into my neck. I felt the moistness of a tear.

'Who's that lady?' Clem pointed behind us.

'Manners, Clementine,' growled Fran, still in my arms.

'I'm your great aunt, Clementine,' Daphne said. 'You can call me Daphne.'

'What makes you great?' asked Clem.

'Years, my dear. Many, many years.'

'Can I see your puppies?' She bounced with excitement.

'Clementine.' My sister's remaining kilojoules of energy seeped out with every utterance of her daughter's name.

'Soon, dear,' smiled Daphne. 'They're looking forward to meeting you.'

Daphne exchanged kisses with Fran. 'How was the flight?'

'Fine, thanks. An odd man at Immigration asked if we were related to Ruby. I guess it's a much smaller airport than Heathrow.'

Daphne spotted the fogging around the rims of Fran's sunglasses. 'How about Clementine and I get the car and we'll come to pick you up with the luggage?'

'Sounds like a plan,' I said.

'I'm keeping it all in for Clementine,' Fran said when we were alone, clutching my hand, 'but I'm not sure how long I can do that.'

'I could take you somewhere quiet. Just the two of us.

We can talk about it.' I pushed the trolley towards the footpath.

'I can't talk until I've had time to think. I need sleep first, food, possibly alcohol and room to think.'

In the car on the way to the Yarra Valley, Clem sang every line of 'Just You Wait' complete with hands on hips and finger wagging, Fran made small talk with Daphne about the weather and I tried to attend a conference call with Melissa Hatton.

'The worse I look, the more Donaldson loves me, Roo,' said Melissa. 'We've got the front page of the paper today as well as a vox pop and editorial on dirty campaigning.'

Reluctantly, I un-muted my BlackBerry. 'Sounds like a decent turnaround.'

'Oh ho ho, 'enry 'iggins, just you wait!'

'Where in God's name are you?'

'Down you'll go 'enry 'iggins! Just you wait!'

'Community event.'

'Sounds torturous,' said Melissa. 'Thanks for everything. I'll let you get back to it.'

'Feel free to call if I can help at all.'

She hung up.

'Did you like that song, Aunty Wooby?'

'Very much so,' I said. 'The ending was my favourite part.'

Finally, following a deafening rendition of 'The Rain in Spain' for which Clem adapted her accent to both parts of the duet, we made our way up the driveway. Debs stood cradling a tiny pup on the deck.

'Who is that lady, Daphne?' asked Clem.

'That's my friend Debs.'

'Does she live here too?'

'Yes, this is her house.'

'What's that puppy's name?'

'JFK.'

'Where are the other puppies?'

'Inside.'

'Where are the puppies' mummy and daddy?'

'Pansy, their mummy, is inside. I don't know where their daddy is.'

'He's probably with my daddy at the Jewish Poodles Conference in Bang the Desk.' Clem leaped out of her seatbelt and marched towards the deck.

'Bang the Desk, indeed,' muttered Fran.

'Hello, Debs,' Clem said before anyone could introduce them. 'My name is Clementine Genevieve Gardner-Stanhope. Your friend Daphne is my great aunt because she has so many ears.'

'Nice to meet you, Clementine Genevieve Gardner-Stanhope.' Debs bent to shake her hand.

'You don't have to call me that, silly,' she said. 'Aunty Wooby calls me Clem.'

'Righto,' said Debs, 'Clem it is.'

'This is my mummy,' said Clem when the rest of us had caught up with them.

'Thank you for having us in your beautiful home,' said Fran.

'Pleasure. Shy kid you've got here.' Debs lowered herself to Clem's level. 'Want to pat him, Clem?'

'He's very soft,' Clem whispered.

Debs took Clem by the hand and led her inside. 'Let me introduce you to the others.'

While Fran and Clem showered, Daphne insisted on doing my washing and Debs and I made a pot of tea.

'So, are you legal yet, kiddo?'

'Yes, thanks to you. Your fee is at the dry-cleaner's.'

'Good to hear. So, you and little Lukey Harley, eh?' She slapped me on the back as if we were blokes on barstools.

'What about me and Luke?'

'No need to be coy,' she said. 'He's a good guy.'

'I know he is. He's my boss.'

'He's the Chief of Staff. It's a week out from polling day and he left a meeting with his boss to rescue you. You seriously expect me to believe you're *not* doing him?'

'Excuse me?'

'It's fine. I won't judge you for it. I mean, he's not my type.'

'Clearly,' I said as Daphne joined us.

'Hot cross buns, anybody? The dough should have risen by now. I'm adjusting my recipe this year—using lime zest instead of lemon to mix it up a bit.'

'Sounds delish,' said Debs, kissing Daphne's forehead. 'In the meantime, I'm trying to figure out whose hot buns Ruby's been crossing.'

'Oh, very droll,' I said, not even thinking about it. *Much.*

'Has Ruby got a boyfriend?' probed my aunt.

'No, I don't have a boyfriend. I did accidentally slip and fall on a journalist though, which in hindsight wasn't my wisest move.'

'Did you hurt yourself, Aunty Wooby?' My stealthy niece's ringlets were tucked up into a towel-turban almost twice the height of her.

Debs cackled. 'Good question, Clem.'

Bollocks. 'Not really,' I said, 'just a little bruised, that's all.'

'And the journalist?'

'The journalist is fine. He wasn't hurt at all.'

'Who wasn't hurt?' asked Fran. Bollocks squared.

'The journalist who Aunty Wooby slipped and fell on.' Debs was gleeful with the salaciousness of it all.

'I see,' said Fran with a disapproving big sister look. 'Why don't you go and find the puppies, darling?'

With Clem at a distance the interrogation intensified. 'You're sleeping with a journalist?' The three women gathered around, cornering me against the kitchen bench.

'It's more past tense and singular an episode than that,' I said. There hadn't really been time since leaving Canberra on the previous Monday to dissect the Oscar incident over a box of Kleenex and a *Sex and the City* marathon, as any right-minded female would have done.

'Which one?' asked Debs.

'Not a chance,' I said.

'They're mostly feral,' she said. 'Did you sleep with a feral one?'

'No.'

'Then you slept with a hot one. That narrows it substantially—pretty much rules out print and radio.'

'I didn't say that. It was a stupid mistake anyway. I don't want to relive it, if it's okay by all of you.'

Debs whipped out her BlackBerry.

'What are you doing, Debs?' asked Daphne.

'Googling TV journos from the national press gallery.' Bollocks cubed.

'Now, darling, leave poor Ruby alone,' said my aunt. 'I'm sure she'll tell us if she wants us to know.'

'Tell me,' said Fran. 'I'm your sister.'

'I suppose that makes you a bastion of confidentiality?'

I could recall countless examples of merciless teasing over high school beaus, including one my family affectionately dubbed Lumpy Liam.

Cue the emotional blackmail. 'I'm going through an exceptionally difficult time in my life at the moment, Ruby, as you're well aware, so I think I have the right to know who my baby sister is bonking.'

Debs and Daphne exchanged concerned glances.

'Bonked. Single occurrence. Past tense.'

'Okay,' said Debs, scrolling sadistically. 'There are only four possible candidates—the rest are female, unless...?'

I shook my head.

'Okay, so that leaves us with Michael Joyce?'

'Is he still alive?' asked Daphne, checking the buns in the oven.

'Apparently so,' said Debs.

I stood still and silent.

'What about that Patrick man from Network Six?' asked my aunt, dismounting the moral high horse she'd only just saddled.

'No, he's screwing the proprietor. Everyone knows that. What about that Oliver what's his name?'

'Oh, I know who you're talking about.' Daphne clicked her fingers and bit her bottom lip to make her brain work faster. 'Oscar Franklin!'

Debs stopped scrolling. All three of them stared at me. The oven timer buzzed.

'Bingo!' squealed Fran delightedly, high-fiving Debs. 'Show me a picture!'

Naturally I was pleased to see my discomfort bring such renewed vivacity to my sister. 'He's *hot*, Ruby!'

'I'll set the table,' I said.

It was both impressive and amusing to watch three grown women find a plethora of sexual innuendoes in religious buns at teatime. Thankfully, halfway through, my phone rang.

'Roo speaking.'

'Roo, it's Oscar.'

My shoulders tensed. 'Hi.' I stepped outside.

'How are you?'

'Completely fine,' I said, a little too convincingly.

'Good to hear. Are you in Melbourne?'

'No.'

'Oh. Listen, I feel really bad about this, but...'

This is your time to shine, I said to my head.

'Oscar, you don't need to explain. Really. It's nothing. I was tired. Let's just move on.'

'That's not what I feel bad about.'

'Excuse me?'

'Roo, I've had a tip-off from a source at Immigration that you've been working in the country illegally and I wanted to put it to you for comment.'

'I'm sorry—are you telling me you're calling as a journalist who's doing a story about me?'

'I tried calling Di Freya first but her phone was busy. I thought the least I could do after, well, you know, would be to let you know that this is what we're running with tonight and see if you wanted to comment.'

'No.'

'Are you the same person who wrote the email, by the way? The banker?'

I threw my BlackBerry onto the paved pathway. It disintegrated. My body shook with rage as I bent down to pick up the pieces. Pansy came over to help me. She sniffed the battery and licked the gravel from my quivering fingers.

Fran approached cautiously. 'Is everything okay, Ruby?'

'No, everything is not okay.' I ran into the house and picked up my bags. 'I have to go. Can I borrow a car?'

'Darling, you've only just arrived,' said Daphne.

'Ruby, I'm sure whatever it is we can work it out from here,' said Fran.

'I'm really sorry; I know I said I'd be here, but I must go.'

'I'll drive you, kiddo.' Debs handed me my reassembled BlackBerry.

'Thanks.'

Fran hugged the breath out of me. 'I'm not leaving you,' I told her. 'I'll be back later.'

I tried to compose myself as we zoomed down the drive in Debs' Aston Martin.

'Di,' I said when I got through to her, 'I need to talk to you about a media issue.'

'Roo, you're supposed to be having a day off.'

'Oscar Franklin has had a tip-off from Immigration that I've been working in Australia unlawfully. I'm on my way back into the city now. He's going to run with the story tonight.'

There was a pause. 'Are you here unlawfully?'

'No, and I wasn't working unlawfully because I wasn't technically employed.'

'Why not?'

'I forgot to sign my employment contract.'

'Who else knows about this?'

'Luke knows—he got me out of it—and long-socked Bruce from Immigration.'

'Why do they wear long socks?'

'Not sure, but if we win this election let's make long-sock prohibition a policy priority.'

'Agreed. What did you tell Pretty Boy?'

'Nothing—I ended the call. He did mention something about an email I wrote.'

'What about?'

'When I was made redundant in London, I replied to the bank and it went a bit viral.'

'I know. I Googled you. Great email.'

'Thanks.'

'Let me handle it from here, Roo.'

'No, I'm on my way in.'

'Go home and let me handle it.'

'No. Can't we have him whacked or something?'

She sighed. I could see her face. 'You told me not to shit where I eat and I didn't listen.'

'Tastes bad, doesn't it?'

'Tastes rubbish.'

'Look, this didn't happen because you screwed the crew. Pretty Boy's just doing his job and now I need you to let me do mine.'

'Okay.'

'And a word of advice: do not under any circumstances watch the Channel Eleven news, and, if you do, make sure you don't have access to sharp or blunt objects at the time. Screen damage is irreversible. Take my word for it.'

'Thanks, Di.'

'No worries. Now piss off.'

I told Debs to turn the car around. We drove in total silence while I seethed with self-loathing. You nincompoop. You elementary fool. You've done this to yourself, you know. First with the visa, then with that wretched unconscionable creep. Now you're about to face public humiliation and there's nothing you can do about it. You might even derail the campaign.

'Hey, kiddo, you're not beating yourself up, are you?'

'Of course I am,' I groaned. 'I fell for a creep.'

'It's human, Ruby. He's the moron. Fancy letting a great chick like you slip through his fingers. I hope he suffers in his jocks.'

'Thanks, Debs.' We pulled up at the house.

'You're welcome.' She gave me a bone-crunching embrace. 'Now, you'll be pleased to know it's wine o'clock.'

Fran kissed me hello and led me to the kitchen, past Clem, who was singing to an audience of puppies on the deck.

'Just you wait, 'enry 'iggins, just you wait.'

Tug of war

For once I took Di's advice. Granted, I had intended to watch the six o'clock news, but at 5.47 p.m., when simmering slate-grey clouds overhead came to a sudden boil, a thunderstorm clapped across the Yarra Valley, blacking out everything in its path.

Debs and Daphne snuggled under a tartan blanket on deck chairs to watch the lightning illuminate pockets of the countryside. Fran had been fast asleep on the couch since lunch, leaving me with a jet-lagged Clem, who doesn't much like the dark, let alone without her mother.

'Come on, Clem. Let's tuck the puppies in.'

We took a torch from the kitchen and led Champagne to the laundry. Clem gave her a kiss goodnight and Pansy welcomed her little girl back to the familial basket. The Widdler was trying his hardest to steal a holey old sock from JFK. They growled unconvincingly. Pansy looked on disapprovingly.

'What are they doing?' asked Clem.

'Playing a game.'

'Like toggle ball?'

'A bit like tug of war, yes.'

'JFK sounds angry.' Clem yawned.

'Well, he had it first.'

I picked Clem up and slung her around my hip, carrying her to the bedroom and tucking her in.

'Aunty Wooby, do you want me to look after you so you don't get frightened?'

'That would be nice, Clem.' I crawled into bed next to her. Two yawns later, she was snoring like a Harley-Davidson. I fumbled for the torch and, when I couldn't find it, I decided to stay and rest awhile.

There was a particularly sharp pull on my right arm and a lapping sound in my left ear. 'Aunty Wooby, you're making funny noises,' said Clem, dislodging a puppy from my neck.

I jumped out of bed, giving The Widdler a catastrophic fright. 'What time is it, Clem?'

'Ruby, darling,' yelled Fran, 'there's a chauffeur car here for you.'

'The Widdler wet the bed,' announced Clem.

'Bugg— bother. I need to pack. And I need to wash the dog drool out of my ear and hair. Now.'

'Clem and I will pack for you, darling,' offered Fran, rushing in. 'Get in the shower.'

'What day is it?' I called out.

'Tuesday,' yelled Debs.

'Wednesday,' corrected Daphne.

Silence. 'Is it...ouch...Tuesday or Wednesday? Fuck, shit, bother.'

'Ruby!' shouted Fran.

'Sorry, I got shampoo in my eye!'

'Count to ten and the stinging will stop, Aunty Wooby.'

I turned the shower off, wrapped myself in a towel and counted to eleven. Still stinging. Twelve. Stopped.

'Thanks, Clem.' The steam rushed out of the bathroom and into the hall as I made a near-naked dash to my bedroom.

'G'day,' said a suited man.

'Hello,' I said, picking up my pace. 'Bollocks, who is that?' I asked Fran.

'That's your driver: George.' Fran was changing the sheets. 'Daphne has given him a hot cross bun and cup of tea while he waits.'

'Has anyone seen my shoe?' I pulled skinny jeans over damp skin.

'What colour is it?'

'Black.' I was on all fours looking under the bed. 'It's a black pump. It looks much like this one except it's for the left foot.'

Debs poked her head around the door. 'Is anybody missing a shoe?'

'Aunty Wooby is missing a shiny black one just like this one except for the other foot.'

'Bad news, mate. Champagne has demolished it. I think she's teething or something. She's taken to chewing the underwire from our bras too.'

'Sh—'

'Language, Ruby,' anticipated Fran.

'Right, I've got to go.' I stepped into a pair of wedges which I knew to be uncomfortable. 'The launch is tomorrow and we're preparing today. Love you all.'

'May I please give your other shoe to The Widdler?' asked Clem. I nodded, kissing the top of her head.

'Good luck, darling,' said Daphne. 'Have a great week and remember to enjoy it.' She handed me a thermos and a large warm paper bag.

'Thanks.'

'See you, kiddo. Try not to get deported.'

Fran carried my handbag to the car. 'When will I see you next?'

I threw my arms around her. 'You should all come to the election after-party or wake, whatever the case may be. It's a bit more than a week away. Sorry we didn't get a chance to talk.' I kissed her cheek and let go. She smiled, her upper lip trembling. She contained her emotions by looking up to the sky, proclaiming it a glorious day, just as our mother had always done when she dropped us off at boarding school.

George lowered his sunnies and drove off. 'Great buns,' he said. I think he was referring to Daphne's baking.

It was time to face the music and dial in. 'Morning people, sorry I'm late,' I said to the conference call.

'Hi, Roo,' said Di. Everyone else was silent. 'We're just doing a coverage wrap-up from last night and this morning.'

'We had a blackout in the Yarra Valley, so I didn't see it,' I explained. 'Was it awful? I'm really sorry, everyone. It was stupid of me.'

'It was barely a story. Pretty Boy gave it a damn good go, and everyone's seen your wife-beater and thongs now, but there's been no follow-up this morning because it's been swamped by...this other thing.'

Brilliant.

'You can all go now,' said Luke. 'Archie, stick around.'

I hung up and called Maddy. 'What other thing?'

'The government has a copy of a leaked email from Archie to someone else in the party sourcing dirt on Gabrielle Brennan,' she said. 'They gave the story to the papers and the PM has slammed us for it, calling us hypocrites for running the whole dirty politics agenda against her.'

'Shit,' I said. 'How bad is the email?'

'Disgraceful,' said Maddy. 'He writes "Married or not, everyone knows she's the village bicycle, but nobody has the balls to come out and claim having had her. Get me something concrete on her."'

'That's terrible. What did Max say?'

'Not a word. Speechless, I suppose. Archie told us to calm down. "Clean campaign?" he said. "Do you still believe in Santa too?" It's as if he's completely disconnected from what we're doing.'

'Did he apologise?' I asked as we drove past a newsagent where a *Herald* newsstand poster read MASTERS OF DIRT.

'He apologised for putting his request in writing but wasn't at all sorry for doing it. Where are you? Are you coming in for the launch prep?'

'Yeah, I'll be there soon. I've got another call coming in.'

It was Melissa Hatton. 'What the fuck are you pricks playing at?'

I held the phone at a safe distance from my ear.

'Here I am, on your advice, running a campaign denouncing gutter tactics, and your deputy press sec is on email scouring for grot about the Prime Minister's sex life!'

'Melissa, I assure you we had no idea about this. Everyone is pretty shocked.'

'I don't give a shit how you all feel. I'm drowning in interview requests. Blobby's going to have a field day in tomorrow's papers. My opponent is doing a press conference about it. I'm screwed.'

'Leave it with me, Melissa. I'll get back to you as soon as I can.'

I called Di. 'How are we handling this?'

'Not sure yet. We're working on a few lines to put distance between Archie's role and the campaign, but that'll be pretty tricky because everyone knows him and has seen him on the media plane, the bus—'

'Is Max doing a doorstop somewhere today?'

'Not really. We're supposed to be doing launch prep all day.

'I think he needs to cut Archie loose.'

'But then it will look like he's not taking responsibility for his staff, Roo. He can't do that. It'll look like he's making excuses.'

'Then Archie should resign.'

'Preaching to the choir,' said Di. 'Let me get back to it, Roo. My phones are going crazy.'

'Thanks for handling things for me yesterday.'

'No worries, mate. By the way, I thought you said Luke knew about your little issue?'

'Huh?' I took a cautious sip of Daphne's scalding tea.

'Didn't you say that Luke knew about you and Pretty Boy?'

'No, I said Luke knew about my visa issue.' I added 'pick up visa' to my To Do list. 'Why?'

'Sorry, mate. No wonder he was knocked for six. Gotta go.'

Now he thinks you're a trollop.

Not that my head should care what my boss thinks of my sex life. Although, it would be nice if he didn't think I was a gullible idiot. Or, for that matter, a promiscuous one. I drafted a text to clear the water.

Sorry for Oscar and visa issues...

I backspaced to the blank screen.

Thanks for your support on the visa...

No, that wouldn't do.

I know you're busy, but I'm not seeing Oscar. He's a wank...

What's he supposed to say to that? intervened my head. *Dear Ruby, yes, I know he is a wanker. The entire world knows he's a wanker. You slept with a wanker. What does that say about you? Kind regards, Luke, Your Boss, Whose Opinion of Your Personal Life Shouldn't Matter.*

'We're here,' said George. I thanked him and went inside.

The auditorium was abuzz. A purple backdrop was being fitted on the stage. The lectern was plain with a simple, light oakwood finish. Young party members roamed the room in purple T-shirts.

A girl approached me. 'Oh my God, you're the illegal immigration staffer, aren't you?' Her excitement was the sort usually reserved for encounters on the Oscars red carpet. 'Sorry, I'm a total news junkie.'

'What does your T-shirt say?' I ignored her question.

She pulled it flat over her stomach. 'VOTE NO TO DIRTY POLITICS.'

I spotted Maddy adjusting the giant white-felt P for Party onstage and made my way towards her. 'What are we going to do about the T-shirts?'

'It's too late now. They're everywhere.'

'Is Di here yet?'

She nodded, texting simultaneously. 'Di, Luke and Theo are backstage figuring out what the fuck they're going to do next.'

I picked up coffees for everyone and took them to the backstage room. Theo and Luke were at the whiteboard, sketching out ideas, while Di sat in the corner attached to her charging phone. Theo greeted me with a nod; Luke kept writing.

'Who wants coffee and my aunt's homemade hot cross buns?'

'Fuck, yeah,' said Di.

'Just give us some time, please,' snapped Luke without looking at me.

'Ease up, Luke. Have you got your period or something?' asked Di.

'I'll have Luke's coffee,' said Theo. 'And buns.'

'Sorry.' I put their coffees on a table and closed the door behind me.

Maddy was in an adjacent room. 'Can I do something to help?' I asked, handing her a coffee and bun.

'I need someone to inflate three thousand balloons.' She pointed to a tall cylinder of helium in the corner.

'Sign me up.'

My fingers might have ached from all the knot-tying, but it was indescribably satisfying to perform a task with such limited capacity for error. Fix balloon to nozzle. Check. Turn tap to release helium. Check. When balloon inflates, close tap. Check. Tie balloon. Check. Tie ribbon. Check. Next balloon.

Theo came to join me. 'Can I play?'

'Sure.' I handed him a balloon. 'How are things going?'

'Badly.'

'What's the strategy?'

'There isn't one.' He accidentally released an untied balloon, which went whizzing around the room before it landed limply in the corner. 'Any more buns?' He helped himself to the paper bag.

I wanted to ask him about Luke, but as Theo had the emotional and social intelligence of a lawn mower it would have been a pointless pursuit. 'Has Archie resigned?'

'Nope.'

'Why not?'

'Because I've got nothing to apologise for,' said Archie, emerging from behind a balloon bouquet. He seemed lost, like a jester with no court.

'Sorry, Archie, but I disagree.' I resisted the temptation to be mean about it.

'I did what you guys should've been doing,' he said, clearing a path. 'It's neck and neck. This new PM offers about as much change as people can stomach at the moment. It's a case of same horse, new jockey—that's what mums and dads want. We need something big to bring her down and so that's what I tried to do. You don't think they're not out there looking for exactly the same stuff to shoot Max with?'

'That's not the point,' I said. 'We've campaigned in earnest on this high moral ground and now you're what they're going to shoot us with. You dug for dirt and put it in writing and you did so when there was no need to. We were doing fine on policy grounds. I think that warrants some remorse, don't you?'

He considered it for a second. 'No, I really don't. I get

it, Roo. This is your first shot at politics, but I've been doing this my whole life. This is how it works. Don't like the game? Don't play.'

'You're right. This is my first time. Maybe more people like me would get involved in politics if people like you weren't. You're a walking stereotype. You're the lonely, bitter cynic who has never done anything else but spin, and this is the result—you can't see right from wrong anymore.'

'Is your aunt single?' Theo looked into the empty paper bag.

'No.'

'Bummer.' He scrunched the bag and turned to Archie. 'Look, just do the right thing or you'll be sacked. At least you maintain some integrity by offering your resignation; otherwise, your career will be even more fucked. That's my advice.'

Archie kicked the A-frame I had been using to anchor my inflated balloons, and stomped off. The balloons floated to the ceiling. Teetering dangerously on my wedges, I bounced up and down, clutching at dangling ribbons while cursing my father for the short gene. Theo shrugged and left.

'Excuse me,' I said, chasing a passing conference centre attendant down the hallway, 'you wouldn't happen to have a pair of kitchen tongs, would you?'

'Try catering. Ground floor.'

The enormous commercial kitchen was full of chefs with their bouffant hats. There must have been fifty of them. I cleared my throat. 'Excuse me,' I hollered, 'does anyone have a pair of kitchen tongs I can borrow?' They either couldn't hear me or didn't want to.

I moved between two long stainless-steel bench-tops and repeated my request. Nothing. Was I invisible? I cupped my hands around my mouth to perform Di's megaphone trick. 'EXCUSE ME, DOES ANYONE HAVE A PAIR OF—'

The man stationed behind me must have been preparing to feed delegates of the International Vegans Convention because in his fright he upended a steel vat full of vinaigretted alfalfa sprouts all over me, coating my face, neck and chest in a slick of forage.

'My garnish!'

The white coats parted, making way for a smaller one. 'Oo is *ziss*?' he thundered.

Alfalfa man shrugged.

'My balloons have floated to the ceiling. Do you have any tongs?' I licked the over-seasoned dressing from my lips.

'Security!'

I trudged through the sprout sludge and made my way to the lift. It pinged open, revealing Max, Shelly and Luke. Of course.

'Roo, you're covered in salad,' pointed out Shelly.

'Garnish,' I said as we passed the first floor.

Max laughed. 'Mind if I ask why?'

'Long story.'

Luke shook his head.

Ping, went the lift. I scurried to the Ladies to scrape the sprouts into the loo; that's where I learned that vinaigrette stings when it makes direct contact with your eyes.

'Roo, are you in here?' It was Maddy. 'I just bumped into Shelly. She said you were covered in'—I emerged from the cubicle—'salad.'

'Garnish.'

'Archie just resigned,' she said, sniffing my cheek. 'His own decision. Press conference at the hotel in an hour.'

'I'll do it,' I said. 'Can you call Melissa Hatton and tell her to sit tight until Max has spoken?'

'Sure.'

During my second shower for the day, I thought about what I should say to Luke. It was inappropriate to apologise. I used my finger to draft a text message on the fogged-up shower glass.

> Luke, sleeping with Oscar was stupid. I regret it. I just thought you should kno...

No, that was even more stupid than sleeping with Oscar. I turned off the tap, stepped out of the shower, and continued on the mirror.

> Please don't think I'm something I'm not.

The fog subsided and I was faced with my own flushed reflection. I erased my handwriting with a towel, dressed and ran to set up the press conference.

An hour later, the media were rolling in. The cameras, the snappers, the journalists. Serious ones came first and used the time to study the media release, jotting down notes here and there. Then came Oscar, strutting like a peacock.

What on earth did we find attractive about that man?

A lady I barely recognised sat in the front row. She did not read the release. She had her eyes closed, like she was meditating. 'Who's that?' I asked Di.

'That, my dear, is Anastasia Ng. She's only the greatest journo on our planet. Pretty Boy's boss. She's been on leave because her husband had surgery.' Di sighed. 'If I wasn't doing what I'm doing now, I'd want to be her. She's incredible. Incisive. Balanced. Lethal when she disapproves. Genius.'

That's the 'batty' one Oscar is going to replace?

'Is she the one who's on her way out?'

'Ng? I don't bloody think so. Sharp as a tack, that chick. There's no way anyone else could even begin to fill her shoes.'

Max strode in. 'Thanks for coming,' he said when he took to the lectern. 'I wanted to say a few quick words about my former staff member Archibald Andersen. Mr Andersen has offered me his resignation following a unilateral decision on his part to try to dig into the Prime Minister's personal life. I have accepted his resignation.

'I want it to be known that I have enormous respect for the Prime Minister. She is a competent politician and should be judged as such. I have no interest whatsoever in her personal life. It is none of my business or anybody else's.

'That is why Mr Andersen was right to offer me his resignation. Gutter politics have no place in my office or any public office. In fact, as you all know, I denounce it. My party and I are capable of tackling the government on policy and policy alone, and that's what we intend to do.

'I apologise to the Prime Minister and seek the forgiveness of the Australian people and hope we can put this behind us.

'Of course, I will take any questions you might have.'

I watched Anastasia Ng.

'Mr Masters,' said Gary Spinnaker, 'how do you expect to maintain your advertising campaign against the government's dirty tactics in the light of this scandal?'

Max answered. Anastasia was the only journalist in

the room looking and listening rather than scribbling in her notepad. She was like a photojournalist, absorbing every word as though it was an image.

She took the last question. 'Did you ask for Mr Andersen's resignation or did he offer it? And if he hadn't offered it, do you think you would now be calling him a former staff member?'

Not exactly a batty question.

Max stumbled. 'I'm not going to speculate on a hypothetical. What's done is done.' He thanked everyone for their time and left with a smile plastered on his dial. Ouch.

'See what I mean?' whispered Di. 'Slice.' She followed Max out.

Oscar was too busy staring into the Mirror app on his iPhone to witness Anastasia's incision, let alone understand it.

Surely you're not going to stand by and watch Pretty Boy screw over another smart woman, are you?

No. I'm not.

Hallway of shame

I rolled over: 2.53 a.m. Blast. I begged my bladder to hold out for another hour. I tried to get back to sleep, but when my smooth leg encountered a hairy one I wondered whether it might belong to someone else. No such luck: just a fatigued shaving omission from the night before. Grumpily, I staggered out of bed and felt my way around the dark hotel room. My bare hip hit a sharp corner. 'Ouch.' I rubbed the newest bruise of my collection.

Mercifully, I had remembered to leave the bathroom light on, a trick of the trade to help steer weary campaigners through uncharted hotel rooms.

I edged towards the lit strip of carpet before me, closed my eyes and opened the door. It sprang shut behind me. 'What sort of daft designer carpets a hotel bathroom?' I wondered aloud. I blinked the coloured stars away, waiting for my pupils to adjust.

This was either the longest bathroom known to man

or I was standing in the seventeenth-floor hallway. I tried the door to my room behind me. No joy. In vain, felt my side pockets for the key. No key. No pockets. No bottoms, in fact. Just frayed cotton knickers, a buttock-scraping Financial Services Authority T-shirt and one shaven leg. Crap.

Using both hands to stretch my T-shirt down to micro-mini level, I waddled to the lift and prayed for an empty lobby. Ping pong, sang the lift. Its doors opened and I stumbled in. My nose hit the G button. I pictured the security guard spraying his coffee at the screen as he watched my misfortune unfold. Mirrored walls gave an unflattering multifaceted view of my sleeping ensemble. Two knotted tufts of hair stood at an acute angle to my scalp. A rivulet of drying dribble had escaped my mouth. Still holding down the FSA, I made use of my shoulder to wipe it off. Mission impossible.

Ping pong. My shaven leg held the lift open. A vacuum cleaner growled around the corner, followed by a uniformed young woman.

'Hello,' I yelled above the hullaballoo.

'Hullo,' she said, turning off the machine.

'Oh, thank God,' I said. 'Would you mind asking them to cut a new key for room 1707?'

'Hullo?' she asked, looking very concerned.

I raised my voice. 'Hello again. I've locked myself out of my hotel room. Would you—'

'No speck in goulash. Surry.' She looked very nervous.

It's remarkably difficult to use body language hands-free. With thumb and forefinger I tried to indicate pushing the keycard into a slot and removing it.

'No key. Key. I need key.'

'Surry, no, funk you.' She shook her head and wheeled her vacuum away.

'Funk you too,' I said. Crappest of craps.

'Hello? If someone is there, please come to the lift.'

Why preface it with 'if someone is there'? If someone is there, they'll hear you. If no one is there, they won't.

Shut up, head.

I thought we were going to the loo.

Shut up, bladder.

'Hello?' said a voice, probably male, but I hoped female with laryngitis.

'I'm in the lift.'

Footsteps approached. Salvation nigh, I gripped the hem, yanking it as low as it would go without warping my unconstrained boobs.

'Roo?'

Crappest crap of craps. 'Luke?'

My elbow reached for a button bearing two inward-facing arrows. Success, albeit accompanied by Luke's laughter. I pressed 17. INSERT CARD HERE, read a sign beneath an empty slot. Crappest crap of crappest craps.

Ping pong. The doors opened, revealing the lobby once more. There was a mixture of pity and amusement in Luke's smile.

I did my best to tuck myself into the corner so that he could see only my head around the doors.

'Um, your reflection...'

'Avert your eyes.'

He obeyed. 'Here, put this on.' He handed me his suit jacket. I closed the lift and put on the jacket.

My head laughed. *Don't you think it's ironic that you've been saved from a dire wardrobe malfunction by something that should be on the set of* Miami Vice?

Instinctively, I pushed up the sleeves.

Ping pong.

'Hi.'

'Hi.' He blushed, bringing colour to his ashen, unshaven face.

'I locked myself out of my hotel room,' I said, putting my smoothest leg forwards. Then I shuffled out of the lift to escape the hall of mirrors. 'Don't ask.'

'I'll get another one cut for you.'

He left, giving me enough time to hide my bottom half behind a well-placed umbrella stand.

'Shouldn't be long,' he said when he returned. 'I feel overdressed.' He undid his collar and slid off a pink gingham tie.

'Why are you in the lobby at 3 a.m.?'

'I just got back from the LOO's place. We've redrafted the launch speech.'

'Good?'

'Brilliant.'

'You look shattered, Luke.'

'No offence, Roo, but you're not really in a position to be commenting on appearances...not that you're... because you're...'

'Listen,' I chanced, 'I understand that Di told you about me and Oscar Franklin.'

'Roo, I don't need to know.' His smile evaporated. 'It's none of my business. You don't need to explain.'

'I know, but I'd like to. It was the kind of mistake you make once. I choked on—'

He held up his hand to mute me.

But it was an important sentence to finish, so I said,

'Eye candy—I choked on eye candy and it didn't even taste good.'

That sounded much better in here, said my head.

There was a terrible silence. If my hand hadn't been helping gravity with his jacket flap, it would have slapped my forehead.

He slid down the wall he was leaning against and sat on the floor in front of me, holding his head in his hands. This was a good thing, because if he had been looking up, my bristly shin would have been in full view. I swapped legs again just in case.

'I missed my kid's parent–teacher interview tonight,' he said finally. 'Again.'

'Your kid?'

The finger painting. Sun, house, cat, man, child. Woman?

'Yep. Daniel. He's nine. I missed it.'

'I didn't know you have children.'

'Child. Just the one.'

'Well, Daniel probably appreciated it as a gesture of trust. I used to dread parent–teacher night.'

His smile returned. 'You're right: Dan's fine. Bella, on the other hand—'

'Your wife?' I breathed in.

He rubbed his bare finger. 'My ex.'

I breathed out. 'How do you cope doing your job and being a parent? I don't even have a goldfish and find it difficult enough to balance things.'

'That's the point—I don't cope. I suck at multi-tasking. I can't keep going like this.' He sighed. 'Win or lose the election, this is it for me.'

'You can't be serious,' I said. 'If we win, you'd walk away? Just like that?'

'No, not just like that. Don't get me wrong: it's a bloody tough call, but it shouldn't be a tougher call for me to walk away from my job than it is to walk away from my son.'

'Sir,' said the man on the front desk, 'Miss Stanhope's room key is ready.'

'Thanks, mate.' He dragged himself to his feet.

In the lift, Luke said, 'I shouldn't have said all of that. I don't want to stress Max out before the election so I haven't told him yet.'

'My lips are sealed.'

Ping pong.

'Thanks for the jacket.' I handed it back to him.

'You're welcome. See you in an hour.' He walked towards his hotel room. 'And Roo?'

'Mm?' I said, looking over my shoulder.

'Thanks for listening.'

'My pleasure.'

I inserted the new key. The green light flashed approvingly. I turned on the lights, ran for the loo and added 'buy pyjama pants' to my To Do list.

The Launch

'Why are we launching the campaign twenty-five days in?' I whispered to Maddy backstage.

She rolled her eyes. 'Shhh.'

'Definitionally,' I said, 'a launch marks the commencement of something. A rocket can't go into orbit until somebody says "We have lift off." This campaign has already lifted off.'

'What about ships?'

'What *about* ships?'

She leaned in closer. 'Are you telling me that every time a boat named after one of her ancestors is built, Her Majesty steps into her overalls, picks up a bottle of Yellowglen from the Windsor bottle-o and pops up to a Liverpudlian dry dock to scream "bon voyage" over the PA system?'

'Yellow what from the Windsor what?'

'Shoosh,' she said. Max stood beside us. The pages of

his speech were tightly rolled into a tube. He stared at the floor, his fingers fidgety with adrenaline.

An elderly man approached the stage. Abigail got out of her seat to help him up the stairs. He wore a grey suit with a purple MASTERS FOR PM badge on his lapel. The audience clapped. When he reached the lectern, he said, 'Hello, everybody, my name is Frank and I'm pleased to introduce a boy who loves his country.'

The crowd went quiet.

'When he was eight, he had to write an assignment for school about careers. The other kids wrote that they wanted to be ballerinas or firemen. This particular kid said he wanted to serve his country. He got a C on the assignment because apparently that wasn't a career, but, boy, did he prove them wrong.

'At age seventeen, he borrowed my late wife's Datsun and drove to Melbourne to join the navy. There, he served for decades, both here and abroad, before an injury made it difficult to continue.

'But his assignment was still clear. Now he seeks the highest office of service for his country, and I couldn't be prouder of him.'

Max looked up, his fingers still.

Frank's voice broke a little, but he re-established composure. 'He's a man of conviction, courage and integrity. He's my son, Max Masters, the Leader of the Opposition and next prime minister of Australia.'

The crowed erupted into spine-tingling applause, the kind you could feel. Max moved across the stage and into his dad's arms. The flashing cameras were blinding, but I could just make out the tear stains on Milly's emerald silk tunic as her dad introduced her baby brother.

'Thanks, Dad,' said Max, when we had all calmed down.

I studied the audience as Max spoke. People laughed, nodded, clapped, cheered and, at the end, stood up. Hardened hacks were stirred to their feet. When our hands tingled from being smashed together, Shelly, Milly, Abigail and her grandpa joined Max on stage, so we clapped until our palms throbbed.

Afterwards, Max sat calmly in a chair with a salad sandwich and cup of tea. 'How do you think it went?'

Luke, who like Max and Theo was operating on no sleep, could scarcely contain himself. 'It couldn't have been better.'

Shelly squeezed her husband's knee. 'It was the best speech you've ever given.'

Max smiled. 'Thanks, sweetheart.'

'I'm glad we did the redraft last night,' said Theo. 'There was a standing ovation when you talked about gutter politics. It could have been a disaster after the shit sandwich Archie served us.'

Maddy nudged him, gesturing to Abigail.

'Sorry,' he said. 'After the poo sandwich...'

Abigail giggled.

'Roo, can I borrow you for a minute?' said Di, barging into the room.

'Sure.' I excused myself and closed the door behind me. 'What's up?'

'What do you know about social networking sites? How permanent are things once they're on there?'

'As permanent as black shoe polish on white carpet. Why?'

'Gary Spinnaker is running the only negative angle he

can find on the launch. Abigail said something online this morning. Apparently her friend posted something like, "How come you're not at sports day Abs?" She replied, "Dad's making some boring speech and Mum said I have to go."'

'That seems harmless enough.'

'Wrong,' said Di. 'All the happy, clapping pictures of Abigail next to Shelly today will look fake in tomorrow's papers. And the wowsers out there will say she should have been in school.'

'Firstly, she's just turned thirteen, so of course she acts cool with her friends. I would have eleven nose piercings and an eating disorder if I was thirteen and my father was Opposition leader.' I shuddered at a flashback of my father making a speech at my school careers fair entitled 'The Merits of Banking', which became known as 'The Merits of Wanking'. 'Secondly, every parent can relate to pulling their children out of school for an aunt's wedding, a sibling's graduation, a holiday.'

'Roo! We need to fix this. The LOO can't do much without belittling Abigail, which he would never do. Abigail can't exactly retract because it'll look forced. The PM hasn't had her campaign launch yet. She might decide to leave her kids in school to make a point, then this becomes an issue about parenting...Hi, Shelly.'

Di and I stared at our shoes.

'What becomes an issue about parenting?' Shelly moved closer.

'Would you mind if I talked to Max about it first?' pleaded Di.

'Yes,' she said, 'I would.'

'Can we perhaps talk to you both at once?'

'If you must. Max, can you come out here for a minute, darling?'

He was utterly exhausted. It seemed unfair to give him this news.

'What's up?'

When Di explained, they laughed before realising what it could mean for their daughter: unnecessary public exposure. Max flopped onto a chair. The adrenaline crutch that had been holding him upright gave way. He was too tired to think. Shelly stood next to the window. Outside, Melbourne was grey and stormy.

'Let me talk to Spinnaker.' Shelly unfolded her arms. 'Give me his number. I'll call him.'

'With respect, Shelly, I'd need to know what you were going to say,' said Di.

'I'm going to remind him that she's thirteen years old, just a year older than his son, the one he told me about at Christmas drinks.'

Di pondered it. 'But if Spinnaker doesn't write it, someone else will.'

'I'll talk to them, too.'

'I think you should make light of it,' I said. 'Max is lucky to have such a savvy critic in the family. This time, she says, her grandfather made the better speech.'

'Yeah.' Di closed her eyes to capture her thoughts. 'How about you say something like, "Max and I consider ourselves lucky to have such an honest and savvy critic in the family. We encourage her to have her own opinion on things and are immensely proud of her." If Spinnaker presses you on why you took her out of school for the event, tell him you made the decision to pull Abigail out of sports day for the same reason his wife pulled his kids out of school to attend the Walkleys.'

'I'd do it again in a heartbeat,' said Shelly.

'We might need to keep a bit of an eye on what she says online in future,' said Di.

'Let her be,' said Max through closed eyes. 'I wouldn't be where I am today if Mum and Dad had told me to shut up when I was a kid, and that's what I'll say if anyone asks me about it.'

'Come on, love,' said Shelly, 'let's get you home for a nap.' She helped him to his feet and led him to the door.

'Thanks, guys,' he yawned.

'I'll text you Spinnaker's number and let him know to expect your call, Shelly,' said Di.

'Ta,' said Shelly.

'You're not bad at this, you know, Roo,' said Di, before her phone rang. 'G'day Gary, I was just about to call.'

A dish best served with mini-pies

Archie's final contribution to the campaign shaved two whole points off us in that Saturday's Southpoll, dampening Max's post-launch high. The two-party-preferred count put us at fifty-one to Brennan's forty-nine, giving her the perfect underdog status with which to start the final week of the campaign. With the finish line in sight, Max and Shelly found new energy. We spent the weekend visiting key marginal seats like Donaldson in Tasmania to shore up support. Now, in our seventh city in four days, Max read his brief as I sponged oily make-up onto his sweaty face.

'Do I really need that?'

My head was unkind. *With those eye bags and crow's feet, he could probably audition for the before shot in a Botox commercial. The polls open in less than four days.*

'We just need to make sure your face isn't too shiny for the cameras.'

'I'm at a defence base in Woop Woop,' he said. 'It's thirty-four degrees. If I wasn't shiny I wouldn't be human.'

'Isn't Woop Woop in Tasmania?'

His laughter made my hand slip, printing a lightning bolt of concealer across his forehead.

'Keep still. You look like Harry Potter.'

'Woop Woop is a generic description of somewhere a long way from anywhere.'

Oh.

My phone rang.

'Hello, Aunty Wooby, I saw you on the television yesterday wearing a yellow Bob the Builder hat, an orange vest and white trousers with mud on them.'

Yesterday's mine visit had been a brutal lesson in allowing the day's schedule to inform wardrobe selection. 'Mummy said orange isn't easy to wear. Debs said you are very brave to wear white trousers to the ironing mine. I thought your hat was a bit big for you because I couldn't see your eyes. How did you get on the television?'

'Sorry, Clem, I can't talk right now,' I whispered.

'Why not?'

'Because I'm painting someone's face.'

'What colour?'

'Skin colour.'

'Boring. At my birthday party Mummy painted pink stars on our cheeks with itchy violent glitter.'

'Violet,' I corrected. I covered the phone. 'My five-year-old niece thinks I should paint you pink with glitter.'

'Can I talk to her?'

Splendid idea. Maybe Clem can tell Max how you tripped and fell on a journalist.

'Sure,' I said. 'Clem, I'm going to put you on to my

boss, Mr Masters. He might be the prime minister soon. He wants to say hello.'

Max took the phone while I prayed.

'Hi, my name's Max...That's a very long name for a little girl. Do you mind if I call you Clementine?...You're right, it does get itchy up the nose...That's good advice. Thank you for that, but I'm not sure if they'll let you vote yet...Bye, Clementine.' He handed me the phone and I said goodbye to Clem.

'She's an incredible interviewer,' Max said. 'She makes Anastasia Ng look shy.'

I dusted Max down and plucked the tissues from around his collar. He went back to his brief while I washed my hands. 'I thought this was supposed to be a $3.7 billion announcement,' said Max, scanning his copy of the media release. 'This says $4.7 billion.'

Fuck. 'Good point.'

'What time's this press conference?'

'In ten minutes,' I said. 'Let me check if the release has been distributed.' I called Luke.

'You've reached Luke Harley, Chief of Staff to the...'

'Godspeed,' said Max, reading my next move.

I scampered down the steps out to the lawn where the press conference was to be held. It had been a civilised morning tea until my arrival. Under a shade cloth, the local candidate and press pack chatted with their hosts, a pride of sickeningly handsome uniformed officers, the kind you can't help but unbutton with your eyes. I paused to fully appreciate the visual feast before me.

Focus, Ruby.

A hundred yards across the lawn stood Luke, shuffling a pile of paper. The press releases. I waved my arms to catch his attention. 'Yoo hoo!' If I'd had the fluorescent green tie he was wearing I could have used it as a signal. 'Luke!' Nothing. To stop him, I would have to make it across the grass in thirty seconds. This meant discarding my Up Yours, Oscars, a pair of red platform patent peep-toes christened by Maddy on the plane that morning. I bolted barefoot towards Luke, my floaty bias-cut skirt puffing up like a hot-air balloon.

Luke turned to Gary Spinnaker and licked his index finger, poised to release the release. My pace quickened from trot to canter.

There's Pretty Boy.

I attempted a nod, which would have conveyed the perfect cocktail of professionalism and nonchalance if I hadn't felt a crippling spike in my right foot.

'Ugh!' The pain felled me. 'Fuck,' I screamed when my patella pressed against the nest of prickles. Onlookers gasped; teaspoons clinked against saucers. I put out my hand to steady myself, which, with hindsight, was unwise given the ferocious clusters surrounding me. 'Fugh.' Having spotted the causal relationship between movement and pain, I adopted a pose resembling a wounded crab, the kind one might strike in an epic Twister showdown. I couldn't see the expressions on the thirty-five or so faces, but I could imagine them.

A pair of knights in matt camouflage rushed to my aid. 'Gotta watch out for bindies, ma'am,' said one, lifting me off the ground.

'Watch out for *what*?' I retracted my landing gear for fear of further attack, electing to hang from his arm like a Christmas ornament.

'Bindies,' said the second knight, as if it might make

more sense to me at greater volume. They deposited me on the platform beside the lectern.

'Roo,' Luke said, suppressing a grin when he reached me.

I looked around to see Gary Spinnaker underlining. I was too late. 'The press release is wrong.' I plucked at the thorns embedded in my knee cap. 'It's supposed to be 3.7, not 4.7.'

'No, it's not,' he said. 'The new costing came through this morning.'

The pain worsened. 'Do you think someone could have told me that?'

'It's in the brief.'

'Oh.' I collected myself, stepping back into the Up Yours, Oscars.

'I haven't stood in a bindi patch since I was about twelve.' He helped me up.

'Why give a vicious predator such an adorable name? How about Nature's Land Mines or Grasstards?'

He pulled a blade of grass from my hair. 'I guess I should go and get the LOO.'

'You do that,' I said. 'I'm off to the airport.'

It was half three in the afternoon and I hadn't eaten all day. By the time I reached the lounge, the crockenbouche of tepid mini-pies could have been a Michelin-stamped smorgasbord. I settled into a corner couch with a magazine and chowed down on soggy pastry and processed meat. Heaven.

Over the top of *Vogue Australia*, I spotted a familiar woman. Spiral notepad under arm, thick black hair streaked with silver. Anastasia Ng slung a beaten leather satchel over her shoulder and approached the desk.

'Welcome back, Ms Ng,' said the receptionist.

'Thanks, I'm going to need the remote.' She made her way to the television area via a fruit bowl, switched the football to *Two Cents* and turned up the volume. 'Sorry,' she said to the startled gentleman on the couch beside her. She wasn't sorry at all. He picked up his beer and stormed off. She crunched into an apple and watched.

I moved to sit beside her. Oscar appeared with his regular late-afternoon segment, focusing on the PM's launch, which had been full of fanfare. The PM presented as a strong person of sterling intellect with marital integrity and a mother's warmth. Talkback radio hosts had been bombarded with calls crying shame on Max for trying to smear such a lovely lady.

There wasn't time for contemplation. I was on that couch for a reason. When Oscar signed off, I said, 'Anastasia, we haven't met; I'm Ruby Stanhope.' She didn't turn. 'New to Max Masters' office,' I persevered.

Her almond eyes widened in acknowledgement. 'Yes, of course.' She shook my hand. 'I thought you looked familiar.'

'Where are you off to?'

'Back to Melbourne. How are things at Camp Masters during the final days?'

'I don't speak for anyone else, but I'm excited,' I smiled. 'As your network pointed out the other day, this is my first campaign.'

She closed her eyes for a second longer than a blink in order to track down my file. I could visualise it. A manila folder, thin. Stanhope, R. Age: 28. Background: English banker, infamous emailer, political virgin, migrant worker.

'Yes,' she said. 'For what it's worth, had it been up to me, I doubt I'd have run that story.'

'It's worth a lot,' I said. I took a deep breath. 'I was saddened to hear that you're winding down your role. The gallery will seem empty without you.'

She turned to face me fully. 'Winding down?'

'Yes, handing over your role.'

'I think you must be confusing me with someone else,' she said. 'I'm not going anywhere—I took leave to be with my husband, who has been ill.' Anastasia raised the apple to take a bite.

'I'm sorry. Perhaps I misinterpreted him. As you know, I'm new to this game.'

She spared the apple mid-crunch. 'Misinterpreted who?'

'Never mind.' I tried being coy. 'I hope I haven't put my foot in it.'

She paused, lids closing to hide those gleaming black eyes. Inside my Up Yours, Oscars I crossed my toes, hoping the bait would be too tantalising for her to resist. The eyelids opened. 'I'd be interested to know who told you.' Hooked.

'I wouldn't want to cause any internal friction.'

She flinched at the word. 'Not at all: it would remain between us.'

'Well, if you must know, it was your colleague, Oscar. He told me that his superior in the network was on her way out, hence his hosting the debate and taking on a bigger role. Something about ratings...Anyway, I've said too much. I'm glad to hear he was mistaken.'

Crunch. The blood rushed visibly beneath the surface of her porcelain skin.

They called our flight.

'Do tell me if I'm asking too much,' she said, 'but I'd appreciate it if you could keep this information quiet.'

She seemed uncomfortable with her request, but I decided to put her at ease. 'Of course,' I said. 'I like to keep the sisterhood strong.'

'Ditto.'

As we made our way to the departure gate, I catastrophised about the consequences of my disclosure. What if she confronts him and he denies it? What if I get a reputation as a loose woman?

No objections up here, said my head.

In any case, a squirt of vengeance was the perfect condiment to accompany my cold party-food feast.

One more sleep

I woke up early on election eve between a snorer and a tooth-grinder having barely slept a wink.

The night before, Fran and Clem had invited me to join them for supper and a sleepover at Daphne's apartment in Melbourne. Clem had fallen asleep to a singalong DVD of *My Fair Lady*. Fran had cooked and talked. I had poured wine and listened.

'I've been approached by a headhunter to establish an intellectual property practice as partner at my old firm,' she had said, apportioning pasta bake.

'Fran, that's brilliant. Are you going to take it?'

'No, but I'm going to do the bar exam in September. Mummy's friend has offered me space at his chambers.' She grinned. 'I'm going to be a barrister.'

'I'm so excited for you.' I clinked her glass with mine. 'It'll be a walk in the park after five years of Clem.'

'I'm excited for me too.'

I'd had to ask. 'Have you and Mark spoken?'

She nodded. 'I don't know what to do, Ruby. I hate what he's done, but I don't hate him.'

I couldn't bear the thought of her going back to Mark or the idea that Clem might grow up with two bedrooms. 'Take all the time you need and know that I will support whatever you choose to do.'

She squeezed my hand. 'When are you coming home?'

'My new visa expires in twelve months.'

'That's not an answer.'

She's right, said my head.

'I know, but I don't have a better answer than that at the moment.'

I had tossed and turned all night, pondering her question. Now, it was time to start the day.

Maddy and I were in charge of election eve drinks.

We had booked a roof garden at a pub in St Kilda. The sun was gentle and the sea breeze reviving. Shelly had made a special request. Unbeknown to the rest of us, she had been photographing the campaign at her husband's side. She'd asked Maddy and me to put together a presentation of the photographs as a surprise.

'Isn't there something more important for us to be doing right now?' I asked Maddy.

She smiled. 'Nope. That's what sucks about the last day of the campaign. It's kind of like the Melbourne Cup. You can train the horse and jockey, but the night before the big race there's nothing to do but rest and pray.'

So that afternoon, with a pair of mango daiquiris, Maddy and I bundled up our nervous energy and injected it into a slideshow, set to Elton John's 'Tiny Dancer'— Shelly's request. The photos were brilliant. Theo asleep on the plane using an empty packet of Tim Tams as an eye mask. Milly laughing hysterically on a white studio floor covered in a rainbow of ties. The cops throwing a football in a hotel corridor. Maddy showing off the holes in her riding boots. Di on a phone attached to a power source in the dress-ups room at a childcare centre. Max playing snakes and ladders with residents at an assisted care facility in Mildura. Luke, suit trousers rolled up, on the phone standing ankle-deep in the water at Airlie Beach. Me in the paper wearing my wife-beater.

By the time we were finished, it was 7 p.m. and we were, as Maddy put it, 'maggoted'.

'Cheers.' She charged her daiquiri. 'Twenty-four hours until the polls close.'

'Cheers,' I said, thinking that this wasn't something we should be drinking to.

Maddy checked the news online. 'Shit. One of the snappers has a shot of a shadow minister holding a brief face-up. They've zoomed in on it—it's full of lines. We always cover this in media training. Do not under any circumstances be photographed holding a document face-up. Any camera will be able to pick up content. She's a shadow minister, for crying out loud.'

'Did they get anything controversial?'

'Just bits and pieces to do with her portfolio. She's got stuff in there on family law, unemployment benefits, adoption for singles and gay couples.'

'What does it say about gay adoption?'

'Just party policy. What we agreed at national conference.'

'Which was?'

Maddy looked up. 'We don't support adoption—

300

international or local—for gay and single parents.'

My stomach churned. 'Why not?'

'I dunno, Roo. We just don't. The other side doesn't either. It's contentious. I guess if anything we're lucky her stupid brief stuck to policy. Nobody's picking it up—it's a pretty small story in the scheme of things—'

'I'm sorry, why does the party have a problem with single or gay people adopting children?'

She looked at me like I was losing the plot. 'Seriously, mate,' she said, 'I've got no bloody clue. I'm just the advancer.'

'Well, who can I talk to about this? It's ridiculous and it needs to be fixed.'

'Um, Roo.' She put her hand on my shoulder. 'I know how you feel—we're all a bit jumpy at the moment. Let's get another daiquiri.'

'I'm not jumpy,' I said. 'If you'd told me this on Day One I'd have said the same thing. I'm not going to support a party that doesn't support the rights of people to parent.' The churning fast became nausea. 'I need to get some air.'

'How much more air do you need? We're on the bloody roof!'

'A lot,' I said. I ran inside and into the Ladies. Sitting on the loo lid in the corner cubicle, I came to terms with what I had done. How could I have been so stupid as to not ask the fundamental questions before throwing my weight behind something like this? There was so much more I needed to know. Where did the party stand on the environment? And what about higher education? Affordable housing? Genetically modified food? It felt like I'd married a stranger in Vegas.

Pull yourself together, Ruby, said my head. *This doesn't change anything.* But it had. Everything was different. That lovely man who'd taken time out of his day to speak to my five-year-old niece was the same man who would deny my aunts the opportunity to love a child of their own. It was baffling.

I called Daphne to confess.

'Ruby, darling, it's so wonderful to hear from you. What should we wear tomorrow night? Is it likely to be formal?'

'I can't do it anymore, Daphne. I'm truly sorry. I didn't realise...I didn't realise I was working for a bunch of bigots.' A simmering tear plopped onto my lap.

'How so?'

'You mightn't have seen the news, but today I learned the party's position on gay adoption,' I sniffed. 'I can't keep working now that I know.'

'Ruby, that is the sweetest and most stupid thing I've ever heard,' she laughed. 'What difference can you possibly make by heckling from the outside?'

'But, by staying here, aren't I endorsing their position?'

'I don't think so,' she said. 'In fact, you'd be doing us all a favour if you kept going. Stay there. Be a challenging voice. So long as you know that your team would do a better job than the other team, I think that's something worth fighting for. Don't you?'

'I suppose.'

'Now, let's get onto some important questions. What should I wear tomorrow night?'

I laughed. 'You look beautiful in purple, which happens to be the party's colour.'

'I have a plummy beaded wrap dress. Would that work?'

'Sounds lovely.'

'Now get back to work—we want to have something to celebrate tomorrow night.'

'You'll be the best mum one day, Aunt Daphne.'

A square of loo roll absorbed the dampness on my cheeks and I went to rejoin Maddy. Beryl and her husband had flown up from Canberra. Senator Flight, her husband, various offspring and bursting belly hovered around the chips and dip.

Theo was wearing a Hawaiian shirt. 'We're going to win this, Roo,' he said. 'I've got my lucky shirt on.'

As the sun went down, the roof heaved with colleagues, most of whom I knew by email only. The LOO, Shelly and Abigail arrived with Luke. Max took to the centre of the roof with beer in hand. He seemed reinvigorated and opened his mouth to address his supporters.

'Shoosh, darling,' said Shelly, moving to stand in front of him. 'It's my turn. Thank you for all your hard work. If we don't win tomorrow, it won't be for want of trying. People think this is Max's journey alone. It's not. It belongs as much to you and your families as it does to Max and his. Abigail and I, with the combined technical prowess of Maddy and Roo, wanted you all to see *our* journey. And, if you don't mind, I'm going to ask my husband to dance, because this was the song we danced to on our wedding day. I'd encourage you all to do the same. Kill the lights.'

'Yeah,' said Max, 'what she said.' He kissed his wife and accepted her invitation, collapsing into her arms. Against the soft light of our projected journey, they danced like newlyweds to Elton and his ivories.

Di took Luke; Maddy, Abigail; and Hawaiian Theo, me. The rest followed. Too tired to bust a move, we swayed in each other's arms, occasionally joining in for the chorus.

'Wanna swap?' asked Di at the bridge. 'You're welcome to Luke.'

A dejected Luke extended his hand. I kicked off my Up Yours, Oscars and went with it.

His bad suit smelled like the promise of rain. His fingers played my lower back like a piano. He hummed the tune, his chin on my head, the sound reverberating between his jaw and my crown.

'Luke?'

'Hmm?'

'What's our position on genetically modified foods?'

'Shut up, beautiful.' He held me closer, so I did.

Desperate and voteless

I didn't wake up because I didn't sleep. Two things kept me awake. First, Elton John. Second, the fact that I was thinking about Elton John and not about the election. It was an insane-making cycle. The tune would play (mostly without the right lyrics) then my head would scratch the vinyl.

Why in God's name are you awake? Tomorrow is the biggest day of your career and you're lying here with a forty-year-old ballad on loop in your frontal lobe...

And then we'd go back to the piano interlude and so on until 4 a.m. when the newspapers thudded onto the carpet outside my hotel room door.

I pulled the curtains along their runner to reveal the overcast Melbourne morning. The rich brown river was perfectly still and the streets were dotted with zigzagging party-goers making their way home. I grabbed the papers and dialled in.

MAYBE MASTERS, said the *Herald*. CLIFFHANGER, said the *Weekender*. The poll was disgustingly close. We were even with the government. If I could have opened the windows at the hotel, I'd have called out to the revellers and reminded them to vote. I was still alone on the conference call. Just me and Mozart. They were seventeen minutes late. Eighteen. I hung up and texted Di.

Where are you guys? R

No reply. I tried Maddy.

Are you joining this morning's hook-up? R

My phone buzzed.

Dude, no hook up—it's D Day. I'm making sandwiches for the booths in Pratt. Where are you handing out? M

Don't we have work to do? Where's Max? R

Sandwiches don't make themselves. Max is hitting the radios from home. He'll be voting at nine. M

There must be something I can do. R

Find a booth and work. See you tonight. M

The lack of structure did my head in. *Hang on*, it said, *I thought we were going to do the phone hook-up and race around trying to convince people to vote for us like usual. And now you're telling me we have nothing to do?*

Which booth? All of my favourite candidates were in other cities. Melissa was in Launceston, Felix in Adelaide, Felicia in Cloncurry. I didn't know anyone in Melbourne. Not a soul.

We need wine, said my head.

Good thinking. I showered, packed, checked out and hailed a taxi.

'I need to go to the Yarra Valley,' I said, jumping into the back seat.

'I'm clocking off in half an hour, love. Sorry.'

'I'll give you two hundred and fifty dollars cash to take me there.'

He thought about it. 'Righto.'

We drove past countless polling booths—churches, schools, community halls—each replete with bunting and other paraphernalia from both sides. Rolls of flimsy plastic bearing Max's smiling face were being unfurled by volunteers along fences. Full body shots of the Prime Minister glistened on A-frame stands in the dewy dawn. Our campaign workers wore purple T-shirts and caps with MAX FOR PM in white block letters. Theirs were in black and white.

'You look familiar,' the driver said as we went through Lilydale.

I looked at the rear-view mirror to examine his face. 'Really?'

'Yep. I must have driven you before.'

'I've only been in Australia for just over a month and in Melbourne intermittently.'

'I never forget a face. What do you do?'

'I work for Max Masters.'

'I don't bloody believe this.'

'What?'

'You took your duds off in my cab on the way to Tullamarine, remember?'

It can't be.

'No, I think you're mistaken.'

'Nope, I told you. I never forget a face.'

Or other body parts, for that matter.

He winked. 'You've got my vote, love.'

'You can drop me here.' I got out at a tiny weatherboard primary school in Warburton and paid him through the window. 'The polls open in two hours,' I said.

'Good luck, mate!' He sped off with a smile on his face.

Mums and dads were setting up trestle tables. SUPPORT THE WSS LAMINGTON DRIVE, read a handwritten sign. A man in a deck chair dozed under a purple cap, his thermos holding down a pile of newspapers. I cleared my throat. 'Excuse me.'

He stirred, adjusting his hat to see me. 'Yes?'

'Sorry to disturb you,' I said. 'My name is Ruby Stanhope and I work in Max Masters' office.'

'Yeah, right,' he said. 'Why would Max Masters send a flunky to an unwinnable seat? What are you, media?'

'No, I'm a financial policy advisor, except I've never done any financial policy advice; I seem to play a more miscellaneous role, but that's not the point. I'm here because I want to be. My aunts live locally. And no seat is unwinnable.'

'Do you have a card or something?'

I showed him my parliamentary security pass. He rubbed his forehead in disbelief. 'Sorry about that,' he said. 'We don't usually get much interest in this electorate, especially not at'—he looked at his watch—'a quarter past six in the morning.'

'I didn't know what to do today and I needed to do something, so I got in a cab and came here. I hope that's okay.'

'Sure,' he said. 'I've been manning this booth solo for twenty years, so it'll be nice to have a bit of company. I'm Graeme, by the way.'

'Everyone calls me Roo.'

Graeme and I stood there all day. We ate lamingtons, drank tea and talked politics under the shade of a purple and white umbrella.

'Max Masters for PM,' we would say, handing our how-to-vote cards to passers-by.

'Give Gabrielle a go,' said Phoebe, our competitor.

When the midday sun was burning my shoulders, Daphne, Debs, Fran, Clem, Pansy and the pups brought us homemade rye rolls with smoked salmon and watercress. Graeme said all his Christmases had come at once. Clem had tied purple ribbon to the pups' collars, which wooed about seven voters by my count.

'Well,' said Graeme at five, 'I guess we had better vote and pack up—why don't you go first.'

Trembling with excitement, I approached the school hall. In London, election days had always seemed so inconvenient—I'd rarely found time between conference calls to cast my vote—but this was different. I couldn't wait.

Inside, under the ceiling fans, eight cardboard cubicles stood proud with Australian Electoral Commission pencils attached. There were two ballot boxes in the middle of the room near a long trestle table, at which sat three plump ladies. Each had a name tag and a cheery smile. 'Hi, love,' said one, 'what's your surname?'

'Stanhope.'

'Do you live in this electorate?'

'No, I don't think so,' I said. 'I don't know which electorate I'm in.'

'Well, where do you live? You can absentee vote from any booth in the country if you give me photo ID with proof of address.'

'London.' I realised the privilege wasn't mine. It was devastating. 'I'm not Australian.'

The lady exchanged puzzled glances with her colleagues. 'In that case, you don't have to vote.'

'But I really, really want to,' I said. 'I've been working on the campaign for weeks.'

'Sorry, love, this isn't an application process. You have to be a citizen on the electoral roll.'

'What if I wait until five to six? Maybe there will be people who don't show up and I could use their vote.'

'That's what we call a rort.' Her tone hardened.

'What's up?' asked Graeme when I rejoined him.

'I can't vote,' I said. 'I forgot I'm not Australian.'

'Oh, Roo, I'm so sorry.'

'That's okay, just try to make your vote count for me too.'

'I'll tell you what, you can have half of it, presuming we vote the same way.'

A lady walked up the footpath towards the booth. She was barefoot, in shorts and a T-shirt, wearing aviator sunglasses, car keys in hand. When she neared us, I said, 'Max Masters for PM' with a smile, handing her our pamphlet. 'Give Gabrielle a go,' pleaded Phoebe, whose handful of how-to-vote cards was diminishing faster than mine.

'Hmmm,' said the lady, a finger poised. 'Eeny, meeny, miny, moe.' She landed on me, taking my card. 'They're all the same—vote for a politician and you'll get a politician.'

I had a hankering to slap her right across her vote-squandering face, so it was serendipitous that Daphne arrived to pick me up.

I thanked Graeme (who had come over in an enviable

post-vote glow) and invited him to the after-party in the city. He got a bit emotional, but it was the least I could do for a stranger who had given me half of his precious democratic right.

We had done everything we could. Now for the result.

This is it

'How did Aunty Wooby get butterflies in her stomach?'

'It means she's nervous about something.'

'Why is she nervous?'

'Because tonight she'll find out if all of her hard work has paid off. Tonight, you might be one of the first people to meet the new prime minister of Australia.'

'Will there be face painting?'

The car was still moving when I jumped out, leaving Graeme and my family to find a park.

Max's venue of choice for the evening was his local RSL Club. 'That's where we spend every election night,' he'd said, 'so this one won't be any different.' The media team loved it and the advancers loathed it, as is usually the case with bad ideas.

It was a quarter to seven and the place was already overflowing. People were standing in the car park watching huge television screens broadcasting live from the tally room in Sydney. I pushed past the crowd to the front door and called Beryl, who came to collect me.

'Roo, you look hot. Where did you get those shoes?' She handed me a pass.

I twirled and curtsied. 'A man by the name of Louboutin made them for me. I know it's a bit hot for boots, but they have been good to me before, so I couldn't resist them.'

Debs and Fran had gone shopping to buy me an election-night gift to go with them: a Collette Dinnigan black silk sheath dress, tied at the middle with a loose bow. My hair was behaving as well as it could, my burnt shoulders had settled into a healthy-ish looking tan and red lips and shimmery cheeks distracted from the thirty grams or so of industrial-strength concealer encircling my eyes.

'Please tell me you have two of those shirts,' I said to Hawaiian Theo when I saw him.

'A man would have to be exceptionally lucky to have two lucky shirts,' he said, uncharacteristically kissing me on the cheek. 'You are exquisite tonight, Ruby Stanhope.'

'Has he been drinking?' I asked Beryl as she led me towards the RSL sub-branch president's office.

'Since last night. I hope we don't win this—transition to government might be awkward with an inebriated policy wonk.'

Luke was wearing his inaugural banana tree tie. His worst and my favourite. He and Di sat in opposite corners on the floor of the president's office—a man with two basset hounds, Verbena and Vanilla, and a moggy called Chuck, according to the homemade matchstick photo frames on his desk.

Maddy stood at a whiteboard, marker in hand. She had drawn up a table listing every seat in the country by state and territory in alphabetical order.

'I haven't had a shower,' said Di. 'Don't come near me.'

'Me neither,' said Luke.

'Does anybody have a spare whiteboard pen?' asked Maddy. 'This one's lost its pluck.'

I handed her the one from my Toolkit.

Luke scratched his head. 'The exit polls from WA are in, but they can't be right.'

'Why not?' I asked.

'Because they average out to us getting about fifty-four per cent, two-party-preferred.'

This probably wasn't the time to ask what an exit poll was. It sounded like a horrendous workplace injury.

'They're always wrong,' said Maddy. 'Just discard it.'

'Hang on a tick,' said Di. 'Those results are consistent with the swing we're seeing in South Australia, Queensland and New South Wales. Write it down somewhere.'

I looked at the president's circa-1991 television, which sat atop a crocheted doily. 'Looks like Eleven has changed its commentary team.' Oscar wasn't on it.

'Yep, they ditched Pretty Boy for Ng,' said Di. 'Apparently he's been sent to cover Donaldson, the seat Missy Hatton is running for in Tasmania.'

'A friend of mine who writes for the *Herald* told me Pretty Boy is going to be moving back to Melbourne to cover state politics after this,' said Maddy. 'Bureau chief or some similar trumped-up title.'

My head, heart and body rejoiced in chorus, but this wasn't the occasion for a victory dance.

'Mirabelle just texted me some of the preliminary results for Forster in Darwin,' said Luke. 'It's a four per cent swing to us. That would mean Fred Smythe now has one of the safest seats in the country, even after all that immigration stuff.'

'Four?' I asked. Luke looked up at me and nodded.

Maddy wrote the number on the board.

A private number called my phone. 'Roo, it's Felicia Lunardi calling from Cloncurry. I wondered whether you could do me a favour.'

'Anything, Felicia. How's it all going up there?'

'Mick O'Donoghue has told me that exit polls for Rafter are indicating a clear victory, but I can't get through to anyone at party HQ. Can you look into it for me?'

'I'm on it.' I hung up. 'That was Lunardi. Who should I talk to at party HQ to check exit polls?'

'Give Mirabelle's office a call. What did she say?'

'Something about exit polls and victory.'

Maddy laughed. 'I'd eat my hat.'

'It's Roo Stanhope from the LOO's office,' I said to one of Mirabelle's men. 'What are you seeing in Forster?'

'We're not reading anything into the exit polls,' he said. 'It's not possible. It said something like 47.3 on the primary in key booths. With preferences she'd be looking at...No. That's ridiculous. Just don't read anything into these figures. Keep in mind that the bulk of that seat will come down to postal votes.'

I wrote it down, far-fetched as it was.

'Thanks,' I said. 'I'd appreciate it if you could keep me posted on that seat.'

Felicia, stay calm, but exit polls in some booths say you've got 47.3% of the primary vote. Let me know if you hear anything else. Roo

'Um, Maddy, Mirabelle's office is saying 47.3 on the primary in Forster.'

No sooner had her whiteboard marker squeaked the digits than she erased them.

'Write it down,' I said.

'I need to bring Max and the family in,' Di said. 'Roo, can you give me a hand?'

I followed her out.

'Roo, I want to talk to you about something,' said Di as we walked. 'Two things, actually. One, regardless of what happens tonight, Luke has asked me to step into his shoes as Chief of Staff. If Max is fine with that, I want to know that I can count on you to stick around.'

I opened my mouth to speak.

'Think about it,' she cut in. Her phone rang. 'Di speaking, can you hold for a minute?' She muted her phone and gave me her full attention. 'Two, if you're going to fuck over senior journalists in future, would you mind checking with me first? I mean obviously it worked and all, but Christ that was risky—not just for you but for all of us. We need to be a team here, okay?'

There was no defence. 'Sorry, Di.'

'No worries,' she said. 'How did it feel?'

The answer to that question was obvious in my smile. She took the call.

'Right, they're outside,' she said. 'Let's grab them. There's going to be a scrum and it's a bit dangerous out there with all those people, so I'll need you to steer them in pretty tightly with me and the cops.'

She wasn't wrong. When we stepped out into the mild April night the cicadas' shrill din drowned out the crowd, but as soon as Max got out of his car it was mayhem. The cameras clung to us. 'I love you, Max,' screamed a lady near me. 'Good luck, mate,' said a man with a toddler on his shoulders. Shelly and Abigail cowered, squeezing my hands. Milly grabbed her dad's arm to give him something to lean on. Max smiled and strolled into the building as casually as he could. A purple-clad fanatic shrieked in my ear. 'He looks like a Ribena berry,' said Abigail. Finally, we made it inside.

'It's like the FIFA World Cup out there,' said the LOO.

'Don't flatter yourself, Dad,' said Abigail.

The RSL bar was now full of our friends and family, including mine. Max stuck his head in to say hello to everyone, but fast became overwhelmed. You could see the pulse in his neck.

'Come on,' said Milly, 'let's get you guys some food.'

'I can't eat,' said Max, walking into the president's office, 'but I can't just sit here.'

'Max, I need you to have a look at your speeches,' said Di.

'Plural?'

'There *are* two possible outcomes.'

'Shit, I hadn't even thought about the speech.'

'Get Theo for me, Roo,' Di said.

I gave her a look that I hoped might say perhaps this isn't the most appropriate moment to be throwing a drunkard in a novelty shirt into the mix. The look failed, so I went to find him.

'Where's Theo?'

Beryl pointed to the Gents.

I knocked on the toilet door and covered my eyes to open it. 'Theo?' I called out. 'Are you all right?'

'It depends on who is asking.'

'Roo. Which other Englishwoman would come to find you in the loo at an RSL?'

'I'm fine, Roo.'

'Bullshit,' I said, searching my Toolkit. 'I'll get Beryl to get you some food. And you need a shower. What was the last meal you ate?'

'Kebab,' he groaned.

'I've put my emergency toothbrush next to the sink as well as some shower-in-a-can, a razor and cream—use all of it, wash your face and then join us in the president's office.'

When I went back into the room, Senator Flight was on the Channel Eleven panel. 'Anastasia, I've just had a call from a colleague who tells me that preliminary results from forty per cent of the votes in the Tasmanian seat of Donaldson show a swing to our fantastic candidate, Melissa Hatton. The figure they mentioned was over three per cent.'

'Of course, these are early results and we should be cautious, but it does look like a worrying trend is emerging for the government, doesn't it, Hugh Patton?' Anastasia asked her co-panellist, the former prime minister.

'It certainly does, Anastasia. That's a significant proportion of the vote counted across what I'm told is a representative swag of booths in that seat. Donaldson has always been the one to watch. It's a knife-edge marginal.'

Max's face lightened as if someone was air-brushing him. Melissa's number popped up on my phone.

'Roo, can you believe it? Whatever happens, thank you for your support. I couldn't have done any of this without you.' Her voice was raw and teary.

'Nonsense, Missy. You are a highly capable person and you're going to be a magnificent local member. Good luck and have a great night.'

Theo walked in wearing a clean purple campaign T-shirt and smelling of mint, musk and avocado. 'Shall we go through the speeches?' he asked. Max nodded and followed him into another room.

'Now for an update,' said Anastasia. 'Based on preliminary results, and with a view to the thirteen seats the Opposition requires to win government, we're calling this a narrow victory for Max Masters. There are at least fifteen seats with more than fifty per cent of the vote counted and swings of around four per cent.'

'With respect, Anastasia,' said Hugh Patton, 'it's a quarter to nine and there's a lot more counting to be done—isn't it a little early to call?'

'Does that mean Dad won, Mum?' Abigail removed a headphone from one ear.

'Not yet, darling,' said Shelly. 'The night is young.'

The headphone was replaced.

'How are you feeling?' I asked Shelly, who was having her make-up done.

'Part of me wants to drink champagne and another part wants to steel itself for the possibility that these figures are all just a cruel trick. I want to be strong for him for either speech and at the moment I'm a nervous wreck.'

'Whisky?' I offered her a hip flask of single malt Debs had given me in the car.

She took a swig and screwed up her face as she swallowed it. 'Can we use waterproof mascara?' she asked the make-up artist.

Max rejoined us with two stapled A4 piles under his arm. He put them on the table. One was headed WIN, the other LOSE.

'Roo, can you put this on a charger somewhere?' he

asked, handing me his phone. Di was using all of the power points in the president's office, so I plugged it into the hallway.

I texted Felix Winks in Adelaide.

What's Watson looking like?

I went to find Debs to give her a glass.

'Thanks, but no thanks, kiddo.'

'What's wrong with you?'

'Nothing. Yet. I'm going to the gyno tomorrow to get my oils checked and Daph wants me clean. It looks like we might have a donor.'

'SPERM!?'

People stared at us. Daphne smiled.

'Jesus. Fuck. Say it louder.'

'Sorry, I'm just so excited and I haven't had any sleep and I didn't expect it would happen this quickly and you didn't seem at all inclined to proceed with this the last time we spoke.'

'Yeah, well, I changed my mind. Anyhow, my PA said he'd rub one off for us, so that was nice, I guess.'

My phone buzzed.

The local member has just called me to concede. I've won.
I am going to be the Member for Watson. Felix Winks
(MP)

'Luke!' I ran back into the president's office. 'Felix Winks is the new Member for Watson.' I bounced up and down.

'And Felicia Lunardi is the new Member for Rafter,' he said, bouncing with me.

'I don't want to disturb you two in your Maasai moment,' said Max, who swivelled to face us in the president's chair, 'but it'd be good to get an update.'

Luke steadied himself, remembering he was a grown-up. I did the same, but only because I didn't want to wear down the red soles of my boots.

'I've spoken at length with Mirabelle,' Luke said, handing Max a breakdown of the numbers. 'I think you should focus on your winning speech. The marginals are falling our way and eight of the thirteen candidates have already conceded, even though it's only half past nine. There are four others on a knife-edge. You'll probably get the call within the hour.'

For Max, it wasn't sinking in. 'Would you mind rounding up my family and sending them in? Just knock on the door if you need us.'

Maddy wheeled her whiteboard into the hallway. She had an Electoral Commission map of Australia on the floor and used a highlighter to colour in the seats we had won. 'One, two...four...seven...nine, ten, eleven... fourteen!' Her pitch climbed a few octaves as she counted. 'Holy shit, people. That's government. I'm going to get changed.'

'Me too,' said Di. 'There's no way I'm going to look like trash for this.'

'Roo's supplies are in the Gents,' said Theo.

I sat on the floor. 'Now what happens?' I asked Luke.

'We wait for the call from the PM to tell us she's conceding.' He slid down the wall onto the floor beside me. 'So, Ruby Stanhope, are you glad you did this?'

'Did what?'

'This. The campaign.'

'Meeting you at that dreary fundraiser is by far the best thing that's ever happened to me. Not that it wouldn't have been lovely to meet you in other circumstances. It

321

would have, even with the suit. For the record, I don't have a problem with the suit. It's a little big for you and not a great colour for your skin, which is nice, by the way. It smells wet—your suit, not your skin—the good kind of wet though, not like wet dog or wet wool, but like sprinklers and rain. And the banana tree is growing on me. Pun not intended. Of course, I'm not trying to say the sole reason I'm glad to have met you was the career opportunity that followed, even though they have revolutionised me. Not like the Cultural Revolution, which was horrid, or even the Industrial Revolution for that matter, which was necessary but very dirty...'

And there, on the floor outside the toilets at a Melbourne RSL sub-branch on election night, Luke Harley held me still and kissed me. He kissed me with such intensity that I had no doubts, no noisy objections from my head, heart or body. All of me was into him.

'Yuck! Dis*gus*ting!'

Luke let go of my face and opened one eye to find a five-year-old standing over him. Fran was right behind Clem.

'What is it, Clemen...Excuse me, who are you and what are you doing to my sister?'

'Well, well, little Lukey Harley is getting fresh with my niece, as predicted. Good to see.'

'Awkward,' observed Luke as he helped me to my feet.

'Fran, Clem, this is my friend, Luke Harley. Luke, this is my sister, Fran, and niece, Clementine.'

'Oh, so *you* are Luke *and* Harley,' said Clem. 'I thought you were two people, because I went to nursery with a boy called Harley and our gardener's name is Luke the Gardener. I found a phone on the floor asking for you. It's blue. The lady said she wanted to speak to Luke Harley, so I asked which one—Luke or Harley—because I didn't know who you are. And she said both. So I told her they are in London, but sometimes Harley goes skiing. And then she said she wanted to speak to Max Masters and I couldn't find Max so I said I would give Luke, Harley and Max a message if I found them.'

Luke went white.

'It must have been the PM calling on Max's Black-Berry. Shit.'

'Aunty Wooby!'

'Ruby!'

'Where's the BlackBerry, Clem?'

'The what?'

'The phone, darling. Where did you put the phone?'

'It's not black, it's blue.'

I took a deep breath. 'I know it's blue. Life is confusingly counterintuitive at times. The phone belongs to Max. It's very important.'

'It's in my knapsack,' said Clem, unzipping Dorothy the Dinosaur. She pulled out the BlackBerry and gave it to me. Four missed calls, all from the same number. Bollocks, bollocks, bollocks, bollocks.

I hit callback.

'Good evening, Prime Minister Brennan's office, this is Martha.'

Fuck.

'Good evening, Martha. My name is Ruby Stanhope and I'm calling from the Leader of the Opposition's office. I understand you tried to place a call earlier. Is there something I can help with?'

'Tell me, Ruby,' said Martha, 'are you in some way related to Clementine Genevieve Gardner-Stanhope?'

'Yes, I'm really very sorry about that.'

'The Prime Minister would like to speak with the Leader of the Opposition,' she said. 'That is, *if* he is available to take her call.'

'Certainly, Martha. I will get him for you now.'

Luke and I raced down the hallway to the president's office and knocked on the door.

'Come in,' said the LOO.

'Max,' I said, handing him the phone, 'this is it.'

As Luke and I waited outside, I drafted a To Do list.

1. Practise saying 'Prime Minister' without sounding obsequious
2. Delete 'LOO' from vocabulary, unless referring to the lower case
3. Arrange new working visa
4. Purchase copy of *Transition to Government for Dummies*
5. Draft bill to outlaw long socks
6. Replenish Toolkit
7. Visit Toolangi Winery with Luke to get a case of their finest peanut noise.

Acknowledgments

Thanks: to Lihan at Wain Wain, who brought me iced oolong tea and guarded my laptop during loo breaks.

To Catherine, Fi, Fleur, Kathy, Kristy, Nadia, Nicole, Renee and Rita for their wisdom and support.

To Alice, for improving Ruby's Englishness.

To my friend Sue—advocate, ally and enabler.

To Lou Ye and Nai Nai, for their warmth.

To Mum, who redefines 'busy', for finding time to read and give feedback on each chapter within minutes of receipt, even from Kilimanjaro.

To Dad, Nick and Marcus for their unconditional love and encouragement.

To my grandmothers, Elizabeth and Margaret, for the writing gene.

In a big way, to Ali, Michael, Penny, Jane, Kirsty, Alaina and the other good folk at Text Publishing. Authors write manuscripts, publishers make them books. Ruby couldn't have found a better partner than she has in Text.

Last and by every means most, to my husband Albert, who had faith in me when I didn't.